S0-ARN-120

ACCLAIM FOR
The Solitude of Emperors

"An impassioned plea for tolerance in a country rife with competing interests. . . . *The Solitude of Emperors* refuses to counter the simplicity of fundamentalism with simplicity of answer. Unflinching. Unsentimental. Deeply Moving. I loved it."
– Kiran Desai, winner of the Man Booker Prize

"A kind of compressed, Indian *Great Expectations*. . . . Episodes in which Vijay is involved in the Bombay riots are masterfully – and brutally – written."
– *Globe and Mail*

"Davidar is a true novelist, delighted by details, interested in allowing his characters to reveal themselves. . . . It's a novel of feeling as well as of ideas, and a delightful and thoroughly satisfying one."
– Allan Massie, *The Scotsman*

"The sense of place is remarkable, and the questions Davidar raises about religion, fundamentalism and heroism are all worth raising. . . . Anyone who tackles them in a serious way, as Davidar has done, should be heard."
– *Edmonton Journal*

"*The Solitude of Emperors* is fascinating for its depiction of the subtleties of the complex Indian mindset. . . . It skips along almost effortlessly."
– Glasgow *Herald*

"[Davidar] has a keen eye for detail, and an elegant turn of phrase. This is a daring novel that engages with Indian realities."
– *The Independent*

"The book's plea for tolerance is moving. . . . The novel breathes sincerity as it makes its appeal for change."
– *Quill & Quire*

Also by David Davidar

The House of Blue Mangoes

The Solitude
of Emperors

~❧~

DAVID DAVIDAR

EMBLEM
McClelland & Stewart

Text copyright © 2007 David Davidar

Cloth edition published 2007
Emblem edition published 2008

Emblem is an imprint of McClelland & Stewart Ltd.
Emblem and colophon are registered trademarks
of McClelland & Stewart Ltd.

All rights reserved. The use of any part of this publication reproduced,
transmitted in any form or by any means, electronic, mechanical,
photocopying, recording, or otherwise, or stored in a retrieval system,
without the prior written consent of the publisher – or, in case of
photocopying or other reprographic copying, a licence from the Canadian
Copyright Licensing Agency – is an infringement of the copyright law.

Library and Archives Canada Cataloguing in Publication

Davidar, David
The solitude of emperors / David Davidar.

ISBN 978-0-7710-2591-4

I. Title.
PR9499.3.D384S65 2008 823.'92 C2008-900908-8

We acknowledge the financial support of the Government of Canada
through the Book Publishing Industry Development Program and that of
the Government of Ontario through the Ontario Media Development
Corporation's Ontario Book Initiative. We further acknowledge the
support of the Canada Council for the Arts and the Ontario Arts Council
for our publishing program.

Typeset in Great Britain by Input Data Services Ltd.
Printed and bound in Canada

ANCIENT FOREST
FRIENDLY

This book is printed on acid-free paper that is 100% recycled,
ancient-forest friendly (100% post-consumer recycled).

McClelland & Stewart Ltd.
75 Sherbourne Street
Toronto, Ontario
M5A 2P9
www.mcclelland.com

1 2 3 4 5   12 11 10 09 08

For Rachna
&
Eddy Davidar

The one who stays within the limits assigned to him is a man
The one who roams beyond these limits is a saint.

To reject both limits and their absence:
That's a thought with immeasurable depths.

– Kabir

Contents

PART I

Prologue

They are the invisible ones, the ones who were too small, weak, poor or slow to escape the onrush of history. No obituaries mark their passing, no memorials honour their name and we don't remember them because in our eyes they never existed. Yet we ignore them at our peril, if only because their fate today could be ours tomorrow; history is an insatiable tyrant.

I have never been much good at ritual or ceremonial homage – I blame this on my parents, who never really taught me – so I have had to invent a private rite of remembrance for Noah, a man who was ignored by almost everyone for as long as he lived, but who, in his death, affected me more powerfully than I would have thought possible. I can picture his mocking smile now, for the ceremony I'm about to conduct takes its inspiration from a somewhat bizarre funeral I saw him preside over all those many years ago. It is the middle of winter in this northern city, and even though the bitter cold would deter most from setting foot outside a heated room, I have always been stubborn and determined once I have decided to do something, and so I shuffle through the wind and snow to the cemetery closest to my house.

Once there, I look for a grave with an angel on its headstone; there is a crust of snow on the grave and I scrape it off, unroll the plastic mat I have brought with me, and sit down. Noah wouldn't have liked this cemetery, it's too neat and formal; he believed the dead were entitled to comfortable lived-in surroundings. He would have missed his beloved trees: the great peepul with leaves like flattened spearheads and the jacarandas that flung sprays of blue into the deeper blue of the Nilgiri sky. Here the maples are bare, and the evergreens are too dull and uniform to have appealed to him. But there is nothing I can do about the surroundings, so I begin to unpack the rucksack I have brought with me. I take out a bottle of rum, a cigarette packet (I do not smoke and the cigarettes have been replaced by two joints that I have procured with some difficulty from a Bolivian colleague), a cheap plastic lighter, a CD player and, finally, a manuscript. I sprinkle some of the rum around the grave to propitiate the dead, put the headphones on, and am preparing to light up a joint when I hear the sound of an approaching vehicle. I am grateful for the cover of the snowstorm because I doubt the groundskeeper whose vehicle this must be would understand if he caught me here.

In the twelve years since Noah died, I have performed this ceremony annually – in other cemeteries, other cities, in Madras, Bombay, in London, a city I passed through on my way to Canada – and every time I've carried it out surreptitiously, for it is not something that can be explained away easily. The vehicle sweeps past, its driver an indistinct figure in the cab, and silence descends again. I apologize to Grace MacKinnon (1902–1972), whose grave I have temporarily taken over, switch on the CD player, and to the sound of Jim Morrison singing 'Riders on the Storm' I light the joint. The first drag sets me coughing uncontrollably; I wait for my agitated lungs to stop protesting, take another hit, then perform the final part of the ceremony. I pull out a torch from the rucksack, switch it on, shake the snow off my manuscript and begin reading aloud the last chapter. I have neither the effrontery nor the imagination to make this the sort of book Noah would have admired, but my years as a journalist have equipped me with enough tools to thread together a coherent, sturdy narrative. In the course of the decade it has taken me to complete the book – by any accounting that would be deemed slow, slightly over a chapter a year, but I should point out that it has gone through five drafts – I think I have finally put down a version of the events of the winter of 1993/4 that I am satisfied with. More importantly, I feel I understand the man at the centre of them better.

Noah told me once that the dead remain with us for as long as we need them and I have begun to see what he meant. I sensed his presence from time to time as I attempted to recreate his life and the events leading up to his death, and the book has benefited as a result. I should say at this point that I am aware that this account is different from the version put out by the police and the government commission of inquiry that investigated his death; in my defence all I can say is that nobody else recorded the witness of the dead.

I

The final kick

I am of the school that believes a journalist should never become part of the story he is covering, and the only time I broke that rule, the consequences were disastrous and signalled the beginning of the end of my career.

I did not set out to become a journalist. I hadn't grown up yearning to write about corrupt government ministers or the daily injustices that took place in our teeming cities and villages. All I wanted was a job, any job that would take me out of K—, the small town in Tamil Nadu that I was born and brought up in. I can write about it calmly now, but back in 1990 when I was looking to escape from K—, I was filled with the desperation that anyone who has sought to leave small-town India with a second-class degree from a third-rate college would readily understand.

K— sprawled haphazardly beside one of the national highways. It had the standard-issue refuse-filled streets, open drains, ugly residential sections, hospitals, a cinema or two, clamorous bazaars, open-air barber shops, temples, mosques, churches, the scanty shade of neem trees, cows, crows, bicycles, beggars and sunlight so intense that by mid-morning everything in town was wrapped in a shimmering skin of heat – a stereotypical small town, then, with little to distinguish it from the dozens of others that were strewn across the great South Indian plain. The two things that set it apart from its fellows were a temple and a hospital. The temple, which was dedicated to Lord Shiva, had been constructed sometime in the eighth century by a minor ruler of the Pandyan dynasty, and possessed an unusual architectural feature – in the courtyard that fronted the main shrine stood a dozen stone columns that, when struck, produced the saptha swarangal, the basic notes of Indian classical music. The temple at K— was not as well known as the Nellaiyappar temple, with over a hundred musical pillars, which lay an hour and a half to the south by bus and attracted hordes of tourists and pilgrims, but it was a source of pride to us and its annual festival during the Tamil month of Aani was the cultural and spiritual highlight of the year.

Our pride in the Shiva temple didn't extend to its surroundings. It stood at the end of a street full of litter, and just beyond its precincts cows munched placidly on discarded banana leaves and flower garlands, while beggars and stray dogs fought over the right to occupy the best spots to importune worshippers for food and alms. In the evening, their ranks were swelled by what appeared to be the entire male population of K— between the ages of fifteen and twenty-five, who waited for the young unmarried girls to appear, chaperoned by their mothers, for evening worship at the temple. The girls would arrive at a set hour, their jewellery and the corrugations of their richly coloured saris catching the dying light and turning them into worthy handmaidens of the Lord. In a marvel of contrivance and skill, they would manage to peer up from beneath their eyelashes at the waiting boys, while simultaneously affecting not to notice them – for the benefit of their mothers – and delicately picking their way through the garbage strewn in their path. The boys would giggle and shuffle their feet and the girls would press on towards the entrance of the shrine, their mothers waddling along beside them, looking severe. The entire process lasted no more than a few minutes but neither side could have done without it, it was the closest thing to public contact between unmarried men and women in town.

If the temple was the epicentre of the arts, spirituality and romance, The Balaji Medical Centre represented the height of modernity. The gleaming new hospital complex on the north-eastern edge of the town had been completed in 1975, seven years after I was born, by a native son who had made good in Austin, Texas. Unacknowledged by his adoptive country, he had decided to memorialize himself in the town he had always congratulated himself on escaping from – until he had turned sixty and had begun to think about how he would be remembered after he was gone. Being a good self-publicist and an even better businessman, he disguised this giant act of the ego with the trappings of patriotism ('I have long felt the need to do something for India') while quietly taking advantage of the cheap land prices and tax breaks extended to him by grateful municipal and state governments. Nobody in town had ever been treated in the hospital's private wards, it was too expensive, but its high white walls and celebrity patients certainly gave K— something to boast about. To find work at the hospital was the goal of the more ambitious of my college classmates.

Neither the temple nor the hospital complex made me like the place of my birth any better. There were things in general that contributed to my disenchantment such as the lack of opportunity, the slow pace of life, the petty jealousies and small concerns of the people I associated with, but besides these there were specific things that stoked my desperation.

The first of these had little to do with me but with my parents and their romance. My mother taught physics at the women's college and my father economics at the government arts and sciences college I went to, and I felt they lacked the ambition and the guile to advance any further in their careers. Or perhaps they were happy just as they were, muddling along with no real expectations of life, part of the generation of Indians born on the cusp of independence, with no big ideas to fight for, as the previous generation had had, and without the breathtaking ambition of succeeding generations. Their greatest achievement, as far as I could tell, because we didn't talk about such things, was getting married to one another. For they had married for love, and more audaciously across the caste divide – a titanic achievement in small-town India in 1967. My father was a Brahmin, and my mother belonged to the Chettiar caste, and they had attended the same college in Salem, their home town, where they had fallen in love. When they announced their intention to marry, my father's family promptly disowned him, and my mother's father, a thin-lipped old martinet who was the headmaster of a secondary school, and whose progressiveness extended only as far as letting his daughter attend college, locked her up in her room and began scheming with the extended family to send her to the most distant relative he could

8

think of. For three days she had endured the lashings he administered with a belt and a diet of kanji, and then, in a plot line borrowed from Tamil cinema, she had sneaked out of the house – aided by her browbeaten mother – while her father had his afternoon siesta, wearing two saris and carrying a bottle of scented coconut oil and a large black umbrella, the only things she could think of taking with her in the nerve-racking excitement of her escape. Soon after they were married in secret, the couple left Salem for K—, where they had lived quietly ever since. In my more charitable moments I would grant that the drama and tension of their marriage might have so depleted my parents that they had no option but to spend the rest of their lives just getting by.

My father's family eventually came round, especially after he assured them that I would be raised a good Brahmin, although he didn't intend to do much about it, a legacy of his having been a closet communist as a student. My mother's father never forgave her, not even when I arrived on the scene, which she'd hoped would be the occasion for at least a modest reconciliation. I never met my maternal grandfather as a result, and the few memories I have of my grandmother, who died a few years after her husband, are of a faded woman who dressed always in white, and took me to the Murugan temple every time we visited her in Salem.

My parents' crossing of caste lines had not only largely cut me off from my extended family – something that everyone else in town seemed to possess – it also marked me out as an oddity, a mongrel. It wasn't so bad because I was still a Brahmin and did not have to endure the various humiliations someone lower down the caste ladder would undoubtedly have had to put up with, but I would never fit well into K— society. This was a condition somewhat exacerbated by my parents' unconventional attitude to religion. My father's brief flirtation with communism had further diluted any lingering effects of his religious upbringing. I cannot remember him ever going to the temple in the years that my mother turned her back on religion, but neither did he believe in communism enough to delete religion entirely from his life. My mother, from whom I have inherited my stubbornness and a slow-burning temper, had been so enraged by her own family's treatment of her that she shut religion

– which she blamed for her father's inflexibility – out of her existence and mine for the longest time. She allowed my mild-mannered father to fulfil his promise to his family by investing me with the sacred thread and other outward accoutrements of Brahminism, but beyond these token gestures I grew up without religion except for my periodic visits to my grandmother in Salem. By the time my mother had got over her fury, and the house began to fill with the strains of M.S. Subbulakshmi singing bhajans through the speakers of a cheap two-in-one cassette player, and the sweet scent of incense filled the store-room that had been converted into a puja room, I was in my teens and it was too late. I would occasionally accompany her to the temple, and dutifully munch on the sweet prasadam that was handed out, but I developed no more than a nominal interest in religion.

This, more than anything else, kept me from feeling completely at home in K—, for it was around caste and religion that the lives of its families and community revolved. In school and in college the Brahmin boys hung out together, the various non-Brahmin Hindus, depending on their numerical strength, formed their own groups, the Christian boys were separate, and had there been any Muslims in the educational institutions I studied in I have no doubt that they would have stayed within their own community. Most of the boys I knew went to the temple regularly and observed without question the myriad prohibitions and injunctions imposed upon them by the hierarchy of their faith. I was only tolerated, as I have said, because I was still an upper-caste Hindu.

I faced numerous little indignities, none of them dramatic or interesting enough to dwell on, but over the years they deepened my sense of alienation, and made me even more eager to escape to the big cities where I'd heard you could do as you pleased, marry who you liked, go wherever you wanted. An incident that took place during my second year in college made my decision to leave emphatic.

The results of our year-end exams had just been posted on the college noticeboard and I was mortified to discover that I had only managed a second class. Although I didn't yet have a clear idea of how I was going to find employment once I had graduated, I knew these marks weren't good enough.

The boys who had done well were planning to celebrate with ghee dosais at Saravana Bhavan, a popular restaurant in the main bazaar, before going on to a film at Gaiety Talkies, a ramshackle three-storey cinema painted a lurid shade of pink that was the best of the movie theatres in town. Although a couple of boys I knew invited me to join them, I declined. I simply wasn't in the mood.

Disconsolately I set off for home. We lived about a mile away from the college, just off a large open stretch of ground called Gandhi Maidan on the western side of town. Although it was just after five in the evening, it was still very hot. The road ran straight as a ruler between the dirty red shell of earth and sky. All about me, the town moved to its usual torpid rhythm. Farmers rattled along in bullock carts, clicking their tongues and twisting the tails of their bullocks as they attempted to get the ponderous beasts to move faster, an occasional auto rickshaw buzzed past and everywhere there were dense throngs of people on bicycles or on foot returning from work or going to the bazaar or temple whose gopuram towered over the buildings that surrounded it. I noticed none of this. My mind was wrapped around the low marks I had scored, and how much harder I would have to work in my final year if I was going to raise my percentages.

I reached the maidan and briefly surveyed the scene in front of me – a group of boys playing cricket in the middle distance, a fiercely contested hockey game in the far corner of the enormous field, a buffalo herder travelling along in the wake of his lumbering beasts, elderly gentlemen taking their evening constitutional either singly or in pairs. I heard the tinkle of a bell behind me, and stepped aside to let the cyclist pass, but he dismounted instead. It was Srinivas. We had been through school and college together, and a shared dislike of sports like cricket and hockey and the mindless pranks of the more boisterous elements among the Brahmin boys had fostered our friendship. Both of us were very studious and determined to succeed, but while my ambitions were still rather vague, Srinivas had focused with remarkable intensity on getting into the Indian Administrative

Service. He was not fazed by the fact that hundreds of thousands sat the entrance exams to the IAS each year; he was sure he would get in and if his marks were any indication, there was no doubt that he would, because he always came first in class. When he heard about my results, he commiserated with me, and then to my surprise he invited me over for coffee. In all the years I had known him, he had never once invited me home, which I'd found odd because one of the features of small-town life was the amount of time people spent visiting each other to trade gossip, news, and just pass the time. Even I, despite my mixed-caste status, was a regular in the homes of the boys I was friendly with.

Srinivas's parents were ultra-orthodox Iyengars who lived deep within the agraharam, the Brahmin quarter. I had been introduced to his father, an ascetic-looking schoolmaster, whom I would see from time to time around town, resplendent in a turban, caste marks, and a long, high-collared coat that he wore buttoned up to the throat even on the hottest days, but I had never met his mother, and so as we plunged deeper into the twisting lanes of the agraharam my gloom began to be replaced by a sense of anticipation. When we arrived at his place, a row house indistinguishable from the others that surrounded it, except that the kolam drawn outside the front steps was more elaborate than any of the others in the street, Srinivas put his bicycle on its stand, preceded me up the steps into the house, and asked me to sit in the enclosed front veranda while he went and got the coffee. This was the usual practice during visits to the homes of non-family members, and I thought nothing of it. I made myself as comfortable as I could on the stiff-backed folding chair, balanced my bag against the wall so that its contents wouldn't spill out, and waited.

I could hear Srinivas talking to his mother inside the house. A short while later, he came out bearing two plates on which there were squares of the halva the town was famous for, a deep honey colour and glistening with ghee. He handed me a plate, sat down, said the coffee wouldn't be long, and indicated that I should begin eating. I had just taken my first bite when the coffee arrived. Srinivas's mother didn't come out to the veranda, but held out a small round stainless steel tray to her son. He took the two glasses of coffee and before I could get up and greet his mother she had vanished into the depths of the house. Srinivas had handed me my glass, taken his own, and begun blowing noisily on it preparatory to taking a first sip, when I was struck by something about the scene. In any other context I might have set aside what I was witnessing with a shrug, classifying it as yet another aspect of K— that displeased me but not something to make much of. But coming as it did on top of my despondency over my marks, that afternoon in Srinivas's house was what finally made me determined to leave town, just as soon as I could. And it was all over a plate and a glass, it is often on such small things that lives turn.

I was about to drink my coffee when I noticed how pretty the glass was. It was obviously expensive, with a pretty yellow pattern scrolling around the top half, its sides free of the air bubbles that were common in the cheaper glassware hawked in the bazaar. The plate, which was also made of glass, had the same elaborate texture and scrollwork in yellow, and had I been a visiting professor from Germany, say, here to do research into the musical pillars of the Shiva temple, I might have felt honoured by the fact that my hostess was offering me my coffee and snacks in expensive, virtually new glass crockery while her son made do with a stainless steel tumbler and plate. But I was from K— and I knew exactly what my plate and glass signified – that I was not clean or non-polluting enough to eat and drink from the same crockery that members of the household used. Because I was sort of a Brahmin and a friend of her son, Srinivas's mother had served me with the glassware I was using, but its fate would be the same as that of anything used by a person who didn't belong to their religion or their exact caste and sub-caste – it would be gingerly taken to a separate shelf in the kitchen, where it would await the ministrations of a servant who would clean it and put it back in its segregated shelf until it was drafted into use again when the next unclean visitor arrived.

In my rage and humiliation it was all I could do to restrain myself from hurling the plate to the floor. Gently setting it and my glass aside on the small table between our chairs, I rose and left Srinivas's home without saying goodbye. He knew precisely why I was leaving, and made no move to stop me, nor did he offer me an apology; this was the way things were and you either accepted them or walked away if you could.

I wandered aimlessly for a while, trying to get a grip on myself before I went home. Through my anger I wondered at the fortitude of my parents. What must they have had to put up with, how had they coped with the incivility and insults that would almost certainly have been their lot when they had arrived in K— a couple of decades earlier? Presently I found myself beside a large rectangular tank that abutted the temple. Although it was intended principally for devotees, it was also used by the poor people in town, and the boys from the college would often come here to gawk at the younger prettier women as they bathed fully swathed in their saris. It wasn't much, but the sight of taut firm buttocks and nipples outlined against thin wet cloth haunted the dreams of K—'s youth, and on certain days it was hard to find standing room on the steps of the tank. It was deserted this evening except for a couple of male devotees who were bathing a little distance away – standing knee deep in the water stripped down to their sacred threads and dhotis, scooping the green scummy water over themselves. But the bathers weren't what held my attention, it was the fish which lived in the tank and were fed iddlis by the devout. I had once observed a young woman, barely out of her teens, feeding the fish, her hands cupped and delicate as conch shells, flowing out and over the water with the grace of a classical dancer and I had been entranced. But today the pale and monstrously bloated fish revolted me as they writhed like snakes in the opaque water, between the legs of the bathers, over and around themselves, coiling and uncoiling in a gelid white mass. They should have been gliding through some fast-flowing river, I thought, instead of circling sluggishly within the confines of the tank. They seemed to symbolize everything that was wrong with K—.

I spent all of the next year studying with a vengeance, and narrowly missed a first. It was a better result than I might otherwise have hoped for but who was going to hire someone with a second-class degree in economics? Nevertheless, I began frantically applying to every company I could think of. I wasn't discriminating in the least – anyone who advertised for candidates with an undergraduate degree received an application from me, along with perhaps a hundred thousand other small-town graduates. I didn't receive a single invitation to even a preliminary interview for any of the positions I applied for.

Months went by, and then, in the way these things sometimes happen, everything fell into place quite accidentally. Besides his glancing interest in communism, there was only one thing that truly interested my father, and that was the news. Before he set out for college every morning, he would spend an hour with *The Hindu* and his morning coffee, and not even my mother, who ruled his life in every other way, dared to interrupt his daily communion with his newspaper. He would pore over every page, reading aloud editorials he thought were well fashioned, disagreeing vehemently with others, excoriating the paper's subeditors for lapses in grammar and style and finishing off the exercise by tackling the crossword. Although he would dutifully plod through the business and sport pages, he was only really interested in the news and the editorial page. He would scrutinize and ponder every word in these sections carefully, to the point that I sometimes wondered if he should have been a journalist and not a college professor. Perhaps that was what lay behind the eagerness with which he fastened on to the newsworthiness of our disappearing servant, seeing a story there that none of us had quite thought about.

Raju had come to us when he was fourteen – a sullen, clumsy boy who had run away from his poverty-stricken village, some sixty miles south of K—. The third son in a family of fourteen and therefore entirely without prospects, he had been recommended to my mother by Savitri, one of the women she went to the temple with. In the two years he had been employed by us, he had displayed no aptitude for cooking, and cleaned with little or no application, but he came cheap and was reasonably clean and honest, so he was given a mat and some utensils of his own, and wages that he never saw because he was always borrowing against them.

On the morning of his disappearance my father complained loudly about having to drink black coffee, and my mother explained that it was because Raju hadn't yet brought the milk from the government dairy. In fact, she said, she hadn't seen him since the previous night. He normally slept in the courtyard outside the house but he wasn't there and his mat was neatly rolled up and stored in a corner of the kitchen; the utensils he used were still in their usual place but the cheap cardboard suitcase that my mother had bought him for Deepavali the previous year was gone. We hurriedly searched the rest of the house to make sure that nothing else was missing, then I got on my bicycle and pedalled to the dairy to get the milk, cursing Raju for being so inconsiderate as to leave before he had finished his morning duties. What was the world coming to, my mother lamented, servants came and went these days, they had none of the loyalty of retainers of the old school, who willingly sold themselves into servitude for generations, why her parents had had their Gopal for forty-five years, and so on and so forth. We'd heard it all before: Raju was the third servant we'd employed in five years. Someone else would turn up in due course, and there the matter would have rested, except for a curious fact. Two days after his departure, my mother announced, upon her return from the temple, that Raju wasn't the only servant who had disappeared; Savitri's cook had gone as well. Apparently, a recruiter from a Hindu right-wing organization had happened upon a group of young men who were either unemployed or held low-paid jobs and persuaded some of them to participate in a scheme to manufacture and transport consecrated bricks to Ayodhya, a dusty town far in the north, where they would be used to build a magnificent temple to Lord Ram.

For months now we had been hearing about this and other initiatives by sectarian political parties, including a massive procession on wheels that had passed through numerous small towns and villages drumming up support for the building of the Ram temple on the site of a sixteenth-century mosque, which, it was alleged, had been constructed by a Muslim invader after he had destroyed the temple which had originally stood on the spot. This campaign in particular alarmed most of the people we knew, because it seemed calculated to bring ordinary Hindus out on to the streets to avenge themselves on their Muslim neighbours for a centuries-old insult that neither party had had anything to do with. For days my father had muttered and seethed at the breakfast table about 'barbaric northerners whipping up communal sentiments' but now that the issue was no longer academic he exploded. I cannot remember too many occasions on which my father became truly angry, but this was one of them. The first sign that he was about to lose his temper was that his ears would redden. They did so now, and my mother and I braced ourselves.

'Abominable,' he ranted. 'These people are giving every one of us Hindus a bad name. But now they have gone too far, pouring their poison into the ears of a simpleton like Raju who can't read or write or count. What do they intend to do with him, transform him into someone who can be controlled at will? Their plan should be exposed.'

This wasn't the moment to point out that my father wasn't being original; it was precisely what a number of editorialists and TV commentators had said, so my mother and I simply exchanged glances and did not contradict him.

'We must do something, get a reporter here to do a human interest story, a view from the front line.'

His audience of two didn't bother pointing out that the national media had other priorities, especially now. Riots had broken out in many of the towns and villages that the procession had passed through, thousands had been arrested, and it was doubtful that anyone would be interested in the story of a sixteen-year-old domestic from K—. But we had underestimated the depth of my father's outrage. He wrote to the editors of *The Hindu* and *The Indian Express* suggesting they send a reporter out to K— to follow the trail of Raju and others who had been brainwashed into making common cause with the extreme right wing. When neither newspaper bothered to send him a response, he had another idea.

'Why don't you write the article?' he said to me one evening while we were gathered in our small, cluttered living room watching the news on television.

'Me?'

'Yes, you. Your command of English is adequate, you can do the research, you're from here, and you're not doing anything at the moment.' He paused, casting around for the clincher. 'And I will help you,' he said. It was thus that I was launched on a career that I hadn't even thought about till then.

Raju's trail had long gone cold, but this was of no importance to my father. He sent me off every morning to interview anyone who might have known him or Savitri's former servant, and in the evening he would bring me books, borrowed from the college library, by famous journalists – Khushwant Singh, Frank Moraes, James Cameron, Kuldip Nayar – all of which he insisted I read to get a feel for journalistic prose and the art of constructing a good piece. Initially it was my father's enthusiasm that propelled the project along, but I was soon fully committed as I began to channel my own simmering rage and frustration into the story.

In the end, it wasn't an especially good article; we were amateurs, and simply did not have the skill to craft a great piece of journalism. I did not keep a copy of it, but I still recall its rather baroque opening line, which owed more to my father than it did to me: 'On 6 October 1990, P. Raju travelled further than he had ever done in his young life, a journey both temporal and spiritual.' I remember we looked in our battered *Concise Oxford Dictionary* to get the exact meaning of 'temporal' and several other words that were much too ornate and ponderous to feature in a normal piece. It didn't exactly surprise me that none of the major newspapers and magazines that we sent the story to bothered to reply, with the exception of *Time* magazine's office in New Delhi, which sent us a standard two-line letter of rejection. Undeterred, my father set his sights lower, and we sent out another batch of photocopies of the article with the same result.

Some months after we had first sent out the article, he came home from work, visibly excited. He pulled from his briefcase a very unglamorous magazine, printed entirely in black and white with no perceptible attempt at design, not even a proper cover, merely the title in a rather becoming shade of green over the table of contents. *The Indian Secularist*, the masthead read, and beside it, in smaller letters, Vol. 20: issue 11.

The magazine, which he had discovered in the college library, comprised forty-eight pages of closely set black type rather like an academic journal. Most of the articles were semi-academic in nature and concerned themselves with issues of sectarian and communal conflict. Besides these, there was a round-up of international and domestic news and on the last page an editorial by Rustom Sorabjee, the paper's editor, printer and publisher. But what had especially caught my father's attention was a column entitled 'View from the Front Line', in which various committed citizens, and occasionally the paper's regular contributors, wrote about instances of communal conflict or amity they had witnessed in their daily lives. 'This is where your article will appear,' he said; 'there couldn't be a better match.'

We mailed a revised and updated copy of the piece to *The Indian Secularist*'s offices on Carmichael Road in Bombay, and ten days later there was a reply. On a postcard, in copperplate handwriting, Mr Sorabjee wrote that he had admired the piece and was willing to publish it if I was open to making some editorial changes.

I was about to dash off a reply, my enthusiasm now as great as my father's at the prospect of seeing our piece about the unfortunate Raju published, when my father stopped me.

'If he likes your article, maybe he wouldn't be averse to employing you. Why don't you write and ask him about a job?'

He brought home a pile of back issues of *The Indian Secularist* the next day, so my letter to Mr Sorabjee could make suitably enthusiastic references to the magazine, and after several attempts he finally approved my letter of application. My wait for the post from that day on took on the same sort of intensity it had in the days when I had first sent out applications for jobs. This time Mr Sorabjee did not reply as quickly, and I began to lose hope. However, three weeks later I received a response. In his neat script Mr Sorabjee apologized for the delay in getting back to me, but said he'd had to attend to a personal matter out of town; if I was still interested, he would be pleased to invite me to an interview in Bombay. I would be reimbursed second-class train fare to and from the city, and as soon as he had the dates of my arrival he would have me booked into a lodge near the office.

The day before I was due to leave for Bombay, my father suggested we go for a walk in the maidan. This was unusual because we didn't often do things together; there was always a certain distance between us. We walked for a while in a somewhat awkward silence, then my father began talking about inconsequential things – it was clear that this was quite difficult for him. I wondered whether he saw in my departure from K— to the big city something that he should have done twenty years ago; was his hope that I make something of myself intricately bound up with his own long-abandoned dreams? It is often true that the most profound things surface at the end of a protracted conversation, and so it was that after we had completed a circuit of the maidan and were walking back home my father began telling me a story about a cousin of his back in Salem who had been a brilliant athlete in his youth, a long-distance runner. He participated in and won his speciality, the 10,000 metres, in every inter-collegiate and amateur sporting event in the district. His greatest rival for the mantle of top distance runner in the state was a man who studied at Loyola College in Madras. The two had raced against each other once before, but not since they had each grown to be so dominant in their event. The big showdown would take place at the annual inter-collegiate event in Madras, and there was an extra honour the athletes would vie for – a chance to try out for a spot on the Indian Olympic team.

My father told me that his cousin decided to add an extra element to his training routine – he travelled to Madras a month before he was due to compete and ran every morning on the soft shifting sands of Marina Beach, dragging a rickshaw behind him. His endurance had always been a feature of his athletic excellence but now he raised it to a different level.

On the day of the race, the stadium was packed. The Madras man had the stands full of raucous supporters, while my father's cousin ran virtually alone, with just my father and another boy to cheer him on. He ran a magnificent race, and as the runners came up to the last lap, the crowd fell silent, for the Salem boy looked as fresh as when he had started out, whereas his rival looked exhausted, the breath heaving out of his slender body in great waves. My father's cousin was in the lead by a few feet, a position he had held for most of the event, and as the gong sounded he raced confidently into the last circuit. His rival held on, barely, and then midway through the lap came the moment the fans had been waiting for, the final kick that would carry one of them to victory. The athlete from Madras, who until then had looked on the verge of collapse, reached deep within himself, found one last pocket of energy, and began accelerating forward. He drew level with his rival, and then began to surge ahead. When my father's cousin looked for his own kick he found nothing there. He could have run another 10,000 metres without any problem – he had enough stamina to spare – but during his long hours of training on the beach with the rickshaw, which had invested him with prodigious endurance, he had neglected to practise the final sprint that would separate the victor from the rest of the field.

'What it comes down to in the end is timing and the last push forward. You've done everything you can to prepare, Vijay,' my father said, 'just don't ever forget the final kick.'

2

The Indian Secularist

The cornices and fretwork of Jehangir Mansion were crumbling, scaffolding propped up the west wing, but the grandeur of the five-storey building was still unmistakable 122 years after it was first built. Stately gulmohars and peltophorums kept out the tumult of the city from the wealthy enclave in which the building stood. It was from here that the legendary Rustom Sorabjee had published *The Indian Secularist* for a little over twenty of his eighty-three years. The magazine, still printed on one of the last surviving letter-presses in Bombay, had never missed an issue in this time; neither big events nor small – riots, cyclones, government censors, lawsuits, the death of Mr Sorabjee's wife – had prevented its appearance on the first Monday of every month in the postboxes of its 3,200 faithful subscribers. At its peak, during emergency rule imposed by Prime Minister Indira Gandhi in the 1970s, when virtually all the mainstream media had meekly submitted to government pressure to conform and prevaricate, the magazine's defiantly independent stance had caused its circulation almost to quadruple. Once law and order returned to the land, however, the surge abated.

The Indian Secularist broke no new stories and was printed on cheap paper, but its faithful readership was not buying it for any of these things. They subscribed to it for its mix of informed commentary and analysis of the sectarian mischief of politicians and priests and especially for Mr Sorabjee's thoughtful editorials that he still wrote out in long hand to be typed up on an old-fashioned Godrej typewriter by only the second secretary he had employed since he had started the magazine. Mrs Dastur, who had come on board when his first secretary had died a decade previously, was a small woman with iron-grey hair and oversized lilac-framed spectacles – an unexpectedly ill-judged touch to her attire, which was otherwise restricted to sober skirts, white blouses and sensible shoes. She was devoted to her employer, and guarded him with a ferocity that anyone misguided enough to cross him soon discovered. Mrs Dastur was the one who announced me the first time I met Mr Sorabjee. She led me into a room with high ceilings which, at first sight, seemed overwhelmingly given over to paper. Old issues of the magazine, newspapers, government reports and files stuffed with clippings were strewn everywhere on the sofas, bookshelves, sideboard and desk.

'Don't take too much of his time, he's had a bad attack of gout,' she whispered and left.

Her employer was a small man with a large domed head that was totally bald and spattered with liver spots. He put me in mind of a judge, with his commanding nose and deep-socketed eyes – a figure of trust and authority. He shook hands with me, murmured, 'Mr Vijay,' and indicated that I should sit on the only chair besides his own that wasn't littered with paper. A telephone rang in the outer office, and Mr Sorabjee cocked his head as if to hear what his secretary was saying. Then he said quietly, 'I have published this magazine for two decades, Mr Vijay, and I have rarely despaired as much about the country's future. Not since we put the insanity of the partition killings behind us have I felt things were so bleak; communalism seems to have become an everyday thing. And all because of a small group of people with a self-serving agenda and those who have been taken in by them. That's why I was so heartened by your article – the sense of disgust with the way things are is good to see in someone so young. Although we're one of the world's oldest civilizations, in many ways we are a young country too, so it's crucial we chart the right path for the future.' The large domed head shook as if in sorrow and then he added, 'But I am sure we will have plenty of time to talk. Shall we start the interview?'

I had prepared for this day as I would for a final exam. With my father's coaching I had studied wide swathes of Indian history, ploughed through the scriptures of all the major religions and memorized the sayings of holy men on the universality of God. Most importantly, given the bias of the magazine, I was reasonably informed about the violence instigated by religion in the country – over half a million dead during the partition of the subcontinent, nearly 20,000 dead in riots, the majority of them Muslim, in the country since independence. It had made for depressing reading, the endless catalogue of destruction and death engineered by calculating politicians and holy men, but I had carried on, determined that there should be no question that Mr Sorabjee had that I didn't have some sort of answer to. He was my path out of K—, I was sure about that, and I was determined not to be found wanting in any way. And then, to my chagrin, the very first question he asked stumped me.

'How do you see yourself, Vijay?'

I was nervous so might have been excused my stammering attempts to answer the question, but the truth was I didn't quite know how to. I could have spoken at length on why I wanted to work for *The Indian Secularist*, the evils of sectarianism and the role of the media, but how did I see myself? What sort of question was that? Should I be completely honest and say I saw myself as a twenty-two-year-old unemployed youth with an undergraduate degree in economics who was so desperate to get out of K— that he would do anything Mr Sorabjee wanted – shine his shoes, marry his daughter, carry water from the well, milk his cows ... The seconds passed, and I finally found my voice.

'What do you mean, sir?'

'Don't be nervous, Vijay, take your time. I was just curious to know how you see yourself.'

'As a South Indian, sir?' I hazarded.

He nodded vigorously in approval. 'Yes, indeed, a South Indian. And?'

'A BA in economics, sir.'

'Very good, young man. Tell me more.'

'A Tamil, sir.'

'And?'

'A Brahmin, sir, although I'm no great believer in caste or religion.'

'Do you mind telling me why?'

I told him then about my experiences in K—, about how I had begun to feel oppressed by the very things that seemed to nourish and reassure my peers.

Mr Sorabjee listened attentively, and when I had finished said, 'You have handled your situation sensibly. But, tell me, why didn't you lose your faith?'

I replied that because of my upbringing my own faith had never been so strong that I had felt restricted by it, and therefore tempted to discard it; what I had disliked was the way faith in general had made the environment I lived in claustrophobic.

He nodded and said, 'I'm very glad to hear that, Vijay. Here at the magazine we don't believe in throwing religion overboard. Our stance is that it has its place, it only turns malign when it exceeds its boundaries.'

I was quite comfortable now as I had expected to be asked this sort of thing at the interview, but then, without warning, the questions became unorthodox again.

'If you don't mind, I'd like to set the subject of faith aside for the moment. May I ask who your favourite cricketer is, Vijay?'

'Kris, sir. Srikkanth, I mean.'

Mr Sorabjee smiled. I noticed he had perfectly white, even teeth, and then it occurred to me that they were probably dentures.

'Not Azharuddin, Kapil?'

'Oh, they are brilliant cricketers, but ...'

'Very well, let's move on. I assume you're a movie buff. Who are your favourite movie stars?'

'Kamal Hasan, sir. And I also like the old Sivaji Ganesan movies.'

'Good. What about books?'

'I have read several books by top journalists, sir.'

And so it went for another ten minutes, with Mr Sorabjee eliciting my preferences in song and food, my views on marriage and friendship, the weather and fashion. Apart from the brief exchange we'd had about my personal experience of religion, not once did we discuss the politics of faith or any of the myriad other subjects I had studied. At the end of his questioning, Mr Sorabjee said to me, 'Well, that's all I have for you, young man. Do you have any questions for me?'

I had grown tense as the interview continued to meander along without touching on anything that I hoped would clinch the job for me; now, without intending to be quite so forceful, I blurted out, 'But sir, don't you want to know my views on politics, on communalism . . .'

'I already know everything I need to know,' Mr Sorabjee said with a slow smile that folded the skin at the corners of his eyes like a concertina. 'Let's see, what we have here is a young, single, economics graduate, a Tamil Brahmin from K— who prefers Krishnamachari Srikkanth to Kapil Dev and Kamal Hasan to Amitabh Bachchan, who listens occasionally to M.S. Subbulakshmi and doesn't really know too much about contemporary popular music.

'And this young man wants to work for an old Bombayite with a degree in philosophy from Wilson College, a practising Parsi who is fascinated by every other religion that has taken root in this country, a widower who has had to give up red meat on account of his gout, whose cricketing geniuses stopped with Farrukh Engineer and Sunil Gavaskar, who loves to go to Western classical music concerts, Dvořák and Tchaikovsky preferably, at the NCPA auditorium, who is partial to Shakespeare especially the tragedies, whose favourite hero will always be Cary Grant, and, well, I deliberately didn't bring up heroines, young man, we're all entitled to some secrets . . .

'I might have got the order a bit wrong, but I believe I have covered pretty much everything we talked about. I can see you're puzzled by my apparent lack of interest in your reasons for wanting to join this magazine, Vijay, but the very fact that you are here for this interview is reason enough. In the course of the next few months I will have plenty of time to explore your credentials, nothing you could have said to me in half an hour would have made a difference. I was a student myself once, and we Indians are the best in the world at soaking up information and spitting it out on demand. No, Vijay, I wanted to discover as many facets of you as I could in the time that we have, and tell you in turn as much as I could about myself, because in my long years with the magazine I have discovered that the core of the battle we're fighting is this: the fundamentalists have always sought to pare people down to a single dimension, their religious identity, and in doing so exclude everything else about them.

What we're trying to say, in our stubborn way, is that each of us contains worlds within us; we are so multi-faceted that we will not be put into little boxes, segregated and turned against one another.'

He paused, and then said, 'Do you know why I named this magazine *The Indian Secularist*?'

'Because it champions secularism, sir?'

'Yes, indeed, but I had something more in mind when I was thinking about a title for it. So let me ask you this: how would you define secularism or better still the word secularist?'

This was one of the questions I had prepared for. 'The *Concise Oxford Dictionary* defines it as someone who is concerned with the affairs of the world, not the spiritual or the sacred.'

'Quite so, which is why it was important to me to have both the words *Indian* and *Secularist* in the title because taken together they stand for something far richer and more resonant. The Western interpretation of secularism is the strict separation of Church and State, but as that would never have worked in this country, where religion permeates every aspect of daily life, our founding fathers took it to mean an even-handedness or neutrality towards all faiths. We practise secularism in the Indian sense of the word without quite realizing it – while we remain true to our faith we tolerate every other faith without much of an effort. I don't necessarily mean that we fraternize with one another, but the unique strength of our society is that over the centuries most of us have developed an innate secularism that allows us to coexist fairly amicably. Unfortunately this secularism has always been under attack by people with a less than savoury agenda and that is where we have a role to play.'

With that, to my amazement, the interview concluded, and Mr Sorabjee told me the job was mine should I want it. I would join the magazine as an editorial assistant on a salary of 3,500 rupees; he would make arrangements for me to stay at a working men's hostel run by a charitable trust in Colaba and said that it would be most convenient if I could arrange to come on board in the first week of January.

'You don't need to give me your answer immediately, Vijay; you may wish to discuss this with your parents.'

'But I can tell you right now, sir, I would be delighted to take the job. I know my parents will be delighted too. You will not regret this decision, sir.'

'Very well, then,' he said with his slow smile. 'Shall we spend some time on the article that started it all?' He took my piece from his cluttered desk and over the next forty-five minutes wielded an ancient, broad-nibbed Mont Blanc pen like a scalpel, editing, moulding, shaping, querying, until the article was unrecognizable to me. It was still mine, but it was immeasurably better, I could see that.

'I'm so pleased you investigated the case of Raju,' he said, bringing his pen down to cut out an irrelevant phrase. 'Nothing will illustrate better to our readers what these messengers of hate are trying to do.'

'Yes, sir,' I said, feeling a little guilty that I had no idea where Raju was and that some of the information in the piece had been concocted. What would I say to Mr Sorabjee if he enquired about my sources? I didn't have long to wait.

'Is all the information in the piece verifiable?' he asked me.

I was tempted to try and finesse my way out of the situation, but decided it wasn't worth it. 'No sir,' I admitted. 'I have no idea where Raju is and some of the facts are speculative.'

'Umm, can't have that; let's have another go at it, shall we?' He went over the piece again, and by the time he'd finished, it was a mere quarter of its length.

'We have to be truthful and factual whenever we can, Vijay, because we're fighting lies, half-truths, beliefs, don't ever forget that.'

'I won't, sir,' I said, relieved that it hadn't gone too badly.

'Very well, then, you must be anxious to get acquainted with your new colleagues, so let's go and meet them.' He levered himself out of his chair, grimacing with pain, took hold of a walking stick made of some silvery metal, and limped out of the office.

The three other members of *The Indian Secularist*'s editorial team worked in a large room, their view brightened by an avenue of flowering gulmohur trees, frothy confections of red, green and gold. The assistant editor was a cheerful woman called Sakshi Vaidya; she was assisted by the copy-editor, an elderly man called Mr Desai whose editing skills I would discover were, if anything, even more exacting than Mr Sorabjee's, and a young intern, a recent graduate of Sophia College called Meher, the granddaughter of a friend of Mr

Sorabjee's who was spending a year at the magazine before taking off to Columbia University. Once introductions were made, Mr Sorabjee took me back to Mrs Dastur, shook hands with me formally, said goodbye and hobbled back to his room.

Mrs Dastur asked to see my train tickets, which I had fortunately remembered to bring with me, then efficiently counted out a small stack of rupee notes as reimbursement. She then added 400 rupees to the pile.

'It's your first time in Bombay, isn't it?'

When I nodded, she said, 'Mr Sorabjee thought you should have a little extra money to go out and enjoy yourself.'

An antiquated lift, manually operated by an old man in a Gandhi topi and khaki uniform, serviced the five floors of Jehangir Mansion. You could hear it coming from a long way off, the sound of its iron gate being opened and shut echoing through the lift shaft as it rose, slow as melting tar, towards you. That afternoon it was much too slow for me. I took the wide, shallow stairs, one, two at a time, and rushed out on to the road, anxious to share my good fortune with someone. I smiled and nodded and tried to make eye contact with passers-by and was not put off in the least by the fact that nobody in this most indifferent of cities would return my smiles or my desire to establish a bond. I was free of K— that was the most important thing. Bombay belonged to me, whether anyone cared or not. At the bus stop, waiting for the bus to Chowpatty and Marine Drive, I gave a legless beggar perched on a low wheeled platform fifty rupees, much more than I could afford, but it didn't matter, and I was beside myself with delight to see his warty, sour countenance soften with pleasure for just an instant.

At Chowpatty, I merged into the crowds milling about the beach, bought sweet and frothy sugar-cane juice from a man who fed the purple sticks of cane into an enormous hand-operated juicer, ate pav bhaji and bhel puri and walked until I was exhausted. Night was falling when I took my place on the sea wall among amorous couples, retired people and other solitary men like myself, all looking out to the horizon where the colour was fading from the sky. Behind us Marine Drive circled the bay in a necklace of light and over to the east more lights began to come on in the tall buildings of Nariman Point and Cuffe Parade. Night fell abruptly and the massive promontory of the city that extended into the sea began to resemble nothing so much as a great ocean liner ploughing steadily through the black water. My journey, I thought, had finally begun.

3

In Bombay

Bombay is not an attractive city. It has few tourist sights, its architecture is functional for the most part, the salt air from the Arabian Sea takes its toll on the most expensive buildings, and slums, noise, dense crowds, humidity, crime and pollution further deplete its charms. But it is one of the world's great cities with a vitality that defies belief, derived from the fourteen million people who call it home. I felt that charge from the minute my train deposited me in the early hours of the morning at VT station; all about me lay what looked like sheeted corpses, transients who slept on the railway platforms because they had nowhere else to go. I took a taxi to the hostel, an expensive luxury but unavoidable because of the enormous suitcase I was carrying, peering out of the window at the people who swarmed the streets, although it was barely light. These were my people, I thought; I was a Bombayite now. I could hardly wait to take the city by its throat. That didn't happen of course because, as I soon discovered, Bombay's sense of possibility and adventure was largely an illusion – none of the pretty girls who waited for the buses or the trains showed the least interest in me, no strangers walked up to me on the street and revealed mysterious worlds, but even as I scaled down my expectations the thrill of living in the city did not leave me.

And I had my own niche, the magazine I worked for, without which I might have felt the indifference of the city more keenly. Every morning at 8.15 I would take the bus from Colaba Causeway to Tardeo, which was a short walk from the office. And every day, even when it was very hot or traffic was slow or the queues for the communal bathrooms at the hostel had been very long, the sight of Jehangir Mansion never failed to lift my spirits. Just a few hundred feet away was the unceasing roar of Warden Road, but in this blessed corner of the city there was peace – the squirrels flickering their tails as they raced up the trunks of the gulmohar trees, the harsh cries of crows clattering down on the delicate gold tracery of fallen leaves and the passage of the occasional car were the only things that disturbed the tranquillity of the place. The creaking lift would deposit me on the fifth floor and I would make my way to the office, where I was usually the first to arrive. I would head straight to my desk to read through the thick files bulging with government reports or newspaper clippings that Mr Sorabjee or Mr Desai had cut out and marked for my attention as one of my jobs was to put together a brief digest of sectarian violence in India and around the world.

Once a month I was expected to put the magazine to bed. On press nights I would eat supper at Olympia, a local restaurant famous for its brain masala, perfectly cooked and soaked in rich gravy. I had only begun to eat meat in Bombay, because it wasn't cooked at home, but I had developed a liking for it very quickly. Finishing my meal with a paan that I would purchase from a vendor across the street from the restaurant, I would leave at about ten for the press, which was located just behind the paper merchants' quarter in the Fort area. During the day the place heaved with noise and activity – squadrons of businessmen and clerks and secretaries scurried to and from the cliffs of office buildings that surrounded the open square on three sides, while traffic flowed slowly and noisily through the clogged streets – but at this hour it was usually deserted. I would walk in through the loading dock at the back of the building, nodding to the chowkidar, who no longer bothered to check my pass, and negotiate my way carefully up a rickety wooden staircase to the compositors' room where the typesetting machines clattered away, lead filings drifting down like silver rain. The press where the magazine was composed and printed was one of the very few that had survived the onslaught of computerized phototypesetting, and it had about it an almost prehistoric air. The typesetters, dressed in shorts and banians because of the oppressive heat of the room, their eyes protuberant and enormous behind the thick lenses of their spectacles, would pound furiously at their keyboards and small boys would run off long sheets of coarse paper on which the proofs were printed, and bring them damp with ink and sweat to a long ink-splotched table at which I would read them. At around two in the morning I would finish up and go home, passing through the colonnaded archways of Flora Fountain as the city swooned in a half-sleep, deserted except for a few freelance whores who were either too ugly or too old to have a pimp or room of their own, and other people of the night – homeless petty criminals and those whose shifts started early. I was entitled to the day off when I was on press duty, but I couldn't bear to sit around in my room at the hostel so I would doze off for a few hours and then make my way to Jehangir Mansion at noon.

It was at the magazine that I began to develop a real appreciation for my own faith and the other religions that had flowered in India. Sakshi, who was working towards a PhD in comparative religion, would spend hours talking to me about the evolution of Hinduism, the various reform movements that had swept in, the ways in which Islam and Christianity had become Indianized, the origins of Buddhism, Sikhism and Jainism. I even started to look upon K— a little more kindly when she told me that she would love to see the musical pillars at the temple. One of the rooms at Jehangir Mansion had been converted into a library. It was crammed full of books on religion, and under Sakshi's tutelage I began reading translations and interpretations of the Vedas, the Upanishads, the Koran and the Bible among others with greater insight than I had back in K— when I was preparing for my interview with Mr Sorabjee.

As the months passed and I became an integral part of the editorial team, I no longer had much time to read because there was always work to do, research for Sakshi and Mr Sorabjee, sub-editing under Mr Desai's expert guidance, correspondence to be dealt with, phones to be answered and files to be kept up to date. As the two most junior people in the office, Meher and I quickly formed a bond. We would help each other out and often take a few minutes during the morning tea break, when Divakar the peon served us all tea and Marie biscuits, to chat and joke and trade harmless gossip. But even my liking for her and my appreciation of my other colleagues paled into insignificance when compared with the presence of Mr Sorabjee in my life.

I had never really had such a role model before, nobody in my family or my immediate environment had possessed the requisite stature, and I found myself craving his approval and attention. He dealt mainly with Sakshi and was otherwise well protected by Mrs Dastur, but it was enough for me just to have him around, and on the days he singled me out for praise I was exhilarated. If Sakshi had sparked my interest in religions it was through Mr Sorabjee that I began to understand just how insidiously faith was being politicized and perverted in the country. 'We should consider ourselves fortunate that the two religions that have dominated India's history, Buddhism and Hinduism, are two of the most benign and inclusive religions ever conceived by man. That is why, no matter what they do, the fundamentalists can never change the basic nature of our country. But they can do plenty of damage and that is why we must never stop speaking out,' he said to me one afternoon while discussing the forthcoming issue's cover story, a brilliant essay on Indian identity by a famous economist. That day, on my way home, thinking about the single-minded purpose that had informed his life, I wanted it for myself. And gradually, what had started as a desire to emulate Mr Sorabjee evolved into a genuine belief in the ideas and philosophy that motivated my mentor.

﹏❦﹏

The seasons wheeled and turned in their heedless way, the brief spring was followed by summer and then a particularly severe monsoon. The city's services broke down almost immediately. Gutters overflowed, houses and apartment buildings fell down, parts of the city flooded drowning cars, lorries and the occasional drunk, and after a few weeks of this, my health began to give way. I had a cold or a mild fever almost constantly, and for the first time since I had arrived in the city I began to feel low. I found my night shifts especially trying. In the badly lit streets around the press it was impossible to avoid wading through stretches of stagnant water polluted by sewage, muck and industrial waste. One night on my way home, in weather so foul that even the most desperate whores and street people had been driven to find shelter, I was subjected to a final indignity: I fell through an open manhole, and was plunged up to my throat in foul-smelling sewage. Fortunately I wasn't hurt in any way and managed to scramble out, but that night I caught a chill and was laid up for four days with a high fever.

My room-mate, an advertising executive called Rao who spent most of his nights out drinking and sleeping with an assortment of girlfriends, could only care for me in an abstracted way; his assistance, for which I was not ungrateful, consisted of buying me some strips of Crocin from a local pharmacy and bringing me tea and a couple of slices of toast from the mess in the morning. Thankfully I was befriended by Deepak, my next-door neighbour, who I discovered was originally from a town not far from K—. He would look in twice a day, once in the morning before he set off for work, and once in the evening when he returned, usually bearing a packet of food – baida rotis from Bade Mian, uppuma from the Udipi on the corner or mutton korma from the Afghan restaurant behind the Taj. I usually wouldn't have the appetite to eat anything, especially when I was running a fever, but I was glad to have Deepak's company. He worked for a large engineering firm located in the western suburbs and was saving up to buy a flat when he turned thirty a year from now; at this time he intended to marry one of the young women that his mother kept throwing at him, have two children and then concentrate on his career and his family. A short man with skin so dark that his thick bristly moustache hardly showed up against it, Deepak had lived in Bombay for eight years and loved every aspect of it. He promised to take me out with him in the evenings when I got better.

My illness underlined the fact that I was friendless, alone in the city and had little but my work to keep me going. It was while I was in this fragile emotional state that I began to think more about Meher. She had continued to be friendly and perhaps even mildly flirtatious with me in the confident way that seemed to come naturally to rich, attractive Bombay girls, but it was still an office friendship, nothing more. Then, one day, during our lunch hour, she suggested that we walk over to a trendy restaurant by the Kemps Corner flyover for a cold coffee. She had heard that morning she had been granted a partial scholarship by Columbia, and was in a mood to celebrate. That little excursion outside the office was when my feelings towards her changed from friendship into a mild infatuation. I suppose I should be able to recount every aspect of the drink we had, after all it was the first time I had ever gone out with a girl, but unfortunately over time most of the details have thinned away. What I do remember is the unconscious habit she had of flicking back her straight, glossy hair every time she leant forward to sip from her glass. She was intensely pretty in the way petite women can be, and I can recall her even today as she bent over her drink in the dimly lit restaurant, her long slender fingers tucking wayward strands of hair behind her ear, from the lobe of which a single oval of lapis glowed a mineral shade of blue.

On our way back to the office it began to rain fitfully – it was still the middle of the monsoon season – and she playfully grabbed hold of my arm and suggested we make a run for it. I am sure she meant nothing by the gesture, but the touch of her fingers burned their way into my senses. Although I realized the impossibility of my infatuation – the difference in our status was much too great and she was due to leave for the States in a little over a month – a lifetime of deprivation, when it came to women, distorted my sense of reason. I fantasized about her, intensely, purely, but I did not reveal my feelings to her; I was both too intimidated as well as too proud to lay myself open to rejection.

And so what began as an infatuation quickly turned into an obsession, in the way that only a first love can. My world turned brown and desolate when the workday ended, and brightened again the next morning. On the days she didn't turn up at the office I would rage with jealousy at the thought that she might be with someone else, although she had never mentioned a boyfriend. If I were a poet I might have plaited my longings into creative work – after all great art often springs from the chasm that lies between longing and fulfilment – but I was no artist, and so I passed day after day morose and angry for the most part, cheering up when our eyes met or she laughed at something I said. Was she aware of my passionate longing? I think she must have been; I believe beautiful women are always able to sense when men are interested in them. But whether Meher knew or not she gave no outward indication that anything between us had changed. And then the day came for her to leave. We bought a chocolate cake from a patisserie on Nepean Sea Road for her farewell party, Mr Sorabjee made a short speech to thank her for everything she had done and to wish her well in life, Meher giggled prettily through her own speech, and then she was gone, and my loneliness deepened, grew immense.

I took to leaving the office exactly at closing time and boarding buses to various parts of the city – Bandra, Khar, Malabar Hill, Chowpatty, Juhu – where I would spend an hour or two aimlessly wandering among the crowds, nursing my unhappiness, eating fried foods from the hawkers' stalls, eyeing women more beautiful than I'd ever seen, with the sole exception of Meher, as they made their way self-consciously and skilfully through great swells of male attention. But unrequited love is usually not a fatal affliction, and gradually I began to grow more positive in my outlook. I immersed myself in my work, and reasoned to myself that somewhere in this city of endless possibility there would be a woman for me.

Towards the end of the monsoon Deepak came to my room and discovered I had no plans for the evening. He suggested we go out. As he possessed neither the sophistication nor the connections that enabled my room-mate Rao to wander among the beds of the princesses of Cuffe Parade, Deepak made do with the whores of Shuklajee Street. When he discovered I was still a virgin, he swept my protestations aside and, after a few shots of Old Monk in his room, we found ourselves in a leaky taxi crawling through the flooded roads towards Shuklajee Street, where the madam of one of the brothels was expecting a consignment of fair-skinned, moon-faced, 'almost virginal' whores from Nepal.

The taxi dropped us off in one of the poorest areas of the city. Deepak, who could barely contain his excitement at the prospect of the women who awaited him, tipped the driver a hundred rupees and we floundered through dirty water to a building that seemed in imminent danger of collapse. The bouncer at the door looked astonished to see us, it had obviously been a day without customers, but his demeanour changed in an instant when he recognized Deepak. With a cry of 'Palang-tod Master' he hauled us in out of the rain and up a narrow staircase to a parlour where five girls lounged on two sofas. The attempts to make the place alluring were depressing. The sofas were covered in green Rexine, nylon saris had been strung up as curtains, garish posters of corpulent actresses torn from film magazines were stuck to the walls, and the glare from a cheap multicoloured chandelier from Chor Bazaar only served to accentuate the hopelessness of the place. But Deepak seemed to notice none of this, and the madam, a gargantuan woman casually draped in a sari, more than made up for the deficiencies of her brothel by enthusiastically crushing him to her shapeless bosom.

'Ah, Palang-tod Master, not even the weather could keep you away, could it? Today you get two girls for the price of one.'

'You said there would be new Nepali cheez,' he said in his Tamil-accented Hindi.

'The rains have stopped everything, alas, but there's Shalini and you haven't tried Neeta yet, have you? Her nipples are the size of rupee coins.'

Two of the girls got up obediently at a signal from the madam, and it was then that Deepak asked the mistress of the house to look after me.

'He'll be taken care of, Palang-tod Master, he'll be taken care of,' she bellowed jovially as he was led away by the two girls. I had been feeling more and more uncomfortable as Deepak and the brothel keeper bantered on, but now that he had vanished I wanted nothing more than to leave the place. To make matters worse, a blurry vision of Meher in the restaurant, the glow from her earring misting her face in blue, came to me, and it was all I could do to keep from bolting down the staircase and out into the rain. The madam must have sensed my discomfort because something approaching pity entered her voice.

'You're new to this, aren't you? Think nothing of it; I have seen many young men like you. There will always be a first time, and it is my duty to make it memorable for you. Think of me as your own mother, I'll make sure you're cared for. Anita is very experienced, she'll be gentle and loving, or, if you like, Bindu is a spitfire – after you have had her, you will never want to look at another woman again.' I was so unsettled by now that I didn't even react to the madam comparing herself to my mother; instead I was furious for landing myself in this situation, I was furious for not being firm with Deepak.

'Take your time, beta, it's a slow night, take all the time you want.'

And that's when it struck me that I was the one in control here – the brothel keeper couldn't do anything that I didn't want her to do, and for 300 rupees she was mine to command. Decisiveness entered my voice, and I said clearly, 'I don't want Bindu or Anita, I want you.'

She couldn't have been more than thirty-five, but her years of whoring had coarsened her. She was gross, with a triple chin, vast shapeless breasts, bad skin and a behind that had a life of its own, yet suddenly a huge desire grew in me to have my way with her.

Her self-confidence faltered when I made my demand but she recovered quickly enough. 'Ah-ha, the young stallion wants to ride a mare with enough capacity to swallow a whole ship of lesser cocks. I like that spirit, beta, chalo.'

The whores on the sofa tittered as she led me away. But by the time she had drawn the curtain around the cubicle and motioned to me to sit beside her on the plank bed in that tiny space that reeked of semen, incense and stale food, my sense of power and the surge of desire I had felt had ebbed away. Her small shrewd eyes, bagged in layers of flesh and kohl, missed nothing.

'You're terrified aren't you, beta? But there's nothing to be scared about. I'm so pleased that you have chosen me. I feel like a young girl again, waiting for the first thrust of your manhood, I never thought I'd experience that sensation again. Come now, let me take off your clothes.'

If her words were practised, they didn't seem like it. Her heavily be-ringed hands went to the top of my shirt but I pushed them away nervously.

'Fine, let me take off my clothes, then maybe you'll want to take off yours.' She unwound her sari, slid the blouse from her shoulders, and her breasts swung into view. They were not a pretty sight, cumbrous and falling almost to her navel, but I had never seen a grown woman's breasts before, so I gaped at them. 'Do you want to touch them? If you're really nice to me I'll let you,' she said in a high-pitched little girl's voice, then guffawed, revealing her paan-stained teeth.

I was beginning to feel bilious – the Old Monk I had drunk earlier in the evening, the whore's cheap perfume, the close fetid air of the cubicle and my own nervousness were beginning to come together in an unpleasant way and my stomach began to churn. The woman didn't seem to notice my discomfort. She raised her hips and slid her petticoat off, then turned to me.

'Do you like what you see, you little badmash?' she asked coquettishly as she stood and shimmied her hips. She then did a slow pirouette, her belly following her hips just a fraction slower, swaying like a sack with the movement. The vast masses of flesh almost covered her incongruously neat pubic thatch, and as she revolved in front of me I caught sight of an angry red pimple high on her massive behind. I could take it no more. The bile that had been steadily rising in me ever since we had entered the cubicle now surged up and I began to retch.

The fabled humanity of whores is overrated. Abandoning any further attempts at seduction, the madam lifted me up and marched me across to a washbasin in the corner of the cubicle. 'Don't dirty my room, you useless bakra. That chutiya Deepak should know better than to bring me babies who haven't outgrown their mother's breasts.' The warmth had gone from her eyes, they were hard little seeds of anger in her ravaged face. Quickly rinsing out my mouth I stumbled from the room.

After the fiasco at the brothel Deepak kept his distance from me, and my craving for company vanished for the moment. I was still at an age where I believed every setback should only be seen as a spur to advancement, so I attacked my work with a new ferocity. In time

I might have tried to do something about my situation, but that was not to be. I and all the other inhabitants of the city were about to see our world rearranged in a way that would drive everything but fear from our minds.

4

City of fear

In Mr Sorabjee's cluttered and utilitarian office there was a single decorative object. The room faced east and on the wall opposite the window was an antique mercury wheel barometer. When the morning sun slanted in, it would kindle a deep caramel glow within the instrument's satinwood finish. Catching me staring at it one day, Mr Sorabjee told me that he had bought it cheaply almost thirty years ago in Chor Bazaar. He had been advised to get it valued because it was a fine example of the work of Francis Pastorelli, a renowned maker of scientific instruments in the mid-nineteenth century, but as he had no intention of selling he had done nothing about it. When I remarked on the fact that the pointer seemed to indicate that it was stormy when it was in fact a fine day he said that a barometer told you what the weather was going to be, not what it was like at the present moment; then he smiled and said the needle had been stuck in that position for as long as he could remember.

A week after we'd had our conversation I would have occasion to think ruefully that my employer's barometer may not have been very good at predicting the weather but that it was prescient when it came to the political situation in the country. The Hindu right-wing organizations bidding for political power had embarked on the final phase of their campaign and the stage was set for what Mr Sorabjee's editorial later described as the fourth greatest tragedy to befall independent India since the partition riots, the assassination of Mahatma Gandhi and the 1984 massacre of Sikhs in Delhi.

On 6 December 1992, as a supine government watched, hundreds of rioters demolished the mosque in Ayodhya that had been the object of their venom. Immediately, a long comet's tail of violence swung across the country and tens of thousands of lives were affected.

In the past Bombay had always taken a sensible view of riots elsewhere in India. It believed that it was its own country, and if it was going to have riots and other disturbances it would manufacture them itself – it had its own crooked politicians and gangsters, it had no need to follow the lead of some politician from the Hindi heartland. Also, as the city's riots were usually restricted to the poorer sections of town, nobody you knew, except perhaps the office peon or the dabbawallah who brought you lunch, was affected. Work went on as usual in the great steel and concrete canyons of Nariman Point and Dalal Street, the parties continued in Malabar Hill and Cuffe Parade, and the great ship of the city would rock briefly on the swells caused by the commotion and then continue to sail serenely on.

This time, the riots were different. Immediately after the mosque was demolished, there were reports of scattered cases of stabbing or assault by Muslims outraged by this insult to their faith. The reaction from Hindu mobs, egged on by fundamentalist political parties, was unimaginably savage. Muslims were sought out and killed wherever they could be found – in crowded tenement buildings, slums, mosques where they had sought shelter, trains and buses. They were burnt alive in their shops and places of work. If the victims were young and pretty and female they were raped before they were killed. Older women were merely beaten up before they were murdered. Milkmen and bakers, neighbours and people who had been part of the same local cricket team, no one was spared in an orgy of violence that was unlike anything the city had ever seen. To make matters worse, with some exceptions, the police either looked the other way or even encouraged the rioters. People had been killed in the past, often as a result of religious bigotry, but it was in December 1992 that Bombay lost its way.

I was working harder than ever because Mr Sorabjee had decided to put out a special issue of the magazine to decry the demolition and the sectarian violence it had unleashed everywhere in the country. On the third day after riots broke out in the city, I came home from work a little earlier than usual and noticed that the reception area and the courtyard in front of the hostel were unusually full of people. At any other time I might have stopped to see what was going on, but I was very tired so I continued on to my room. Just as I was walking up the stairs I heard a familiar voice call out my name. It was Rao, my elusive room-mate, who was at the centre of one of the groups animatedly discussing the riots. It rapidly became clear why there was such a crowd. In the evenings most of the residents of the hostel would go out as was to be expected of single men in a big city, but now no one was sure that it was safe to do so. The night belonged to the rioters, and although so far most of the victims had been Muslim, there was always the likelihood that the flames could reach out to others, especially those who belonged to other minority communities or were newcomers to the city. As a sizeable percentage of the residents of the hostel were non-Hindu or from outside Bombay, few of them wanted to find out if that was indeed going to happen.

Rao was part of a gang listening to Deepak, who was describing a killing he had witnessed from his office. A window in his firm's building overlooked a Muslim slum and he was telling the group how it had been ransacked by a mob frustrated by its inability to find anyone to kill.

'I could see them milling around, with lathis and choppers, trying to figure out what to do next. The streets were so deserted it was eerie. The last time I saw something like that was years ago when there was a total solar eclipse over the city and no one would venture out because it was considered inauspicious.'

'What happened next? Come on, yaar, get on with it,' Rao cut in.

Deepak looked irritated by the interruption but didn't remonstrate. 'The rioters set a couple of buildings on fire, but it was clear they didn't have too much petrol or other weapons; they had just rushed out on to the street to kill as many Muslims as they could, and now they couldn't find any. The leaders of the mob were arguing amongst themselves about what to do next when their prayers were answered. A taxi came pelting down the deserted road, obviously driven by a Muslim – the stupid fellow hadn't bothered to take off his topi or shave his beard. I don't know what the poor fucker was thinking. If I had been him, I would have put the car in reverse and made a run for it, but maybe he thought he could ram his way through the crowd. He didn't stand a chance, a couple of stones were flung at the windscreen, and the car veered off the road. After that there wasn't a whole lot left to see.'

'Did you actually see the guy die?' someone in the audience asked, sounding hopeful.

'Of course I did,' Deepak said, and then reluctantly corrected himself: 'We couldn't see very much; there were about a hundred men trying to get their hands on the taxi driver. I think they beat him to death, and then set him on fire. We called the cops, it took us a long time to get through, and when we finally managed to speak to them they promised to come but no one did.' Deepak had little more to add, and his audience began to drift away, eager to soak up more information about the riots.

⁓ೕ ೪⁓

Back in my room, I let my satchel drop to the floor and lay down on my bed fully dressed, not even bothering to take off my shoes. I took in my surroundings – two iron cots with thin, skimpy mattresses, mine made up and Rao's in a mess as usual, the large unwieldy chest of drawers, its wood scarred by former residents of the room, the oxidized mirror on the nail, the peeling paint, the clothes hanging on pegs driven into the wall – and a feeling of desolation swept over me. I thought about the taxi driver who had been murdered. Deepak hadn't said whether he was young or old, but I imagined him to be as young as I was, and there was a good chance that he, like me, was a recent immigrant to the city, perhaps from Hyderabad, or some smaller place that did not have enough work or resources to hold on to its young. He would have come here hoping to make his fortune, and maybe in time he would have.

Why had he worn the badges of his faith to the very end, I wondered. Even when his life was at stake, why hadn't he thought to take them off? Maybe they were so much a part of him, he hadn't even seen them as symbols to be discarded. They would have helped him link himself to a community, of course, until he had saved enough to bring his family over from his home town because it was

45

likely he had married young. Until this fateful day, his religion would have saved him from the loneliness of the room in the chawl or slum. He would go to the mosque, meet others as lonely as he was. They would do their namaz together, celebrate the great festivals of Id and Ramzan with feasts of biryani on Mohammed Ali Road. Yes, his religion had been good to him, until the day it had devoured him. Just like that. What did others like him feel, to be singled out for no reason other than having been born into a different faith? I wanted to find out just as I wished to understand how faith drove the agents of persecution.

In the course of the past few days, as our work at the magazine had grown feverishly busy, I had become aware of vague feelings of discontentment that had swiftly crystallized. I did not want to merely rehash the reports that had appeared in the dailies; I wanted to do more than sub-edit eloquently worded editorials. I wanted to go out on to the front line where the battle was being fought and report on it. That was what I had imagined myself doing when I had first thought of becoming a journalist, and never before had it seemed more important. I thought of my father telling me about his dreams for me, for himself. I thought of his cousin, the distance runner who had lacked the requisite 'kick' when it mattered, and the feeling grew in me that the time had come to make my move. My job at the magazine did not involve reporting on events but surely, I argued to myself, Mr Sorabjee would not mind me writing a piece for 'View from the Front Line' about what was happening in the city.

Outside my room, the pigeons who made their home in the eaves settled in for the night. Footsteps approached the door. For someone so small, Rao walked with a heavy tread. 'Hey, this is really a bummer, you know all this shit going on in the city – it's putting a dent in my party scene . . .'

I wasn't paying much attention, I was still thinking about how I might get to cover a riot, but Rao didn't seem to need me to participate in the conversation.

'Apparently the rioting is going to get worse, the Sena and others have just got started, they'll be going house to house soon, the cops are with them, the ministers are with them, they are going to play Holi again this year, only with blood instead of colour.'

I could detect no sympathy for the victims in his voice, perhaps my room-mate thought riots were the same as his parties only a little more high concept. As I half listened, an idea began to form in my mind. Although I wanted to witness a riot, I wasn't sure I had the nerve to go it alone, but if I could persuade Rao to accompany me it would be perfect.

'Hey, Rao, want to see if we can find some action?'

'You mean, like, babes?'

'No, riots, I'm a reporter, remember.'

'That's a brilliant idea, man.'

'Do you know where Deepak is?'

'The mad fucker said he was off to Shuklajee Street. Riots or no riots the man needs to get his rocks off.'

'Oh well.'

'Drink in Gokul's first?'

～∂❀～

We left the hostel slightly before nine. There was no breeze, and the night was warm but not unpleasantly sticky as it could be during the summer and the monsoon. We walked briskly down Wodehouse Road, and emerged on to Colaba Causeway, which was inscribed like a great glittering whip on one of the busiest areas in the city. The Causeway was usually humming with people, traffic, light and noise until very late at night but today its vigour was sapped. No crowds gathered in the lobby of the Regal theatre, spilling out on to its steps; the restaurant next to Sahakari Bhandar was deserted, and even the dense throngs that filtered past the pavement stalls filled with counterfeit and stolen foreign goods were noticeably thinner. There was light and music from Leopold's Café as the sailors, druggies and whores continued to party – it would take a nuclear explosion to shut the place down – but otherwise there was no noise. We could actually hear our heels on the pavement, and individual explosions of sound – the receding rumble of a BEST bus, the clanking as a restaurant downed its shutters, a beggar hawking and spitting on the pavement.

I was filled with a nervous exhilaration, afraid yet tense with anticipation at what we might encounter. This was what war correspondents and cops and soldiers must feel, I thought: the rush of adrenalin. At the same time, I felt vulnerable, stripped of the anonymity a city confers upon its inhabitants. I was not Muslim, my penis was not circumcised, I still wore my sacred thread and I could recite the Gayatri mantra, but the thought that my identity could be put to the test by some thug made me nervous. I remembered stories about South Indian and Gujarati immigrants being targeted by mobs in Bombay a few decades earlier, when they were accused by opportunistic politicians of taking jobs away from native-born people of the state, and I worried briefly about these riots losing their focus, turning from one target to another, and then let the thought go. I wondered what Rao was thinking about, he seemed a bit subdued, although I could sense that he continued to be excited by the prospect of witnessing a riot; I had no doubt that it would go down well as party talk. But did it bother him that he was South Indian and therefore at some slight risk? It probably hadn't even occurred to him, I thought, he floated in the bubble that encased the city's elite, far above the netherworlds where the less privileged lived and, from time to time, killed each other.

Gokul's was almost deserted when we got there. Usually, at this time of night, the low-ceilinged main room and the mezzanine that you had to bend over almost double to negotiate would have been thick with a fug of smoke and noise, waiters careening past the densely packed tables with trays of whisky, rum, bowls of peanuts, ice buckets and soda, but today only three tables were occupied and most of the waiters were crowded together at the back of the room, gossiping. We were served as soon as we sat down, and our waiter lingered to chat.

'They're going from gully to gully slaughtering the Miyans, saab. I myself saw three dead last night and tonight there will be more.'

It did not matter whether the waiter had seen three or thirty dead, by the time these riots were finished, every one of Bombay's residents, bar those too young to speak, would have their own impressions of a city gone mad. My imagination was now inflamed by the possibilities – a lead story in the magazine worthy of being nominated for the country's highest journalism awards, anchored perhaps by the words of one of the victims, a man dying from sword cuts or blows from a lathi. I could almost see the article in my head now, but the final piece of the picture eluded me, the dying man, and I realized that I had no visual reference to fuel my imagination. Nothing I had seen of these riots in print or television portrayed images of the dying, all that they showed was the dead. No, there was no substitute for actually being present at the scene of a killing. Rao, who was very talkative, had been chatting to me while I had been lost in my thoughts, and now he shook my arm impatiently, almost upsetting my drink.

'What are you thinking about, man, you've scarcely touched your drink?'

'Oh, nothing really . . .'

'See, I knew you weren't listening, fucker, what's the matter with you?'

The waiter had reappeared at our table, and I noticed Rao had finished his drink. I took a prolonged swallow at my own, gagging slightly as the rum flooded my throat. Although I had started having the occasional drink almost as soon as I arrived in Bombay, I was still in the process of acquiring a taste for the stuff.

'Saab, we're closing in fifteen minutes, manager saab says no more orders after this one.'

'What's wrong with you people? There have been riots before, nothing will happen to us here,' Rao said irritably.

'It's not my rule, saab,' the waiter said stubbornly.

'OK, two large Old Monks each, jaldi,' he said.

'I can't drink that much,' I protested, 'I'll puke for sure.'

'No problem, I'll drink three, man – I need the buzz. This is bloody exciting.'

I was briefly sickened by his callousness, but I needed him, I couldn't do this on my own. And besides, who was I to moralize? I wasn't going out to save lives, I was hoping to use the riots for my own purposes.

Soon, the shutters were clattering down, and the waiter reappeared to tell us it was time to leave. But we lingered, now afraid to step into a world where the old certainties didn't hold. I found my courage ebbing away and was fully prepared to walk back to the hostel but

Rao, fuelled by four rums, urged me on. It took us a while to find a taxi, the black and yellows seemed to have vanished, and when we eventually managed to flag one down the driver refused to take us to where we wanted to go. Finally, we managed to strike a deal – we would pay him a hundred rupees more than the fare, and he would drop us off a safe distance from an area where riots had recently occurred.

The taxi driver was a large man, almost filling the front seat. As we got into his vehicle I was immediately struck by the absence of religious objects the dashboard would normally have been crammed with – depending on the faith of the driver or owner, verses from the Koran, small crucifixes, reproductions of a variety of Hindu gods and goddesses or pictures of Guru Nanak. Sometimes, if the driver was hedging his bets, you would have portraits of the syncretic saint Shirdi Sai Baba, or an assortment of artefacts from every faith, divine protection to guard against suicidal driving and a variety of other dangers that could hurtle out of the Bombay night. As we drove along, I found myself wondering about the faith of our driver. Was he Hindu or Muslim? Would he take to the streets later tonight to kill, or would he be in hiding?

We were dropped off as agreed, and began walking. As we went deeper into the maze of streets, heading away from the storm of light and noise of the main thoroughfare, there were fewer and fewer people. In my memory the streets of the neighbourhood we passed through are a bluish grey, burned a dusty gold here and there by the occasional street lamp that worked. Although it was still only slightly after ten, I had never walked streets so deserted in all the time I had lived in the city. I grew ever more excited. And nervous. Beside me, I could hear Rao breathing heavily. After we had walked for about fifteen minutes, the city still and watchful around us, the tension growing with every step, Rao's rum-inspired courage began to give way.

'Let's get back to civilization, man, this is creeping me out,' he whispered.

'Come on, yaar, we can't go back now, just when things are getting interesting.'

'Two more streets and I'm out of here.'

'Fine.'

That was when we heard the scream, faint and muffled, but quite clearly that of a human being in distress. Grabbing Rao's arm I headed in the direction of the sound. We went down street after empty street but found nothing. It was difficult to pinpoint exactly where the noise had come from and it didn't help that the screams had stopped.

'Poor bugger's probably dead,' Rao said to me in a voice in which excitement and fear vied for supremacy.

We wandered down a few more streets, and just as we were about to give up and go home, I stumbled over something on the pavement. I hadn't been looking down but around, trying to figure out where we were, and in the dim light I hadn't noticed what seemed to be a pile of rubbish. But now, as my eyes adjusted to the light cast by a single street light about thirty feet away, I saw something that was to burn brightly in the nightmares I suffered in the aftermath of the riots.

He was a presentable young man, you could tell that from the lower half of his face, but something had gone terribly wrong with the rest of his features. The left eyeball had been gouged out of its socket, and the right eyeball had been slashed by a knife, and was cloudy and occluded by blood. These injuries hadn't killed him; below the chin, there was a surgically clean cut that had finally extinguished his life. In the few seconds that had passed since we had come upon the dead body, Rao finally found his voice.

'Ah fuck, oh fuck, let's get out of here, man, is he still living, let's call the cops, come on let's get out.'

We ran from there, and then slowed down when we realized we had no idea where we were going.

The very next street we turned down, we came upon what we had been searching for and were now desperate to avoid. Beside an old four-storey building propped up by scaffolding we saw fifteen or twenty men pounding away at something that lay at their feet. Off to one side, there was another figure lying in the street, legs curled up towards his chest, arms splayed out. I didn't feel fear so much as a heightened clarity of vision and perception. The dead man's kurta had been torn from his body and he had been sliced open, the flesh neatly peeled back from his stomach and the internal organs visible as if in a urology lab demonstration. Perhaps because of the position in which he was lying, nothing had spilled out, except a rope of blood that secured him to the dusty pavement.

It's hard for me to describe with absolute precision what happened next, although I learned from the counsellor I saw in the aftermath of the killings that this is a common symptom of post-traumatic stress disorder – victims almost always blank out the most extreme aspects of the violence they are witnessing in order to protect themselves.

The mob beating the man suddenly stopped as though they were reacting to some unspoken command. One of them picked him up with something of an effort as his body was limp – he may well have been already dead – and his arms and legs flopped all over the place. Another man approached the pair; then, as if they had practised the manoeuvre, the first attacker crouched down into a semi-recumbent position, acting as a support to keep the victim upright, while reaching up and pulling the victim's head back by the hair. The second man took up a comfortable stance and raised the weapon he was holding, a four-foot-long-sword. The first man let go of the head and, in the same instant, the swordsman whipped his weapon down and across with blinding speed, cleanly severing the victim's head from his body. It is here that my actual witnessing of the incident grows fuzzy. In the nightmares I was prone to afterwards, I would see the head flying off and the gush of blood, but on the day I saw none of this, only something more obscene than anything else I would witness that night – the neck abruptly collapsing on itself like a flaccid rubber tube.

Next to me I heard Rao muttering obscenities beneath his breath as he took in the scene, and then before I could do or say anything he yelled, 'Come on, let's go,' and began to run back the way we had come.

To this day, I can't tell you why I didn't follow him. Maybe it was some survival instinct telling me that if I ran I would seem guilty, and would therefore be killed, whereas if I stood my ground I might be able to reason with them. Or perhaps the thought had surfaced, no matter how foolhardy it may seem in retrospect, that here was my story, the one that I had come on to the streets to look for.

A couple of men at the fringes of the mob looked up when Rao yelled, caught sight of me, and alerted the rest of the group to my presence. Instantly, all the men turned their eyes on me, including the one holding the sword.

It was too late to move. A man detached himself from the group and ran towards me. He stood no higher than my shoulder for I am reasonably big, just under six feet tall. As he came up he took a clumsy swipe at me with the lathi he was carrying. The blow wasn't well aimed and didn't hurt. I caught hold of the weapon and said firmly, 'I'm Hindu. Don't touch me.' I was speaking in English, and the man, struggling to release his weapon, swore to his colleagues in Marathi, 'Behenchod says he is Hindu.'

The same survival instinct that had rooted me to the spot now told me that I couldn't let go of the lathi and that things would go badly for me if my assailant managed to free himself. It sounds as if I was fully in control of the situation, weighing my options and acting in a measured manner, but it wasn't so at all – everything I did was automatic, controlled by some little-used part of my mind.

A man, evidently the leader of the mob that now surrounded me, came up and slapped me so hard that I almost fell. I relaxed my grip on the length of bamboo that my first assailant was wielding and it was wrenched free. As I staggered back, determined to stay upright no matter how often I was hit, because to go down would be to die, the man who had slapped me said, 'Gaandu, you aren't Muslim, are you?'

I shook my head and murmured, 'Hindu.'

'Behenchod, everyone in Bombay says the same thing. How do I know you're not lying?' My horror deepened when I noticed the man with the sword standing just behind my interrogator, listening to every word.

'Ask him to drop his pants, then we'll see if the maderchod is telling the truth ...' someone shouted.

The one clear part of my brain that was fighting for my survival impelled me to say, in the pidgin Hindi I'd acquired since I'd moved to Bombay, 'Why should I drop my trousers, will you drop yours?'

I was rewarded with another bone-rattling slap, another hand reached for me and I could hear my shirt tearing.

A voice piped up from within the mob, 'Madrasi lagta hai ...'

And then another, 'Behenchod, he's wearing a thread ...'

The tearing of my shirt spared me from further damage. As soon as my attackers saw the sacred thread I wore and realized I was Hindu, they began turning away. Later I would feel ashamed that I had taken refuge in my Hindu identity when my life was at stake – it didn't seem the right way to stand up to terrorism committed in the name of God – but in the moment I felt only unadulterated relief.

'Mind you, don't tell anyone about what you saw here. Remember we can find you no matter where you hide. Chalo, let's forget this pitiful chuthiya ...'

And then they moved away, leaving me in the street with two dead men. Suddenly, one of the mob turned back. It was the little man who had first attacked me. Raising the lathi he carried, he brought it down on me in a fury. I hadn't been expecting this and could do nothing to defend myself The blow landed on my head and I staggered back from the force of it. Mustn't fall, mustn't fall, was the only thought that went through my mind. He struck me a couple more times and I remember thinking for one so small he seemed tremendously strong, but I felt no pain, that would come later; all I was aware of was the encroaching darkness.

'Behenchod, this is for you to remember us by,' he hissed, spittle flecking his beedi-blackened lips. These last blows, I would later realize, had very little to do with religion. The man probably earned a meagre daily wage in a factory or godown, enduring the myriad humiliations of the blue-collar worker without any means of getting his own back. Until now.

'Eh, bewda, come on, let's go,' one of his friends shouted back, noticing his absence. 'We've got a couple of juicy Muslim women for you to play with on the next street.'

My attacker glared at me for a minute more, then turned away. It was over.

My experience of the riots was as nothing compared to the hundreds who died or were tortured and maimed, not to mention their families and friends who would remember the days the evil on the city's streets had invaded their pathetic shelters. There were two major spells of rioting: the first when I was attacked, and the second a few weeks later when gangs of rioters owing their allegiance to fundamentalist Hindu organizations began to kill Muslims even more systematically, aided by sections of the police force. I saw none of this for I was immured in Jaslok Hospital, where I was treated, at Mr Sorabjee's insistence and expense, for a mild concussion and a high fever brought on, according to the doctor, by the shock I had suffered as a result of the attack. There were other symptoms that any victim of trauma would recognize – memory loss, insomnia, stomach aches and depression – as I retreated into a personal darkness, away from a world I couldn't handle. When I was discharged from the hospital, Mr Sorabjee wanted to send me home to K—, but I pleaded with him not to, afraid that if my parents discovered what had happened, they would not allow me to return to Bombay. He came round in the end, but arranged for me to have counselling, and virtually placed me under house arrest in the hostel for nearly two months.

When the grey world I had sunk into was finally dispelled with the help of my therapist and a regime of antidepressants, I became obsessed with the riots. I read every word about them in the papers, watched reports on the television in the hostel's mess, and was desperate to get involved in some way with the peace marches, mohalla committees, fund-raisers and other measures that were being initiated as concerned citizens tried to put the city back together again. Failing that, I wanted to return to work on the magazine, it would give me a measure of engagement with what was going on. Mr Sorabjee was in the thick of the action, working with the energy and focus of a man half his age, but he would not allow me to leave my room and even threatened to dismiss me from his employ if I insisted on getting involved; all he would agree to was my helping with the magazine from the safety of the hostel. Every morning at 11 a.m. his chauffeur would come to my room with a stack of brown paper files and a large Thermos filled with glucose-enriched, freshly squeezed mausambi juice, and would return the following day to pick up the completed assignments and deliver a fresh batch.

During my days of rest and recuperation, although I chafed at the restrictions placed on me by Mr Sorabjee, I marvelled at my good fortune in finding such a benefactor. When we are very young our allegiances are extreme, and I recall that it seemed as if the course of my life was set for the foreseeable future and that nothing would stop me from serving the man who had been so kind to me with unswerving devotion and diligence.

The other person I felt indebted to was Rao. I couldn't have had a more unlikely saviour, this wastrel son of a wealthy Andhra landowner whose only aim in life seemed to be to enjoy himself as much as he could, but somehow he had summoned up the courage to come back for me. He had found me lying on the pavement and had bundled me into a taxi and brought me to the hostel from where he had telephoned my employer. He apologized profusely for running away, but I didn't hold that against him; I was grateful he hadn't left me in that street of dead men.

Of all the problems I suffered in the aftermath of the attack, the nightmares persisted the longest. Almost every night for weeks, I would have a dream that varied little in its essential details: I would be walking down a Bombay street much like the one I had been attacked on, with crumbling buildings and an absence of people. The street lamps on either side were of an unusual design, with human heads surmounting the columns. I would make a great effort to escape but some invisible force would pull me along, the tops of the street lamps shearing off and the columns collapsing in a welter of blood as I passed them. At the very end of the street was a seated figure. At my approach, the man, who was slouched over, would start to straighten up, and then, just as I was upon him, his eyelids would open to reveal orbs of blood. His mouth would stretch in a ghastly smile and he would begin to lift his right hand in which there was a sword ... and I would wake up, drenched in sweat and shivering violently. Fortunately for me, under the patient ministrations of my therapist, the nightmares eventually began to fade, and in a couple of months I no longer experienced them.

As time passed, the riots receded from the front pages of the newspapers, from public memory, from everywhere except the hearts and minds of the victims and the people who had come together to ensure that Bombay would never have to experience that sort of trauma again. At *The Indian Secularist* our mission took on a new dimension – we would try to do everything we could to ensure that the dead were not forgotten. We started a section in the magazine that was wholly devoted to short obituaries of the hundreds of ordinary Bombayites who had died in the riots. After consulting with my therapist and generally satisfying himself that I was completely recovered, Mr Sorabjee entrusted me with the task of collecting as much information as I could on these humble victims. I would travel to chawls, slums and footpaths to interview eyewitnesses and families, a task that was as depressing from the moment I started it to the day I was finally told by Mr Sorabjee to stop, when information became increasingly hard to come by. From then on, the magazine simply ran lists of names of the remaining dead, the only memorials these people would ever have.

Just when it seemed the city was finally getting over the riots, bombs went off in some of its most crowded localities, as the powerful dons of the Muslim underworld sought to avenge the massacre of people of their faith. It was a Friday, and we had already sent the forth-coming issue of the magazine to the printers, so Mr Sorabjee sent us home early, after telling all of us that he did not want us to go anywhere near the affected areas.

I heeded his injunction for as long as I could but by the evening of the next day I could no longer passively watch the unfolding of the tragedy on television. Arguing that I would be more or less following Mr Sorabjee's instructions by not getting in harm's way, all I wanted to do was see things for myself, I walked to the site of the nearest explosion, the Air India high-rise on Marine Drive. This was close to the place where I had watched the sun set on my first visit to Bombay. This time I did not look out to sea but faced the damaged building. Shattered glass coated the road like frost, and smoke black-ened the facade of the structure, otherwise the scene in front of me was strangely calm. But I didn't need to hear the screams of the dying to be assailed by feelings of rage and sorrow. When would this cycle of hatred and bloodletting end? Were Muslim murderers any better than their Hindu counterparts? How could the killing of hundreds more innocents be justified no matter how great the provocation? Perhaps what was needed was for the sea to rise up and flood the city, wasn't that what the Gods did when evil in the world grew too unmanageable, didn't they simply destroy their creation and start all over again?

All through the weekend my despair grew. I couldn't wait to get to the office on Monday, where I hoped that Mr Sorabjee would be able to offer me the wisdom and comfort I needed. But it was not to be for even Mr Sorabjee's determination to keep fighting for what he believed in was shaken by the latest round of violence. After a brief appearance in the office, he locked himself away in his private quarters, leaving word with Mrs Dastur that he was not to be disturbed. He missed his Thursday editorial meeting two weeks in a row, and didn't come back to work for twenty-two days. Sakshi, Mr Desai and I tried to cobble together the next issue of the magazine, but we were making little progress in the absence of the boss, so we went in a delegation to see Mrs Dastur. She was sharp with us. 'Mr Sorabjee is not well, but he expects you all to keep working. If you don't, how will the magazine come out?' We tried to explain the problem to her but she couldn't offer us a solution, so we went back and tried again; however, our desultory attempts were not stellar, and it seemed that *The Indian Secularist* would miss an issue for the first time since its inception.

But the next day when I walked into Jehangir Mansion, I saw to my delight that Mr Sorabjee was in the chair he usually occupied during editorial meetings, dressed in the spotless white drill trousers and long-sleeved white shirt he always wore, scanning the day's papers, ready to start the editorial meeting. I still remember what he said to us that day: 'We have always fought for what is right, and until last month I was prepared to go on doing that for as long as I had the energy and the means to do so. But after the bomb blasts, I wondered whether anything we do is going to make a difference – there are forces massing to destroy the plural masterpiece that this country has always been, and those of us who think this is deplorable don't seem to be doing any good at all. I have told all of you that we can never allow our voice to be silenced but is there any one around to hear us cry out? This is what I have been wrestling with for the past few days. This morning, when I woke up, I finally had my answer: if there is even one person left in the country to whom our message will make a difference, that person is the reason we will keep going. Let us never forget that, my friends.'

And so we went back to work. I was sent out to gather information for a series of investigative reports that the magazine intended to run on how one of India's most secular cities had been destroyed from within. Sakshi would write the articles and I would report them. I interviewed ordinary people accused of murder, the families of victims, volunteers who were helping with the reconstruction of the city, policemen, bystanders ... Often I would think I couldn't go on, the tales of brutality and pathos in my notebook were almost too much to bear. But I kept at it, as did my colleagues, and the tens of thousands who were trying to help, people from every faith and every section of society, all of us doing our best to heal the wounds inflicted on our city.

But Bombay would never be the same again. It was broken, its industriousness and resilience a sham, a thin veil that covered the deep-seated fear and suspicion that had taken hold of its inhabitants. The trains and buses ran packed to capacity every day, office workers and mill hands and shoppers and hawkers and beggars and pick-pockets and policemen went about their daily routine, but it was only because they had no option but to go to work in order to feed their families; they did not have the luxury of staying at home and building bomb shelters and stocking them with mountains of toilet paper and grapefruit juice and low-fat yoghurt as their counterparts in a Western city might have done. Bombay would live and die on its streets, its crowded bazaars and mohallas, and even as they went about their daily lives, its millions watched and wondered if they would be expected to sacrifice themselves for their city. But the same fear that ruled their lives hobbled the venal politicians and criminals who stayed their hands for the time being for fear of retribution from the other side. As the first anniversary of the riots approached we watched, and prayed, with the rest of the city that the fragile peace would hold. It did, more or less, and we went on.

The week before Christmas, Mr Sorabjee invited me to tea in his private quarters after work. This was unusual, and as I walked over to his room I wondered what infraction I had committed. When Mrs Dastur asked me to go in, I was surprised to find Mr Sorabjee had company. His visitor, a large man with thinning hair and a bulbous nose that dominated his face, was introduced to me as Mr Khanna, an old friend of my employer. Without wasting too much time on niceties, Mr Sorabjee said to me, 'Vijay, I know that the last time you took a holiday was nearly a year and a half ago, and you haven't taken any time off since, except when you were ill. I checked with Mrs Dastur and she said you weren't planning on going home this year. Now, while I don't think I should get involved with your personal life, I am concerned about you. Your health has not been the best, but you are a stubborn young man, and you don't seem to want to listen to me. So I've decided to take matters into my own hands. Vikram here owns a tea estate near a town called Meham in the Nilgiris. He has been wintering in Bombay for the past few years, he can't take the cold of the mountains any more, and during his absence he leaves his bungalow in the hands of his servants. I have spoken to him, and he is agreeable to your spending ten days there this winter. I have already booked your train tickets. You leave on the twenty-seventh.'

I was opening my mouth to speak, but Mr Sorabjee held up his hand to indicate that he wasn't finished.

'It's going to be a working holiday, young man, so don't think it's going to be all fun and games. I have two assignments for you. The first is that there is some sort of controversy in Meham surrounding a shrine called the Tower of God, one of the hundreds of brush fires lit by those rascals when they brought down the mosque. There is a Bombay connection, apparently, but Vikram doesn't know very much about that. I know you've been itching to write for the magazine, so consider this your first assignment. But a word of caution: I do not want you to get mixed up in this matter in any way. All I want you to be is a responsible journalist, collect the facts, and write a piece for our "View from the Front Line" column. That's all.'

I left his room elated. I had never been on a proper holiday before in my life, especially not to a hill station as celebrated as the Nilgiris, but more than that I was thrilled by the thought of doing my first proper assignment for the magazine. I couldn't wait to send my father a copy with my byline in it.

In my excitement I had forgotten to ask Mr Sorabjee what my second assignment would be but I needn't have worried because the day before I was due to leave Mrs Dastur, from whom I had collected my train tickets and money for expenses, told me that Mr Sorabjee wanted to see me.

My employer took me to his office. Next to his desk stood a Godrej steel cupboard. Unlocking it, he withdrew a slim manuscript which he handed to me. The title page read: *THE SOLITUDE OF EMPERORS: Why Ashoka, Akbar and Gandhi Matter to Us Today.*

'I've always been fascinated by them,' Mr Sorabjee said, 'the three greatest Indians who've ever lived. And why do they so easily assume that mantle of greatness? Because each of them, along with their other attributes, has embodied the one prerequisite that anyone who wants to be remembered as a great Indian needs to possess – a soaring vision for this country that transcends caste and creed. I wanted to write about them when I retired but then I started the magazine, which soon took up all my energy and passion and I simply didn't have the discipline to write the book in my spare time. However, I have wanted to write it for twenty-three years, and while she was alive my wife Bhicoo never failed to remind me about it. When she died ten years ago with not a page written, it was the biggest regret of my life, and I was determined to do something about it.

'Finally, when I thought it would never happen, a Bombay publisher approached me with an idea. They were textbook publishers but were thinking of starting a new series aimed at high-school students about the key issues facing the country today. I thought it was a very good project. There are so few books written for our children that are stimulating and teach them how to think that I decided to take on the assignment. Each book in the series was to be 10,000 words long, and the publishers were going to commission a famous painter to illustrate the text.

'They wanted me to write on communalism and how the country was going to tackle it. I have spent my life trying to educate adults to the dangers of sectarianism, but it is, if anything, even more important to mould young minds, don't you think? Young people, especially young men who are making the journey from adolescence to adulthood, are so full of energy and desires and the need to make their mark on the world that they will turn to anything that will make them feel fulfilled. This is why the fundamentalists find it so easy to recruit them, especially when they feel rejected or cast aside. But if they could be moulded in the right way, what a force for the good they could become!

'As I was thinking about how I might make the book interesting enough for a teenager, it struck me that this might be the way in which I could finally write about my emperors: I could use them as examples for my argument on how intolerance could be combated. However, I'm sorry to say the book languished; I'm a journalist, and asking a journalist to write a book is rather like telling a sprinter to run a marathon. And it might never have been written had it not been for the riots and the bomb blasts – they so anguished me that I wrote the book in a frenzy, in less than six weeks, pouring into it all my dreams of what I would like this country to become. I'm not at all sure that this is what my publishers are looking for, although there is nothing in it that an intelligent teenager couldn't grasp. But that's not the reason I'm bothering you with it: it's only that when I was rereading it, I wondered if it might not also have some appeal to young people of your generation, Vijay. I would be greatly obliged if you could read it and tell me what you think of it before I send it to the publishers.'

PART II

5

Journey to Meham

In the winter, visitors to the Nilgiris are rare. The gaudy entertainments of the summer are a distant memory, the big resort hotels in Ooty and Coonoor are empty and the mountains are restored to those who live there. I was pleased by this because the relative absence of touts and tourists was very welcome. The Toyota van I boarded to my final destination on the eastern edge of the mountains was almost empty, and I managed to get a good seat by the window. The driver told me that we would arrive in Meham in about an hour, and I settled back in my seat, glad that the journey was almost over. The long train ride from Bombay, an uncomfortable night in a waiting room at Coimbatore station, and the subsequent stretch the next morning by bus up a road that rose by a series of hairpin bends clipped to the mountainside, had left me feeling drained. By the time I changed vehicles in Coonoor, I was looking forward to a bath and the opportunity to rest for a while.

All morning long, as the mountains had loomed like a wall of blue smoke on the horizon, I had looked forward to being amongst them, but they hadn't made any real impression on me so far. This was not surprising given how exhausted I was feeling, but now, as we neared our destination, I began to take an interest in my surroundings, helped by the invigorating eucalyptus-scented breeze that began to flush the dirt and pollution of the city out of my system.

'In the old days, the British called the Nilgiris a sanitorium, you know,' Mr Khanna had told me in Bombay. 'It was where people went to recover, especially when they were run-down from months of living in the heat and grime of the plains.'

As the van made its way through low rounded hills that might have been plucked from a child's watercolour painting, past white-washed houses set in exact gardens, churches pleated into sheltered valleys, a golf course edged by a jade-green stream, all this enclosed in a pipe of air so pure you could feel its passage into your lungs, I could see what my host meant.

A few kilometres past Wellington, the road to Meham branched off to the right. A roadside marker announced that our destination was twelve kilometres away. I shut my eyes and had begun to doze off to the sound of the wheels on the road when a bone-jarring crash brought me fully awake. The van had hit a large pothole but it didn't appear to have been damaged in any way because the driver soon picked up speed again. It didn't seem a very sensible thing to do because the condition of the road had deteriorated alarmingly. It was pitted everywhere with large craters and in some parts had disappeared entirely, submerged under a foot or so of running water. None of this seemed to deter our driver. He drove as fast as before, crashing the vehicle through all the obstacles that were strewn in his path. I had heard it said that these ugly vans were built to withstand terrain even tougher than the one we were traversing but no vehicle could stand the sort of punishment this one was taking for too long. I wanted to get to Meham, so I leaned forward and was on the point of asking the driver to slow down when he brought the van to a stop of his own accord. Peering through the windscreen, it seemed to me that a part of the mountain had collapsed on to the road. I wondered whether this meant that we would have to return to Coonoor. And if this was the only road to Meham, and if things moved as slowly as I expected them to in a mofussil town, how long would it be before the obstruction was cleared?

'Landslides are very common in this area,' my neighbour said unhelpfully, but then uttered the magic phrase, 'No problem. Our driver is very experienced.' As indeed he seemed to be. He began edging the van on to the rubble, and I could now see that a rough passage, barely wide enough for a car to squeeze through, had been hacked through the obstruction. The wheels spun on the loose rock and gravel, and we were all asked to get off to lighten the van. This time the wheels began to gain traction, and the vehicle lurched forward.

As we picked our way through the rock and scree, I noticed that while I had been dozing the landscape had changed completely. Gone were the neatly barbered hills of Coonoor and Wellington with their sprightly cockscombs of eucalyptus and cypress, and sholas in the valleys; everywhere I looked there were towering crags of granite, slick with moisture and almost bare of vegetation. A dirty grey mist that seemed to be drawn deep from within the lungs of the giants that bore down on us poured through the clear mountain air, lessening the visibility ahead. As we climbed back into the van, the dangerous driving conditions began to worry me and I told the driver to go slowly. Either he deliberately chose to ignore me or had misheard, because no sooner were we settled into our seats than he took off at great speed. Fortunately, the road was so bad that it put the brakes on his suicidal notions. Although we were thrown around a fair amount as we ploughed through potholes and puddles, we seemed in no imminent danger of sliding off the mountaintop, and my nervousness subsided, even though the light was dwindling overhead. Perhaps there was going to be a storm. I remembered my host telling me that Meham was prone to more than its share of thunderstorms because of its location at the very tip of the Nilgiris. But I wasn't too concerned, the town couldn't be more than a few kilometres away now, and even if by some mischance we were stranded, help would be within reach. We rounded a corner and all my worrying was washed clean from my head by the spectacle that unfolded before us.

Above, the sky had grown dark and muscular and veined with lightning. Below, the earth fell away from the narrow road in tremendous cataracts of living stone, rearing up occasionally into a confusion of jagged peaks before falling again for thousands of feet into the heat-hazed plains. Between the hard, dark emptiness of sky and stone, thunder rolled and echoed without pause, and thorned whips of lightning cracked time and time again. There was no rain and, as if reading my thoughts, my neighbour said, 'There won't be rain. This is a peculiarity of Meham: often there are storms without rain, sometimes the Gods just need to play. It's not called the Tower of God for nothing.' I looked to where he was pointing and saw, at very edge of the escarpment, dimly visible in the poor light, a smooth almost cylindrical peak rising straight up from the choppy surf of boulders and forest at its base. 'There is a shrine at the very summit of the Tower of God. It's one of the holiest places in South India,' my informant said. 'It's been a place of pilgrimage for almost 300 years; people of all religions come to worship at the Shrine of the Blessed Martyr.' So this was the place that Mr Sorabjee had asked me to investigate. I hadn't expected it to be so spectacular, however, imagining it to be an insignificant place of worship that had suddenly attracted unwelcome attention because of the troubles elsewhere in the country. The van turned a corner and the Tower of God was lost to view. I asked my neighbour whether it was difficult to get to, and he said it wasn't if you approached it from Meham town.

'But the hill itself is very steep,' he added. 'There were quite a few accidents in the past but now the government has installed railings in the most dangerous sections, and it is prohibited to make the climb during the rainy season.'

⤟✵⤞

After the grandeur of the Tower of God the town of Meham came as something of an anticlimax. Growing like a mould at the base of a mountain, it comprised a cluster of small shops, a bazaar, lodges and showrooms that were mostly engaged in the buying and selling of tea, and further back an untidy straggle of houses. The bus stop was at the edge of town, and I immediately spotted Mr Khanna's driver standing next to a gleaming blue Contessa. He looked incongruous in his spotless white uniform and peaked chauffeur's cap but also very grand and I wondered madly for just a few seconds whether I should give him the slip and take a less ostentatious means of transport to my lodging. But the moment passed, and gripping my suitcase a little more firmly than was necessary, I went up to him and identified myself. The chauffeur stowed my suitcase in the boot and opened the back door for me. I climbed in gingerly and sat as carefully as I could on the plush cushioned seat. It was by far the most luxurious car I had ever ridden in. The chauffeur got behind the wheel and the heavy vehicle moved off, its weight soaking up every bit of roughness in the road, so that it seemed as if we were driving on glass.

My host had informed me, back in Bombay, that if ever I got lost in Meham and couldn't find my way back home I should ask for directions to the Englishman's House, because that was the name by which the locals knew Cypress Manor. The retired English tea planter who had built the bungalow over a hundred years ago, when Meham had enjoyed its brief heyday as a quieter, healthier, more scenic alternative to Ooty, had picked his location well. The house was built halfway up a hill thickly clothed with cypress and eucalyptus, and commanded an unparalleled view of the town, the tea estates fitting the low rounded hills in the north-west like skullcaps, and in the distance the great wall of peaks that marked the eastern edge of the Nilgiris. The road leading up to the house, in contrast to the other roads in the area, was in an excellent state of repair – I later learned that this was because all the residences on the hill belonged to the wealthiest, most powerful people in Meham.

Cypress Manor was a long, low bungalow with white distempered walls, doors and windows picked out in green and a roof of over-lapping red tiles. A semi-circular driveway separated the house from the garden, which stretched down the hillside in bright waves of colour. The afternoon was so sunny and clear that the storm that had threatened the Tower of God seemed to have existed only in my imagination.

There were no signs of life anywhere on the property. The driver pulled the car up to the front door, and, precisely on cue, an elderly butler clad in a spotless white veshti and turban emerged and made a deep namaskaram in my general direction. A younger servant followed him out of the house, and bowing if anything even more deeply, took my suitcase away. Unused to such attention, all I could do was stand around awkwardly until the butler asked deferentially whether he might show me to my room.

It is remarkable how quickly you can get used to a life of luxury, especially if there is no one around to observe you and make you feel self-conscious. Within a couple of hours of arriving at Cypress Manor, bathed and clad in clean clothes, including a brand-new sweater that I had bought specifically for my sojourn in the hills, I was luxuriating in a deep armchair in the living room sipping a cup of tea that was incredibly flavoursome compared to the rubbish I was used to drinking in Bombay. When I had finished, I decided to explore the house. I wandered through room after room, each as perfectly maintained as the next, the floors and metal polished and shining, the furniture and windows without dust or watermarks, the very air of each high-ceilinged space denuded of odour. I could have been in a museum. Nowhere did the house bear any traces of its owner; there were no family photographs or personal mementos, even the paintings and vases of flowers on the carved mantelpiece and sideboards were beautiful but impersonal. I contrasted the burnished neutrality of the house and furnishings with the disorder that marked every room of Mr Sorabjee's home, and wondered if Mr Khanna looked forward to his annual visits to Jehangir Mansion simply in order to get some clutter into his life, some balance. The sterile beauty and order of the rooms soon drove me out into the garden.

The scene outside could have been lifted from a tourist brochure – a sky so blue and hard that knives could have been sharpened on it, and light so clear that everything it touched turned to crystal. I am an urban creature through and through, without the least bit of interest in gardens and nature, but even my jaded city eye was momentarily diverted by the beauty that was laid out before me. About half of the garden was given over to flower beds, and the rest was planted with fruit trees. A line of poinsettia bushes, exuberantly coloured, marked the farthest boundary. Paths of beaten red earth laced the garden, and I took one of them. I recognized a few of the flowers – roses of pink and gold, thrusting their petals out for inspection, a blaze of yellow marigolds near the garage, hibiscus bushes lining the driveway, and a multitude of other plants and blooms, each individual leaf, petal and sepal distinct and perfect in the relentless clarity of the light. As I walked among the flower beds, my eye was caught by a row of short stumpy shrubs slathered with flowers in arresting colours. They looked like the cheap gaudy earrings a common whore would wear, but despite their seeming tawdriness, they were quite extraordinary to behold. I wondered what they were called, and looked around to see if there was a gardener I could ask. It was then that I caught sight of smoke rising beyond the thick clump of trees that marked the north-eastern corner of the property. As I approached the trees, I saw a short dark man with white hair and white sideburns that curved like riding boots down either side of his face feeding a pile of bluish-violet flowers into the fire. If he noticed me approaching, he gave no sign of it. I watched him for a couple of minutes, and then coughed to attract his attention. He looked up briefly, and then went back to his work. Unsure of what to do in the face of the man's rudeness, I was about to turn and make my way back to the house, when he said, still not looking up, 'You're the dorai from Bombay. Is there anything I can do for you?'

'No, nothing,' I said, hastily, and then without intending to sound as peremptory as I did, asked, 'Why are you burning those flowers?'

'Because,' he said slowly, 'that's the only way to get rid of them, although you wouldn't think it to look at them.' He plucked a flower from the pile and held it out to me. The petals were pale and almost translucent, so delicate they were already shivelling from being plucked. 'The morning glory is tough. It's the weed every gardener in Meham detests. It'll take over your garden, suck the goodness from the soil and smother every other plant. And it's virtually indestructible. It can survive pesticides, drought, frost ... The only way to get rid of it is to burn it. Very beautiful, very deadly.'

This little rant seemed to have exhausted the gardener, and he lapsed into a moody silence. He wasn't going to be the most helpful tour guide, I decided, so I left him to his task and continued to explore the garden.

The air was alive with the sound and movement of birds and small animals. By the time I left Meham, I would learn the names of the swifts that darted through the air snapping up insects, the green parakeets that flew as straight as jets at a fly-past, and the two varieties of bulbuls that ravaged the guava trees, but on that first afternoon in the garden, ignorant of almost everything that surrounded me, I felt profoundly out of place. The rural setting, the lack of people I could relate to, even the purity of the air and light unsettled me, and I was suddenly possessed by the desire to flee back to Bombay.

The feeling passed. I plucked a guava from one of the overburdened trees, and savoured the tart, sweet pulp and seeds, plucked another, and yet one more, realizing as I ate them that this was the first time I had actually eaten ripe fruit off a tree. Growing up in K— the best I'd been able to do was sample stolen green mangoes from a neighbour's grove. I rambled aimlessly around the garden a little longer, and then for want of anything better to do I went back into the house, ensconced myself in a comfortable armchair and picked up Mr Sorabjee's manuscript. The next thing I knew the butler was gently shaking me awake. Feeling sheepish at passing out fully dressed, I quickly went into the bathroom, washed my face and made my way to the dining room in the centre of which was an enormous teak dining table that seated twelve. A single place was set at the head of the table.

The butler apologized for the simplicity of the meal. He explained that one of his staff was sick and hadn't been able to go to the market, but it was an unnecessary apology – the rice, sambhar, fried mutton and beans kootu that were served wouldn't have been out of place in a fancy hotel in Bombay. I ate well, my appetite sharpened by the journey and the mountain air. After dinner, I strolled once more into the garden. The vast blackness of the night was sprayed with the glitter of stars and it was very quiet. To my city-bred ears, the absence of noise was something that took a little getting used to. I stood there for a while longer, thinking about the series of events that had brought me to this mansion on the hill, and I felt curiously distant from everything. The violence and dissonance of men in the cauldron of the city seemed to belong to a different world altogether. And then I remembered the admonitory finger pointing to the heavens, the Tower of God, which I had seen on the journey into town, and realized the peace of the countryside was probably an illusion.

It was beginning to get chilly, so I went back inside. The servants had returned to their quarters, but my bed had been turned down and a fire lit in the fireplace. What luxury, I thought, feeling a little embarrassed. I shrugged away the thought easily enough, changed and got into bed, but found that I wasn't sleepy because of my unscheduled nap in the evening. Mr Sorabjee's manuscript had been neatly arranged on the bedside table and, picking it up, I began turning the pages.

THE NEED FOR EMPERORS

Our Gods have always looked after us, through the good times and the bad. All 333 million of them - and I'm not talking here just of the Gods of Hinduism but of all the deities of all the faiths that have found a place in this great land - Islam, Christianity, Buddhism, Sikhism, Jainism, Judaism and Zoro-astrianism. It's quite a good arrangement, when you come to think of it, because our surfeit of Gods, one for every three or four of us, more than makes up for the lack of doctors, policemen, school teachers, nuclear scientists and judges. We make a few sacrifices to our deities, show them that we love, respect and venerate them, and in return they are expected to take care of all our needs and aspirations in this life and our lives to come. Our compact with the Gods has worked quite well for thousands of years, but it is broken, every now and again, and that's when we find ourselves in serious trouble.

Why does this happen? If we look at it from the point of view of the Gods themselves, I can think of a couple of reasons. First, our deities have plenty to do in their own world as well as in all the other worlds they are responsible for. As a result, from time to time they take their eyes off the affairs of men and catastrophes result: a tsunami or an earthquake, a train wreck or a building collapse, but these accidents do not threaten the world. More serious are the times when the Gods put forth their power to save mankind and it fails. No one quite knows the reason for this, not even the Gods themselves, and until their power is restored to them, mankind is extremely vulnerable. For this is when the old Gods, the pre-Vedic Gods, the Gods of Jahiliyya, the Gods of Naraham, a few lapsed Gods turned Demons, who were laid off when the new religions arrived on the scene a few millennia ago and

73

have nursed a grudge ever since, stage a comeback. These were Gods of war and devastation whom our distant ancestors worshipped in a time of great turmoil and fear, when a people could be exterminated by any number of things – natural phenomena, more powerful tribes, disease . . . Naturally they needed pahelwan Gods who could be asked to destroy any threat that appeared. The only problem was that the other tribes worshipped similar Gods, so there was a bit of a stand-off until new faiths were brought into being by religious geniuses of the time in order to put an end to the bloody cycle of destruction and regeneration that existed. The old Gods were abandoned but this didn't mean they went away; they just bided their time until the power of the new deities faded so they could rise again.

For rioters are nothing but the children of these unholy Gods. They do not lie when they say God is on their side. He is on their lips and in their hearts, and when they kill they do so on His command, this terrible deity striding out of the mists of time. How else could you explain the fact that, when weapons have acquired the sophistication to kill 'cleanly' and from a great distance, rioters still prefer to kill the old-fashioned way, with lathis, with choppers, with rocks, with their bare hands? Why do they burn their victims alive? Rioters, it is clear, are not making war; they are performing a holy rite, an act of loving worship to an ancient, terrifying God in which both the murderer and the victim are blessed by the sacrifice. This is why rioters feel no guilt, the men who send them out to kill feel no guilt, and the apathetic majority who watch and do nothing feel no guilt. Surely nobody can be expected to feel guilty for being pious?

The tearing down of the mosque and the riots and bomb explosions in Bombay are only the latest manifestations of our genuflecting to the old Gods and there will be more wanton acts of destruction in the name of religion unless we do something about it. So what is to be done? In order to get rid of the old Gods it is evident that we first need to sort out their proxies. But to rob the fanatics of their power we will first need to understand them, then checkmate them, and kick them out.

It is not difficult to understand how the fundamentalists gained power; they have always been around, like their masters the Gods of destruction, and again just like their masters they have had to bide their time before coming to power. When we – men and women of different faiths, classes and castes – gained independence and dreamed of a new India, we would not be swayed by the religious ideologues and mischief makers who threatened our tolerance, pluralism and stability – that way lay the road to another country, a country bedevilled by obscurantism, hate and religion gone mad. This, despite the violence of partition and the assassination of Gandhi. For what the great men who brought us our freedom did not forget was that India had always been the most plural of countries, a country that contained the world. Our people had come from everywhere: they were descended from central Asian tribes, Mongol warlords, Portuguese adventurers, Arabian seamen, Chinese travellers, Buddhist princes, Jewish wanderers, British traders, Christian apostles, Macedonian soldiers, and although it hadn't always been easy to adjust, we had managed to do so. I am reminded here of a story that was told about my own people. When we first landed on the shores of Gujarat, the local ruler didn't want to let us in – his kingdom was already full, and he didn't want his own people to lose their livelihood or have to put up with strange rituals and customs. Our leader asked for a tumbler of milk and a handful of sugar. He dissolved the sugar in the milk and said to the ruler, this is what we will be like. You will notice, Your Highness, that not a drop of the milk has spilled, but that it is now sweeter and even tastier to drink. We will merge with your society and our advent will make it better. If that was true of the Parsis, it is also true of those who came from elsewhere, every community has added its colour and flavour and is essential to this ancient land. Our art, our music, our architecture, our wealth, our philosophy, all this and more has been created by Indians belonging to every faith, every caste and every creed. When you contemplate a great painting, or listen to a great musician, or read a great book, or send your child to a great educational institution, or even buy a bag of cement to build your house, you don't pause to think about whether its creator is Hindu, Muslim, Christian, Parsi, Sikh or Jain; you merely enjoy it for what it is and at some level are thankful that all these great Indians have given generously of their talent for the benefit of us all. That is why when the fundamentalists seek to portray one Indian as somehow being more Indian than another their lies need to be flung back at them, and it is they who should be asked to leave this country, before their nefarious designs spell the end of India.

So why are we facing this time of darkness especially when the country's prospects have never looked so good? It would take a book several times the length of this one to adequately explain all the reasons that have brought us to this place but I will try and provide an overview. There are several proximate causes of course – incompetent, corrupt politicians who have made appalling decisions, local rivalries, ancient feuds that have never been properly resolved – but none of these are enough in themselves to explain the emergence of fundamentalism on a national scale.

Historians and economists tell us that nations are

ripe for ethnic and sectarian war when a combination of things happens at once - the blurring of ethnic boundaries which arouses the ire of puritans, the absence of enlightened government, but most of all the advent of sweeping economic change. It is at times like these that we are at our most vulnerable, and therefore liable to fall under the spell of false demagogues and prophets. This was true of Hitler's Germany and it is true of India today. There is a popular misconception that it is only when a country is on the ropes that citizen turns on citizen and a nation devours its own but history does not bear this out. Rather, it is in periods of great volatility brought about by an upsurge in economic activity when millions of people are severed from their moorings, when the great divide between the haves and have-nots deepens, when large sections of the population begin to feel powerless and confused as the gap between their expectations and reality increases, as the machinery of the state begins to break down, it is then that the rabble-rousers and politicians who promise security in the name of religion come into their own. When you are alone and far from home, frustrated by life at every turn, denied the comfort of your caste fellows and the minutely ordered web of village life, it is comforting to think that things will be better if only those pestilential adherents to a different faith could be shown their place. You don't pause to think how exactly your life would be better if someone else's place of worship were destroyed (does that put food in your stomach, make your own place of worship more sacred?) or an innocent or two from another religion raped (does that make your wife or mistress any sexier?) or killed (will that give you the office job that you have always coveted but aren't qualified for?) or how your religion alone will sort out all your problems because these

77

politicians are clever, they are convincing, and they tell you exactly how to think. But they don't want you to think too much because you might then wonder how almost 800 million Hindus could possibly be threatened by a little over 100 million Muslims, who are often poorer and more wretched than any other community in the subcontinent, or by 20 million Christians whose numbers are actually dwindling, although the fundamentalists would have you think that they are doubling their population every five years through conversion. Or ask how it is that Hindus are any more indigenous than Indian Buddhists, Muslims, Christians or Jews, when most reliable historians agree that the precursors of the Hindus came to this land many millennia ago from the central Asian steppe. Just like everyone else. Or ponder how this country would be any better off as a theocracy when everywhere we find examples of nations which regressed when they took that route – Pakistan, Iran, the Balkans ... Or question how the depredations of past rulers of the country can be laid at the door of fellow citizens whose only crime appears to be that they belong to the same faith. No, the right-wing politicians don't want you to think too much because if you did you would find they don't care as much about religion as they would like you to, oh no, they are as secular as the pseudo-secularists they excoriate. They are modern men who wish to get ahead, get power, get riches, and the easiest way to do that is to come up with religious symbols and populist slogans that will influence the millions who are rootless, impoverished and looking for a quick solution to their problems. However, to be fair to the politicians, it might be too much to expect them to deal with the real problems of this country – almost a quarter of a billion people below the poverty line, many hundreds of millions who are illiterate, several hundred million more without basic healthcare, drinking water and so on and so forth; they are not supermen after all.

But while it is easy enough to understand the motives of these people, how are we to stop them? For they cannot be permitted to rampage around unchecked, they cannot be allowed to turn Indian against Indian in the name of God or anyone else. We could hope of course that the majority of our people, who are by and large sensible and secular, will reject these agents of destruction of their own accord, but often for good sense to prevail there needs to be a catalyst.

The Gods, we have seen, are powerless to help at this point, so until they are reinvigorated, we must look elsewhere for aid. We don't need the assistance of priests or prophets or holy men, no matter how sagacious and wise: their place is in the temple or mosque or church or gurudwara or synagogue. The liberals and hard-core secularists, who are in the front line of the battle against the fundamentalists, are simply not strong enough to overcome the enemy; there are too few of them, and they are often discredited in the eyes of the masses because they seem too impious and as fundamentalist in their views as those they oppose. Who then can lead us out of the darkness? What we need is an emperor of men, someone who is so strong, commanding, brilliant, secular, compassionate and valorous that the forces of darkness will shrink back, powerless to stop his onslaught. What sort of characteristics should this paragon possess? Fortunately, we have a few role models from our own past who did in their own time what we would like our champion to do in ours. Only three men throughout this country's long, long history could be unequivocally declared great: Ashoka, the Emperor of Renunciation; Akbar, the Emperor of Faith; and Gandhi, the Emperor of Truth. Each of these men were not just ahead of their time, through their actions and lives they transcended time, became men for all time. Interestingly, each of them had to deal with religious conflict without losing his own religion, a quality any new emperor would need because no atheist or agnostic could have a vision for this country that would endure. My intention in this short book, then, is to try and understand for myself, and for you, the youth of our country upon whom our future rests, what made these men great and worthy of emulation. I am hoping our study of the essence of these men will help us recognize the new emperor – it occurs to me as I write this that he might well be one of you – when he finally arrives, so we can help him in his efforts to take the country to a place more glorious than anything we could have imagined for ourselves.

6

The plant hunter

I woke to an unfamiliar sound: birdsong coursing through the stillness of the morning. It was not yet light, so I didn't get out of bed immediately but lay there listening and marvelling, in a sleep-hazed way, at my present state. I was closer, in a geographical sense, to K— than I had been in over a year, and I was suddenly assailed by a sharp burst of homesickness. I scrambled out of bed and hunted for a packet of sweets that I'd bought on an impulse in Coimbatore and took out a square of mysore pak, the colour of amber. As I bit into it, I was transported back to Sri Krishna Sweets, a small shop next to the chaos of the main bus-stand in K— that I was taken to twice a month by my father when I was still quite small. The sweetshop was famous for its wheat halva, but the quality of all its wares ensured it was always packed with customers. There was barely enough space for two or three people in the shop, but nobody minded the cramped interior. Every available bit of space was given over to glass-fronted shelves bearing all manner of sweets and savouries – tottering mountains of halva oozing ghee, laddoos, round and golden as the sun, sticks of sweet mixture frosted with sugar, pyramids of murukku, crisp as kindling, athirasam, moonthirikai, kolukkatai . . . no matter how often we went there my ten-year-old self would reel from the choice that could be mine for a couple of rupees.

On my sole visit to K— after I had moved to Bombay, I had gone to Sri Krishna Sweets on the day of my return. The sweets were as delicious as ever but they didn't hold the same attraction, and as there was very little else for me in the town, within days I was longing to get back to the addictive energy of the city.

Unfortunately, my second rejection of K— included my parents as well. In my desperation to leave everything that had formed me behind, I shut the door on them. I compared them to the people I met and worked with, and was ashamed of them: their small-town ways, their lack of ambition and accomplishment. When I think about it now, all I can say is that in this I was not unique; I have found that ambitious small-town boys, unless they are exceptionally loyal and grateful, almost routinely pass through a phase where they discard their family. I had installed Mr Sorabjee in the position vacated by my parents and it was not until the riots took place that they were restored to me as I looked for every form of security I could find. I wanted them back in my life, and the letters that my mother wrote to me twice a month in her tiny handwriting took on a new importance. For much of my first year in the city I had barely glanced at them, and would rarely reply, but in the days after the attack I began to wait for them, pore over their contents, and reply to them diligently. The irony was that I couldn't tell my parents how much I needed them because, even as I longed for them, there was no way in which I could articulate my feelings, because I knew that they would demand that I return home, and perhaps contrive to make me stay in the bovine, unthreatening confines of K— for the rest of my life. As I began to emerge from the despair that had enveloped me, my need for my parents lessened, and although I was no longer as neglectful as I had initially been, they began to fade in and out of my consciousness.

As I lay in bed I thought about my parents, I felt ashamed that I had made up an excuse to avoid going home for the holidays this year. But the feeling didn't linger and my mind drifted to other things. How proud my father would be if he could see me now; could he and I have imagined, as we waited in line at Sri Krishna Sweets for our purchases to be wrapped in newspaper, that I would, one day, be holidaying in a palatial bungalow in the mountains ... about to receive my first real byline ... and dreaming about emperors? For my thoughts had turned now to Mr Sorabjee's impassioned introduction to his book. I wasn't sure how many of today's youth would actually heed his message, but I found his thesis fascinating. Like everyone who had had a measure of education, I knew about Ashoka,

Akbar and Gandhi, but yoking them together gave rise to all sorts of interesting possibilities.

A pale lozenge of grey appeared in the skylight of the wall facing me. I should get up soon, make enquiries about how I could get to the Tower of God. The excitement I had felt when I had first received the assignment returned, pushing the remaining traces of sleep from me.

~&~

There was a knock on the door, and a voice said, 'Morning tea, saar.' Upon being asked to enter, the young servant who helped around the house brought in a tray on which there was a teapot and other tea-making accessories, together with a plate of slightly soggy Glucose biscuits. I drank two cups, showered, dressed and emerged from my room to find breakfast laid out for me – a boiled egg, freshly squeezed orange juice and porridge – on an octagonal table in the enclosed verandah. I was impatient to get going but dutifully ate as much as I could while making a mental note to tell the butler that he shouldn't bother making breakfast for it wasn't a meal I was used to eating.

When he came in with fresh toast, I told him I only wanted morning tea from now on; I also asked if I could have the driver take me to the Tower of God. The driver had gone on a short holiday, he said, but he would try to get me a taxi from town. Taking my cup of tea, I went out on to the front steps of the house. The light was as clear as it had been yesterday and I could see for miles. I had noticed some lights the previous night, and I saw they belonged to a small cluster of huts and shops lining the road to town. The sound of children playing on the road floated up to me through the still air; at this height the shrillness blurred away and their voices took on a pleasing quality. The butler coughed from behind me, and said that unfortunately there weren't any taxis available today but that he had booked one for early the next morning. This was unwelcome news, as I had been looking forward to starting on my story. The beauty of the landscape, the brisk mountain air, the quiet that I was becoming used to, now seemed utterly without charm, as I imagined the day stretching ahead of me with nothing to fill it.

Just then we heard the sound of a vehicle coming up the hill, and

I grew hopeful; perhaps I could get a ride to my destination. But I thought it prudent to wait for confirmation that the vehicle was indeed making for Cypress Manor as I had learned that sound was deceptive in the mountains. More than once that morning I thought I'd heard a car or bus approaching the house when in fact the sound had carried there from some other place. This time, though, I hadn't been mistaken, for a few minutes later an ancient scooter driven by a skinny, old man spluttered up the driveway. The butler went out to meet the visitor, and when I walked over, he introduced himself as Moses, the pastor of the local church. He had come to invite Mr Khanna to their annual New Year's Eve concert, an event that my host had never missed in all the time that he had lived in Cypress Manor. This year, he had told the priest he was taking his holiday early, but that his guest might like to attend in his place.

'Are you a Christian, sir?' he asked hopefully.

'No,' I replied.

'Every faith is welcome at our New Year's concert so you must come,' he said. 'Our church is just across the valley. I'm sorry I can't stay, but there are a lot of preparations I have to attend to.' He pointed out the location of the church on the opposite hill – I could just make out a thin steeple that poked out of a mass of green – and then laboriously turned his vehicle and drove away. After he had gone, I asked the butler if it was possible to walk to town but he said that it was miles away and there were no bus stops close by. Feeling frustrated, I wondered if I should read more of Mr Sorabjee's manuscript, but there would be time enough for that. Excusing himself, the butler went back into the house. I drifted into the garden, plucked and ate a couple of guavas, and then, bored, went back to the house, where I sat down on the steps and weighed my much diminished set of options.

The only other person about was the taciturn gardener, who was weeding among the fruit trees, but there seemed no point in talking to him. Six butterflies flew past me in the next half-hour or so, some hectically, others languidly, and I watched them go by – a large one with blue scalloped wings, followed by two small yellow ones, a violet one with ochre and brown wings, a bright orange one, then another yellow. I began to grow ever more restless, although I kept urging myself to relax; I had barely been here a day, and it would do me good to take it easy for a while.

My conversation with myself was interrupted when out of the corner of my eye I noticed something move. Directly below where I sat was a sunken garden, with rose bushes ringing an oval lawn and a fish pond in its centre. Lying across the lawn, and hidden partially by a rose bush with sagging blooms of dirty pink, was a long brown branch, and it was this that seemed to be moving. Fascinated, I watched it coiling forward into the roses. 'Paambu, Nalla Paambu,' I yelled to the gardener, 'bring a stick quickly, there's a huge cobra in the rose garden.' I looked around for something to throw. Abandoning his hoe, the gardener trudged up the path scowling as I cautiously descended the steps. The snake was still disappearing slowly into the roses when the gardener came up to it, took a look, and then turned to go back to what he was doing. 'Kill the cobra before it escapes,' I yelled, but he seemed not to hear and continued to walk away from me. Prudently choosing a path as far away from the reptile as I could, I made my way to the lower half of the garden to where the gardener had renewed scratching away at the weeds.

'Why didn't you kill the snake?' I demanded.

'It's harmless,' he said, without looking up.

'Harmless?' I said incredulously. 'I have never seen a cobra that big!'

'Cobras don't come up so high. That was a rat snake, keeps the rat population down,' he said irritably. I was instantly deflated. I hung around uncertainly for a minute or so, and then, feeling the weight of the gardener's scorn, turned and made for the gate.

I walked past several barred gates and driveways that disappeared into vast properties, and eventually reached the valley. I knew roughly where the huts lay, and began to walk in that direction. I had no definite plan in mind besides the vague thought that perhaps I could get a glass of tea at a teashop and directions to places of local interest.

The cluster of huts came into view, fronted by the inevitable teashop. As I ordered my tea, I asked the grizzled proprietor if there were any interesting things to see within walking distance.

'Meham,' he said, after thinking for a while.

'But that's too far away, it will take me hours,' I said, immediately regretting the words. All these people, the proprietor, the three old men who sat on one of the benches under the thatched awning of the shop sucking at beedis, probably walked to Meham every day and thought nothing of it. To my relief, the proprietor did not react to my comment. The tea he served me looked thick enough to grow trees in. I took a hasty gulp and almost gagged. Not only was the tea hot, it was so full of tannins from repeated reheating that it nearly took the roof of my mouth off. But I wasn't about to be discomfited yet again, so I forced the tea down, paid, and under the impassive gaze of the customers and owner, strode purposefully away. I had no idea of where I might go but, as I left the huts behind, I saw the steeple of the church, and it occurred to me that I could call on the old pastor. Perhaps I could interview him about the Tower of God; as a priest surely he would have an opinion on the controversy.

The church was farther away than it looked. After walking for half an hour, I finally got to a road that wormed its way through a tunnel of green – cypress, casuarina, eucalyptus. As I emerged from it, I saw the church before me. It was unlike any other church I had seen – bright cherry red for the most part, with red-brick walls and a sloping tin roof and steeple painted red. Behind its impressive frontage of turrets and stained-glass windows was an altogether more modest structure rather like a low-roofed shed. Together the two halves of the church looked like a squatting unicorn. I was about to make my way towards it to examine it more closely when I was stopped short by the sight of a pack of dogs cruising aimlessly around the building. They were all mongrels, the skinny, smooth-haired creatures that fought for scraps at every rubbish dump and bus stop in the country, but the leader of the pack seemed to possess some pedigree – the shape of the head, the powerful jaws, the black and liver colouring and size all seemed to indicate some Dobermann in its ancestry. I've always been nervous around dogs, and my fear of them had increased when I was bitten by a stray about a year before I left K— and had had to undergo a series of painful anti-rabies injections. As I was hesitating between backing away quickly and standing still until they disappeared, the dogs turned and started cantering towards me. I looked around for stones I could throw at them but the hard-packed earth was devoid of anything I could use as a weapon. I couldn't outrun them on the road I had come by, and as I was frantically looking around for some refuge I spotted a high stone wall topped with broken glass. A small sign announced that the wall enclosed St Andrew's Cemetery. Without giving the matter any further thought I sprinted towards the cemetery's gates, hoping they were only barred and not locked. As soon as I began to run, the dogs started to bark and gave chase. We arrived at the gates scant feet apart, when they abruptly opened, and a voice, brimming with laughter, shouted, 'Godless. Bad dog!' I couldn't see the speaker, and the barking had not decreased, so I continued sprinting onwards.

'You don't need to run any more,' the voice said. 'Godless doesn't bite.'

I risked a look back and saw the pack milling around within the gates. A tall, thin man with an abundance of unruly hair and a full beard stepped out from behind a headstone, still laughing, and tossed something to the big dog, which leaped up and caught it in its jaws. 'Good boy, Godless. Now take your bitches and get lost; man can't get peace and quiet anywhere these days.' The barking died down, and the pack wandered off. The stranger shut the gates on them and turned to me.

'That was quite a sprint, I must say, but Godless would have got you if he'd had ten more feet.'

Now that the immediate danger had passed I could examine my benefactor a little more closely, and I wasn't entirely reassured by what I saw. The untamed hair and beard, the wild staring eyes, the torn T-shirt that might once have been green, the lungi casually knotted about his hips, the Bata chappals and his general unwashed air made me wonder if I should be looking to leave just as soon as I got my breath back.

'Don't worry, I'm as harmless as Godless,' the man said smiling, his teeth gleaming against his beard.

'Did you say Godless?'

'Yep, that's the brute's name.'

'It's unusual . . .'

'Just reflects his master's outlook on life. By the way, the name's Noah, what's yours?'

'Vijay,' I said, 'I'm a guest at Mr Khanna's house.'

'Ah, the house-sitter from Bombay,' he said.

'But how ...?'

'Nothing's a secret in these hills, da. If the people don't tell you, the ghosts will.'

I must have looked incredulous, for he winked and said, 'Don't be fooled by the seeming emptiness of the place, there are eyes everywhere. I knew the moment you had arrived in town. So to what do I owe the honour of your company?'

'Oh, I thought I'd visit the priest, Moses. He came to the house earlier this morning.'

'Yes, he's going crazy trying to organize his annual concert. It's quite good, you know, but it drives him nuts.'

We were walking slowly along as I caught my breath. I studied my companion covertly. He seemed as unprepossessing as when I had first seen him, and I would have passed him without a glance in the city or even in the Meham bazaar, but his unaccented English didn't fit with his appearance. A thought occurred to me: perhaps he was the priest's son, although his unkempt appearance remained a mystery.

'Sorry to be asking, but are you related to the priest?'

'Yes,' he said shortly, 'you might say I'm related to him.'

He said nothing more, and I wondered if I had offended him by being too direct. We continued in silence for a while. Then he said, 'Say, do you like gardens?'

'Well I suppose I do,' I said, a bit hesitantly.

'Ah, one of those city boys who prefers his flowers in vases, eh?' he said, his tone mocking.

'Well, I haven't really had much to do with gardens ...'

'Never too late to start, da,' he said. 'This place is famous for its gardens, you know, best in the district, and the Nilgiris, as even *you* must know, is famous throughout the country for its fruit and flowers.'

'Yes, I knew that.'

'But I bet you don't know where the finest garden in all of Meham is, do you?'

'No.'

'Well, then, you're in for a treat, come on.'

I wondered if he was having me on; this was a cemetery and a fairly run-down one at that. Everywhere gravestones poked out of the earth like weathered molars. Several of the headstones had toppled over, weeds grew thickly on the path we were walking down, and none of the graves themselves looked tended in the least. We reached an enormous peepul tree that dominated the place; there was a concrete platform under it and on it was a mat, a smoke-blackened kettle, a kerosene stove, two Horlicks bottles containing tea and sugar respectively, and a small tin trunk. Noah sat down, lit the stove, put the kettle on and asked me if I would like some tea.

I was getting more puzzled by the minute. Even if Noah was the priest's son or nephew just what was he doing in this place? He seemed to live here – perhaps he was a poor relative who was employed as the cemetery keeper or maybe as the gardener? Or maybe his father and he had fallen out – hadn't he made a cryptic reference to being Godless? – and he had been banished to the cemetery, although the elderly pastor, from what little I had seen of him, did not seem to be the type of person capable of meting out such harsh punishment. But Noah didn't seem interested in providing an explanation and I didn't think I could probe just yet. I refused his offer of tea, saying I'd just had some at the teashop down the road.

'Velu's? You must have a strong constitution; he's kept his kettle boiling with the same leaves for about two centuries, if you ask me. Well, sit down anyway, let me have some tea.' I sat down on the platform, and then jumped up again when I realized it was a tomb, surmounted by a weather-beaten angel that was shielded from view by a low-hanging branch.

'Relax, the dear departed May Reston will not be offended if you rest on her grave.' I indicated that I would prefer to stand, and he shrugged, made himself some tea, and when he had drunk it, got to his feet, saying, 'OK, my friend, prepare to be dazzled.'

Past the peepul, the ground inclined steeply. From where we stood up to the far boundary, which was marked by a sagging barbed-wire fence, row upon row of flowering plants tumbled down the slope like flaming opals.

'My garden,' Noah said simply. 'Do you know Pessoa?'

'Who?' I asked.

'Sorry, there aren't too many people I can discuss modern European poets with around here. Are you a poet?'

I shook my head.

'Pity,' he said. 'He was Portuguese, strangely elusive even for a poet, invented a whole raft of alternative identities for himself, called them heteronyms, and attributed his poetry to them. One of them was called Alberto Caeiro, a sort of nature poet, and one of his poems goes *"Poor flowers in the flower beds of manicured gardens, They look like they're afraid of the police ..."*.'

'It's kind of the way I feel, da, which is why I've let my garden grow wild. Do you like it? Do you even have an opinion?' The mocking tone was back, but it was clear that he was proud of his garden. I recognized some of the flowers – roses, lilies, hibiscus – but even my untrained eye could see that these were somehow more beautiful, more richly coloured and showy than the ones I had seen at Cypress Manor.

'It's amazing,' I said.

'It's taken a lot of work,' he said, stooping to pluck a weed from a bed of carnations the colour of clotted blood. 'Many years ago, when I was at a bit of a crossroads, I thought I might become a plant hunter, you know like the guy who first collected the Tibetan blue poppy, Kingdon-Ward. But I was born a century too late, nobody pays you big money now to wander around in exotic places collecting plants ... So I did the next best thing, I just set out to grow the best garden I could. The thing is, you can't simply follow a gardening manual or copy what someone else is doing. Plants have a will of their own, you've got to understand each one of them, empathize with them, know when to coax them, when to be stern, when to be patient, rather like trying to get a gorgeous woman to do things your way. You can't just blunder in and hope for the best, but if you get it right, the results can be astonishing.'

Close by, I recognized a few stalks of the brilliantly coloured flowers I had admired in my host's garden, and I asked Noah what they were.

'Fuchsias,' he said, 'the best you'll find in town, better than anything those old fools at the Fuchsia Club of Meham will ever grow in this or any other lifetime.'

'I was admiring them in Mr Khanna's garden.'

'They're an obsession here. There's something about the climate that makes them grow especially well and the competition among those who cultivate them is fierce. Many years ago the elite of Meham, all of whom were gardeners needless to say, took over a gardening club and renamed it the Fuchsia Club of Meham, which they claim is the oldest continuously active club in the Nilgiris. They are venerable and distinguished every one of them, but when it comes to fuchsias they are as competitive and amoral as a Bombay high-society wife.' He smiled and added, 'But I grow better fuchsias than any of them, except they don't know it. None of them has come up here, and I don't enter my garden in any of the competitions. Take a look at this one, isn't it a beauty?'

The flower he was pointing to was extraordinarily striking, looking like an exotic dancer with her flounced skirts thrown back from long white legs. It had the same delicacy and blazing colour of the other fuchsias but where most of them had straight, elongated blooms, this one's petals were flounced, crinkled and coloured a flagrant pink with flared white and pink sepals and a pure white tube.

'It's called a Wally Yendell,' Noah was saying, 'and it's the only one of its kind in the Nilgiris. Brigadier Sharma, who lives close to you and is the boss man around here, or any of the other members of the FCM would swap their wives and fortunes for this flower, I tell you. In fact, it once belonged to a rich bugger, one of those guys who is not really a gardener but buys a great garden. He lives near Ooty, and the Brigadier paid a friend of mine called Arumugam, the only specialist flower thief I've ever heard of, a sort of cut-rate Kingdon-Ward without the scruples, a fair bit of money to steal it for him; and then he stole it from the Brigadier, and gave it to me because he owed me. The Brigadier was furious, he had the fellow beaten up by the police, but Arumugam never did tell them anything. Quite a place, Meham,' he said with a laugh.

We moved on, walking through detonations of colour that counterpointed the shabby gravestones, Noah expounding on the plants he was growing, and it occurred to me that this was the most unusual place I had ever been, this tumbledown cemetery perched on the lip of a mountain, with its wealth of exotic plants and its reclusive guardian who talked with equal facility of his floral treasures as he did of matters too recondite for me.

We had reached the boundary of the cemetery. Beyond the barbed-wire fence, the hillside fell away in a mass of boulders, lantana thickets and scree. In the distance I could see the towering sentinels that guarded the passage to Meham. Somewhere in their vicinity was the Tower of God. Perhaps Noah could find me a way to get there. Obligingly, he provided me with the perfect opening by asking me what I was doing in Meham. I explained that I worked for a magazine and that my editor had sent me here to write a story about the controversial shrine. I told him I was planning to visit it tomorrow, and to my delight, he offered to take me there.

'So Meham's about to clamber on to the national stage, huh?' he said.

'Well, not quite,' I replied. I told him *The Indian Secularist* didn't have a very large circulation but that its voice was listened to by those who were worried about the direction in which the country was headed. He heard me out, and then said with an edge to his voice, 'Hasn't made much of a difference, has it now, considering what's been done to Bombay? If I had my way, I would have all those who were responsible castrated and tortured to death ...'

He seemed extremely annoyed, and continued to inveigh against those who had destroyed the city for a few minutes. This seemed to take the edge off his anger, and he continued more gently. 'The greatest city in the world, or it was at any rate when I lived there for a couple of years about a decade ago. It was the best time of my life ... It was a city of poets and cafés, and all-night sessions of drinking and versifying, a place to rival Joyce's Dublin or Cavafy's Alexandria or Pessoa's Lisbon: Dom hammering away with one finger at his typewriter in Sargent House, spectacles slipping down his nose, as the poems ran wild in his head, Adil holding court in his eyrie on Cuffe Parade, Nissim spinning his demotic verse in coffee houses and poets' gatherings, Kolatkar with his strange fierce epic about Gods of stone, Imtiaz and the agate-eyed women who glided through her work ... What a time that was, the nights of writing poetry and drinking and partying and fucking the beautiful young women we all shared, the models and wannabe actresses pulled into that vortex of passion, song and metred rhyme ... Some of us more impressionable types were convinced that this was what we were meant to do for the rest of our lives, pluck poems from the moist humid air of the city like the maestros did, drink without getting drunk, fuck without getting trapped into dull, lifeless relationships. And it didn't matter that it was all mere fantasy; we were young and alive and well in Bombay, and were putting whatever talent we had at the service of the Muse, and one day we knew the poetry would well out of us unstoppably fierce and incandescent and beautiful, and some maestro would cast an indulgent eye over it and pronounce us worthy, and the whores and models and party girls who hung around us would have finally realized their purpose, and the verse would continue to flow from our minds, night after night, like a bright shining river out into those dirty pullulating streets, lighting up the city, lighting up the world ...'

Noah fell silent for a moment caught up in his remembering, and then said, 'I am not surprised at all by the violence being done to the city but it is not for the reasons you think. It's because the poetry is gone, da, the Muse has fled the great and the good, not to mention the people around them. Bombay's time is behind it now, just like all the other great flaming cities of the past, their brief effulgence spent, you know like in that Cavafy poem where he compares the future to a row of lit candles, and the past to burned-out candles, and doesn't want to look back because "*how quickly the dark line lengthens, how quickly the snuffed out candles multiply*".'

He paused, and when he spoke again his voice was perfectly even, all the passion leached from it. 'I'm glad I don't live there any more. What's it like now anyway?'

Here was my chance to tell him my stories of Bombay, stories of murderers and innocents, but also of people who were fighting to save their beloved city, but before I could do so he held up a hand, and said, 'No, don't, best to leave things as you remember them.'

93

'Aren't you worried the same thing will happen to Meham? You know this place is so peaceful, but with this Tower of God tamasha ...'

'Nah, nothing will happen, this is Meham, da. Fucking place is inoculated against any kind of catastrophe. Worst thing that can happen here is some kind of pest attacks the fuchsias, then you'll see some real panic, I tell you.'

'But I hear that a Bombay politician is involved.'

'Umm ya, a local who went to Bombay and made good. Fellow by the name of Rajan. Smart guy, very smart guy, I have no idea why he's bothering with this Tower of God stuff. But look, when we go there, I'll introduce you to some people who'll give you all the dope, OK? I've got some business to take care of right now, but we'll meet tomorrow, say eleven. Right here. I'd have offered to pick you up, except the toffs on your hill don't like me. Come on, I'll see you safely past Godless and his harem, they might love you to death.'

Late in the evening I took my mug of tea and sat out on the front steps looking out over the landscape as I had that morning. The sky was the colour of flame but the light was delicate, softening everything it touched.

I wondered about the strange man I had met in the cemetery. It was evident he was no primitive philosopher, some idiot savant of the Nilgiris, but a man of some learning who was familiar with the world beyond Meham. And even assuming he had merely dropped the names of famous Bombay personalities to impress the stranger, how did he know about them in the first place? You didn't get that sort of knowledge from books or magazines; poets were not movie stars. And if he were the priest's son, why had he fallen out with his father? And how and why had he lost his faith? And why did Brigadier Sharma and the other elite of Meham dislike him, was it simply because he had stolen their flowers? There was too much about him that did not make sense. I wondered if it would be safe going with him to the Tower of God, but I quickly put that thought aside; Noah seemed perfectly harmless and besides I doubted that I would be stupid enough to follow him to some remote place to be set upon by a gang of local thugs.

The butler came up and handed me an envelope on a silver salver. A big, untidy hand had scrawled my name on the envelope, and inside there was a note in the same handwriting. The notepaper inside was headed Brigadier N.P. Sharma AVSM, PVSM (Retd). The most powerful man in Meham, according to Noah, was asking if I would do him the pleasure of joining him for drinks and dinner at the Meham Club on New Year's Eve, a couple of days away, to help bring in 1994. Here was the perfect source to discreetly pump for information about my friend from the cemetery, I thought. I went back into the house and scribbled a note to the Brigadier accepting his invitation.

It promised to be a full day tomorrow, and I couldn't wait to get started. After supper, just before I dropped off to sleep I decided to read some more of Mr Sorabjee's manuscript, as I didn't know how much time I would have to devote to it once I began investigating my story.

SAMRAAT ASHOKA

Emperor of Renunciation

In his time he ruled the largest empire in the world, as every one of you who has passed the fifth standard or read an Amar Chitra Katha comic knows: a land mass that stretched from the mountains of the Hindu Kush in the far north, all the way down to the south, ending at the Pennar River. But strangely for such a powerful ruler he made little impression on the minds of contemporary historians, and vanished from view for a thousand years. Then, in 1837, a sickly, obsessive English clerk called James Prinsep, who worked for the British Raj in Calcutta and who had spent the best years of his life trying to decipher the Brahmi script, stumbled across a reference to a king called Devanam-piya Piyadassi or Beloved of the Gods. Prinsep's chance discovery was followed by other revelations about the unknown ruler. As scholars began to understand mysterious edicts carved on rocks and sandstone pillars weighing as much as fifty tons apiece that had puzzled them for centuries, a picture began to emerge of an emperor who was like few others the world had seen. H.G. Wells, the English writer, wrote of him, 'Amidst the tens of thousands of names of monarchs that crowd the columns of history . . . the name of Ashoka shines, and shines almost alone, a star.'

If you are as inattentive a student as I was, you will probably have forgotten most of the stuff you were taught in history class, so I think you will find my recapitulation of a few facts about Ashoka useful. He was the grandson of Chandragupta Maurya, who came to power around 321 BC. With the help of his wily adviser Kautilya, who wrote the manual of statecraft *The Arthashastra* (which Machiavelli is thought to have studied for his own great work *The Prince*), Chandragupta assembled a vast empire. But this story is not about him, so we must skip over his greatness, and that of his son Bindusara, Devourer of Foes, and move on to the third in the Mauryan line of kings, Ashoka (290–232 BC), the one who would be hailed as the greatest of them all. It is appropriate to enter a caveat into the narrative at this point: most of our information about Ashoka's life and times comes from Buddhist texts such as the *Divyavadana* which were not authored by trained historians. Fable, myth and hyperbole were used as liberally as facts, so the best we can do is construct a reasonably accurate picture of the man whose name would be celebrated for millennia.

A second son, Ashoka's beginnings were not as propitious as one might have expected. In fact, the Buddhist texts refer to him as ChandAshoka or Cruel Ashoka. He is said to have killed one or all but one of his brothers (legends say there were 101) in a

96

terrible war of succession; he is also said to have enjoyed killing and torturing people and animals. He was ugly and bad-tempered and was thought to have beheaded ministers for daring to disagree with him and burning alive women who dared to mock his less than pleasing features. He was also supposed to have put down rebellions brutally. But all these stories might just be a way of providing a stark contrast to his saintly later years, as we ought not to forget that the Buddhist texts that are our principal source were not concerned so much with history as with propagating Buddhism through tales of its greatest son. Be that as it may, the Ashoka who came to power was not a gentle soul – he could not afford to be if he was to rule an enormous empire. He may well have killed one or more of his brothers, he was certainly a tough ruler, and his reputation for ruthlessness was not without foundation, as we will see.

We will join him now as he marches to the last battle of his life. The Mauryan army is a terrifying engine of war. Ashoka has at his disposal elephants, chariots, cavalry and over half a million men. The Kalinga force that opposes him has a long and valorous tradition of fighting off invaders but it is much smaller. According to Pliny, the Kalinga army comprised 60,000 foot soldiers, 1,000 horsemen and 700 battle elephants, and even if you double or triple that number (to mesh with other estimates of the Kalinga force) there is no question but that it faced a numerically larger enemy. However, the Kalingas would not back down; they would fight to the very end if need be.

The progress of Ashoka's army is slow, accompanied as it is by a number of support staff and others – the harem of the king and senior officers, traders, prostitutes, cooks, physicians and servants. But it inexorably draws closer to Kalinga.

Battle is joined on the flat plain of Dhauli eight

97

kilometres to the south of Bhubaneshwar in present-day Orissa. It is a pleasant place, fringed by low hillocks and edged by a river, but it will soon become a charnel house. War in Ashoka's time was in many ways a more gruesome business than it is today because it was fought at close quarters and with terrible savagery. The weapons both sides used included bows as tall as men that shot arrows with tremendous velocity, heavy swords that cut through the light armour and shields that the soldiers used for protection, and, above all, elephants, not the most reliable weapon because they could run amok trampling anyone who stood in their way, including the soldiers of their own army.

All that day Ashoka's men massacred enemy troops and officers, chopping off heads and limbs and destroying animals, until their arms grew weary and their weapons were too slippery with blood to hold. Ashoka's own estimate puts the number of Kalinga warriors slaughtered at 100,000. Many times that number from among the army's camp followers died or were taken prisoner. Even allowing for some exaggeration there was no doubt that tens of thousands of warriors died that day. The river ran red with blood, and the screams of the wounded filled the dusty air. It was normal practice for kings to stay away from the forefront of the battle, a sensible precaution for if the king was taken or killed defeat was certain lost, but Ashoka was a skilled warrior and had been in the thick of combat. That evening the enemy army completely routed, Ashoka wandered among the dead and dying combatants, inhaling the smell of blood in the air, exulting in his victory. Kalinga had been won at the point of his bloody sword; there was nothing left for him to conquer. But gradually the terrible cost of his victory began to sink in. He took in the piteous groaning of the wounded, the dazed women who wandered silently among the dead looking for their men, and the dismembered limbs and body parts that the kites and jackals were descending upon.

One of the accounts of the aftermath says that Ashoka was approached by a man dressed in tattered garments carrying the lifeless body of his child in his arms, who challenged the Emperor to demonstrate he was truly powerful by bringing the child back from the dead. The enormity of his crime washed over Ashoka and he cried to the heedless kites and carrion eaters, 'What have I done?' The beggar, who it is said was a Buddhist monk in disguise, saw that Ashoka's remorse was genuine and began to initiate him into the precepts of Buddhism, a faith Ashoka had taken a passing interest in. As he immersed himself fully in the religion, Ashoka declared he would never draw his sword again, and pledged that he would abstain from all killing.

'All men are my children,' he proclaimed in one of his rock edicts. He also pledged that henceforth he would win people over by dharma, which he defined as sinning less and performing actions that were compassionate, liberal, truthful and pure. In time he who was once called ChandAshoka would come to be known as DharmaAshoka, Ashoka the Good.

Ashoka was in his forties when he renounced war and covetousness and devoted himself to the welfare of his people. Our history is rife with examples of men of power who gave everything up to become ascetics and devote themselves to the contemplation of God, but Ashoka was unique in that he gave up the entitlements of emperors but stayed on to serve his people. He encouraged charity, built hospitals, prohibited animal sacrifice, lined the roads of his kingdom with trees, and in many ways set up what was arguably the world's earliest welfare state. Crucially, although he became a devoted Buddhist and spent a lot of time and money proselytizing, he commanded in one of his edicts that no man be interfered with in the pursuit of his faith. It is an edict that deserves to be quoted from at length: 'Beloved of the Gods, King Piyadassi ... values ... growth in the essentials of all religions. Growth in essentials can be done in different ways, but all of them have as their root restraint in speech, that is, not praising one's own religion, or condemning the religion of others without good cause. And if there is cause for criticism, it should be done in a mild way. But it is better to honour other religions for this reason. By so doing one's own religion benefits, and so do other religions, while doing otherwise harms one's own religion and the religion of others. Whoever praises his own religion, due to excessive devotion, and condemns others with the thought "Let me glorify my own religion" only harms his own religion. Therefore contact [between religions] is good. One should listen to and respect the doctrines professed by others. Beloved of the Gods, King Piya-dassi, desires that all should be well learned in the good doctrines of other religions.'

Ashoka was a man well ahead of his time, and our need is for someone like him who will be the perfect antidote to the savage generals of God who dominate our country today.

⁓ℰℋ⁓

I should get some sleep, I thought, and set the manuscript down, drank some water and turned off the light. I liked what Mr Sorabjee was trying to do. It had been a good idea to pare the lives of the emperors to their essential greatness, the profiles were brief enough to hold the attention of even the most restless teenager, and perhaps it would give some of them a moment's pause, a new filter through which to view the country's greatest sons. How far ahead of his time Ashoka had been! Which leader today would consider giving up his power – no matter how paltry when compared to the absolute power someone like Ashoka would have commanded – and devoting his life to the welfare of the people? How many politicians had resigned because of the riots that had broken out in Bombay and elsewhere after the mosque in Ayodhya was destroyed? One? Shouldn't that make people angry, especially the young?

7

The essence of women

I walked to the cemetery the next morning through a world choked with mist. The birds were silenced, and the trees that lined the road seemed as insubstantial as ghosts. I hoped this would not mean that we wouldn't be able to get to the Tower of God; I remembered my neighbour on the bus telling me that nobody was allowed to climb up in inclement weather. Fortunately, by the time I got to my destination, a strong wind had begun dispersing the mist.

When I arrived at the gates, I found they were locked. There was no sign of Noah. To my relief, Godless and his pack of mongrels were not around either. I walked along the wall calling out to Noah, and then decided to scale it. I found a place where it had crumbled a bit, and clambered up. As I dropped to the other side, I heard the sound of giggling coming from the direction of the peepul tree. I hesitated; I wasn't prepared for the possibility that the cemetery might be frequented by others. Just then I heard Noah yelling my name. A moment later he appeared from behind the peepul, his arm around a good-looking young woman dressed in a dirty sari and threadbare blouse. She was struggling coquettishly in his grasp, and he let her go after whispering something in her ear. She giggled some more, darted behind the tree, and the next I saw of her, she was running towards the far wall of the cemetery carrying a large cane basket and a sickle.

'Ah, my friend, have you ever unwrapped a young woman in a sari? Gently, with your teeth?'

I must have looked somewhat scandalized because he laughed and said theatrically, 'Imagine her walking towards you, her thighs working smoothly under the cloth, the pleats of the sari rustling ... each step an intricate movement that inflames the senses. Imagine, yes imagine, your teeth ever so gently plucking at the knot of the sari – tell me now, don't you think that that is quite the most sensual experience you could have?' An image flashed through my mind of the gross body of the whore in Shuklajee Street, and my distaste must have shown on my face, because Noah said, 'Not a sari man, are you?'

'It's not that ...'

'Well then, if you're not partial to the sari perhaps you prefer exquisite bodies clothed in fitting sarong kebayas, or maybe your choice of garment is the flowing kira, or, let me see, a tight-tight cheong sam, slit all the way to paradise, the kimono maybe, taut at just the right places, or perhaps your tastes are not that exotic, maybe you're simply a connoisseur of the little black dress or jeans as tight as skin ... come on, you can tell me what turns you on?'

Somewhat overwhelmed by this flood of oratory, I had nothing to say. Noah smiled mischievously, and said, 'You're a hard man to please, but believe me when I say that nowhere in the world will you find a garment that better celebrates the beauty of a woman than the sari. Flowing like water, settling like rain, tantalizing and bold as it switches and slides off breast and buttock, it's a garment that's untailored and pure, unsullied by the slicing of scissors and the piercing of needles, a garment of the Gods that's lasted, virtually unchanged, for three thousand years ...'

He paused and said in his regular voice, 'Don't mind me, da, sometimes I get in the mood for a bit of heavy declamation. By the way would you like a grass-cutter?'

'What?'

'Here, no two-bit sanctimoniousness from you, one of my grass-cutters is worth a dozen of your city-bred belles. No airs, no artifice, just great fucking, you should try one of them sometime. Have you come across Rimbaud's verse about backsides? Sheer genius, and although he was actually talking about men, we shouldn't quibble. Anyway, I saw Saroja's arse one day when she squatted to relieve herself and I was smitten. Completely. Don't even begin to look appalled, don't you like women?'

'No, no,' I said hastily. 'It's just that I thought it would be good to get to the Tower of God early. The weather's clearing up ... and ...'

'Sure, no problem, let me just have a smoke first.' He produced a joint, lit it and inhaled luxuriously. I refused his offer to take a couple of hits, and he said, 'What, no dope, no women, what sort of life do you lead, da?' He quickly finished the joint and said dreamily, 'What a way to start the morning – a glorious fuck, great dope. Come on, let's go. I have a feeling that today's going to be amazing.'

As we threaded our way through the graves I noticed that the path was littered with used condoms, empty bottles of beer, plastic bags.

'This is where the whores of Meham bring their customers,' he said when I asked why the cemetery was so dirty. 'Quiet, private and the dead don't mind, you know.'

Between the cemetery and the church was a large grassy field, and it was here that the grass-cutters were at work, a group of six or seven women who started giggling and chattering when they caught sight of Noah. He waved to them and then set off in the direction of the parsonage. When we got there he began acting strangely. He cautioned me not to make any noise and inched his way up to the priest's ancient scooter, which was parked outside the house, the ground beneath it darkened by oil. He took it carefully off its stand, put it in neutral and began to wheel it away. He beckoned to me to help him.

'Are we stealing your dad's scooter?' I whispered as I pushed the vehicle along.

'What does it look like to you?' he retorted. 'But don't worry, I've done it before, and as long as we return it in one piece, we'll be fine.'

Once we were on the slope leading away from the church, we hopped on, Noah produced a spare key, turned on the ignition, put the scooter in gear and we were off. I had never ridden pillion on a two-wheeler before, and I was acutely conscious of how close to disaster I was perched. Noah drove very fast and the ancient vehicle protested at every bump in the road, but the fact that he was stoned out of his mind terrified me even more. I tried shouting to him to slow down but my injunctions were torn to shreds by the speed at which we were travelling. I wished I'd told the butler back at Cypress Manor not to cancel the taxi he had ordered.

As we left the church behind and took the narrow twisting road to town, the mist rolled in and visibility came down to a few feet. To add to my discomfort, the horn wasn't working well, and its weak chirp could barely be heard above the noise of our passage. Noah didn't slow down but resorted to shouting at the top of his voice in Tamil to say that we were coming and that approaching vehicles should give way. After about ten minutes of this, I could bear it no longer. I leaned forward and shouted into his ear to stop as I was feeling sick. In response, Noah braked abruptly and I was almost thrown off. 'What's the matter?' he asked innocently, as he pulled the scooter to the side of the road.

'If we drive like this, we'll die,' I said shakily.

'This is the only way I drive, and I'm still alive,' he said cheerfully. 'Do you want to take over?' he asked.

'I don't know how to drive a scooter,' I confessed, adding, 'but if we can't go any slower, I'm sorry, I'd much rather walk.'

He looked at me and smiled, still high, and I thought he might decide to go on without me, but then he said, 'OK, da, have it your way, but I tell you, you're going to miss the adrenalin rush of shooting through the mist like a meteor.'

We set off again, at a pace that was much more moderate although it was still too fast in my opinion. I shut my eyes and prayed that we wouldn't meet another vehicle every time we took a corner, but I wasn't as paralyzed with terror as I had been before. To our great good fortune there was no traffic until we were on the outskirts of town, where Noah had no option but to slow down because the road had been churned up into a quagmire which every passing car and lorry only made worse.

Up close, Meham was a squalid town, in total contrast to the beauty of the landscape surrounding it. The decline in the fortunes of the tea industry, which had been its mainstay for almost a century, was evident everywhere. Its single main street was rutted and muddy. Above it, dingy computer training institutes, minute department stores, shops, bakeries, two inhospitable-looking lodges, the local branch of a national bank, small one-room restaurants, a travel agency, three tea showrooms and a liquor shop clustered together, all looking as if they had been assembled from whatever materials the builders could find close at hand. Rows of small, badly constructed, weather-beaten houses ascended the slope from the shops. On a hill facing the town proper, there were three temples, a mosque and a church – there was obviously no dearth of piety around here. What worried me were the knots of young men I could see standing around aimlessly everywhere I looked. If their frustration and anger were to be exploited by the fundamentalists, then this town could become like all the others that Mr Sorabjee's old Gods had taken over.

Noah wanted to buy some bones for Godless, so we parked the scooter by the side of the road and went into the bazaar that descended from the main street to a dirty river that carried away the town's waste. We made slow progress through a warren of tiny lanes, on either side of which were stalls that displayed all manner of goods; everyone seemed to know Noah, and we were obliged to stop every few minutes to chat to the shopkeepers. Eventually, we arrived at a vegetable market, redolent with the smell of curry leaves, where Noah spent a long time flirting with the fat proprietress of a stall on which mounds of aubergines, bitter gourd, tomatoes and carrots were heaped. From here it was a short walk to the butcher's shop, a low-roofed shack that stood a little apart from the rest of the stalls. Outside, wire cages bulged with quails and chickens, all of them strangely quiet. A mangy black dog slunk out of the doorway as we entered. I was leading but I had barely taken a few steps into the shop when I noticed that Noah was no longer with me. On the far side of the establishment the butcher was chopping up a slab of mutton with a small axe for the only other customer in the place, a well-dressed, pompous-looking man with a high-domed forehead from which a great wave of white hair swept back. The butcher looked up briefly, and then went back to his work, while the customer ignored me. I hastily retraced my steps and found Noah behind the cages of poultry, smoking a cigarette.

'How come you disappeared?' I asked in some bemusement.

'Oh nothing, just didn't want that pompous arsehole in the shop to see me. Great friend of the Brigadier's, would string me up if he caught sight of me,' he said with a shrug. 'Fortunately people like him normally have their noses hoisted so high in the air, they wouldn't notice you unless you bit them on the face.'

'What did you do to make them dislike you so much?'

'Nothing, da. You'll hear about a hundred different versions of what a bastard I am if you stay here long enough, just don't believe any of them.'

He said nothing more. A few minutes later the man he had been trying to avoid walked out of the shop and, looking impassively ahead, disappeared into the vegetable market. As soon as he had gone, we went into the shop. The butcher greeted Noah affectionately: 'Haven't seen you in a while, has that mongrel of yours died?'

'No, he almost took a chunk of meat from my calf yesterday, so I thought I'd get him some scraps. Ismail, this is my friend Vijay from Bombay.'

The butcher smiled and nodded. As Noah and he got chatting I looked around. A whole goat hung from a hook on the roof, and on the long wooden counter, scarred and crisscrossed by cuts from the butcher's knives, there were piles of bones, liver and meat. From time to time, the butcher would flick scraps of fat, white and stretched like parchment, on to the floor, and the eyes of four black cats which occupied various vantage points in the shop would flicker imperceptibly. They were well trained and wouldn't move a muscle until the butcher indicated that they could begin, whereupon one of them would descend noiselessly in a cloud of black fur, scoop up the titbit and return to its perch. The cats seemed to have worked out a system for never once did any of them get in each other's way.

Once Godless's bones were packed and stowed away, we were finally able to make our way to the Tower of God. When we got there, to my disappointment we could see nothing as the valley was filled almost to the brim with cloud and mist. Noah told me not to worry as it never stayed that way for too long; we would make another attempt to get to it the next day. We sat for a while on the parapet looking down into the whiteness beneath our feet and I commented that it looked solid enough to walk on. 'I've never heard of anyone mad enough to try that,' Noah said with a laugh, 'It's over 6,000 feet straight down.'

A taxi drove up, and four people got out, by the look of them tourists from the plains. The man waddled ahead of his family, his little pot belly pushing out the front of his garish, obviously new sweater, inappropriate leather shoes squeaking as he walked. He was followed by his rotund wife, sari- and sweater-clad, with a little girl of about nine clinging on to her hand. A boy who looked slightly older than his sister brought up the rear. The man walked up to the parapet, looked out at the invisible Tower of God and said rather rudely in our general direction, 'When will it become visible?' When neither of us replied, he turned and surveyed us, his small eyes cold above the pencil-line moustache on his upper lip.

'That is the Tower of God, no?' he said, his voice a little more conciliatory, although his air of importance hadn't left him. Surprisingly Noah answered him kindly, even though the man had addressed the question to me. He explained that the Tower of God wasn't going to show itself that day, and that he should return tomorrow when the weather was expected to clear up. Ignoring him, the man strutted back to the waiting taxi, his family following meekly behind. When the taxi had gone, I said to Noah, 'That was good of you.'

'Um, yes,' he said. 'I suppose I was thinking, there but for the grace of God go I, fucking pompous arsehole, apple of his mother's eye no doubt, less than average intelligence but a great mug-pot so stands first in class in his mofussil school and college, gets a job as a management trainee or something, demands a big dowry, marries a virgin, produces two kids within the first two years of marriage, will work for the same company all his life, is sycophantic to his superiors and obnoxious towards everyone he considers beneath him, bangs his wife three times a year, once on his birthday, once on hers and once on the biggest festival day of the religion he belongs to, Christmas or Deepavali or Id. Then if she's lucky, she gets a bonus fuck once a year – how many does that make it? OK, four. The rest of the time she looks after the kids and her lord and master. I guess that's why I was kind to him, little does he know how truly pathetic he is, although he probably thinks the sun rises from his backside. But I could have been him, you know, da, and I ... I just couldn't help myself ...'

He paused for a while, and then said, 'You settled?'

'No,' I said.

'Your mother not bugging you to get married, shoving eligible Tam-Brahm virgins at you?'

'Well, she has brought it up on a couple of occasions, but . . .'

'Resist, my friend, resist with all your might. That way lies mediocrity, a life more harrowing than death.'

❧

That day I was given my first proper glimpse into Noah's life, although it took all my skills as an interviewer to wrest it from him. As the day wore on, the story emerged in stops and starts.

He was the priest's son, he said, and as I had suspected he and his father had fallen out quite early on because Noah had never had much time for religion. 'The quickest way for you to be turned off religion is to have it served to you morning, noon and night,' he said wryly over the best mutton biryani I have ever eaten, hot and perfectly spiced, which we bought from a hawker's cart outside Mitchell Park. He and his father had grown further apart when his mother died. That year Noah had turned ten, and it was then he had finally lost his religion. About two years before her death, his mother had joined a fundamentalist Christian sect, as a result of which she had refused to see doctors or take any form of medical treatment when she was diagnosed with breast cancer, choosing to rely instead on the prayers of her congregation and her Saviour to heal her. His father had failed in all his attempts to make her see reason, and when she had died an agonizing death, Noah had blamed him.

The relationship with his father had continued to deteriorate until eventually the priest had sent him away to boarding school on a scholarship reserved for children of the clergy. 'The school, St Jerome's, is quite close to here, they don't usually allow local boys to be boarders, but my father pulled some strings. He realized that it would be best for both of us, especially with Mum not around to keep the peace.' Things had gone quite well until his senior year, when he had fallen for the most sought-after girl in the neighbouring girls' school, St Catherine's. 'Maya was an almost perfect Punjaban – tall, fair, not the pallor of Europeans but that perfect complexion, you know what I mean, generous-breasted even though she was only sixteen, long

109

legs – she was a queen, da, and I fell hard. It was the worst thing I could have done, but I'd do it again and again had I a chance to relive my life, because you have to fall in love, perfectly, at least once.'

The girl had reciprocated his passion, he said quite unself-consciously, because he had been one of the edgiest boys in school, a high hurdler and the student who was always on the verge of being thrown out for some act of insubordination or the other. Noah and Maya were soon inseparable. Until her father found out. He sent her to live with her grandparents in Delhi and almost succeeded in getting Noah thrown out of his school. His father had managed to enlist the support of the bishop and the expulsion was stayed but the damage was done. Noah began drinking, doing drugs, missing classes repeatedly and, I suspect, having brushes with the law, although he didn't say so explicitly. At this point his father intervened again and gave him an ultimatum – if he didn't pull himself together, it would be too late; he had no more favours to call in, he was just an ordinary pastor. Noah would have to go straight or fend for himself. When I asked him why his father had continued to look out for him, Noah said simply, 'Because he was a good man. We didn't get on, but that didn't mean he was going to abandon me, he was my father after all, and a priest to boot. He didn't really have an option now, did he?'

Noah behaved himself for a while, passed his school-leaving exam, even secured admission to a college in Coimbatore, but it hadn't lasted. Maya's grip on him did not slacken, although he hadn't seen or heard from her in a year, and he began to drink and do drugs again. He was expelled from college and his long-suffering father, his earlier ultimatum notwithstanding, stepped in one last time. 'He explained to me that he couldn't do this any more, although he was a man of God he couldn't find it in his heart to forgive endlessly. I suppose I'd given him a really hard time, but was I in any way remorseful, grateful for everything he'd done ...' Noah shook his head and said, 'Not on your life, da. I was an A-grade arsehole, but I wasn't myself, I was just too intoxicated by Maya, the idea of Maya more like ...'

'Was she worth it?' I asked. In my head danced an image of Meher as I had seen her in the Bombay restaurant, and I thought about what my life would have been like if she had shown even the slightest interest in me.

Noah was saying, 'You don't measure passion and romance with a calculator, da. Was she worth it? you ask. Of course not, but at the same time of course she was. You don't get that sort of pulse-pounding passion too often in life, so you grab it when you find it ... and do you know why? Because even though it may be fleeting, it's the only thing that burns an indelible image on your soul, the only thing you will remember when you're old and spent.'

This time his father tried to solve the problem of Maya by the rather simple expedient of sending his son to study in America. He wangled a scholarship sponsored by the Church on condition that Noah first obtain a degree in India. For eighteen months Noah steadied himself, went to evening classes, studied without a break, passed his examinations and finally boarded a plane to a small liberal arts college on the East Coast.

He loved America, its directness, its essential simplicity and lack of clutter. He read its poets, listened to its music, got caught up in the swirling energy of the country and gradually all the things that hemmed him in, most of all his obsession with Maya, began to fall away. But the freedom he was experiencing was illusory for addiction is progressive, and soon enough his obsession with the woman who had been taken from him returned.

He turned to the girls of America to help him fight off his despair. 'American women were what I needed at that point in my life, da. They are direct, uncomplicated. They want everything clearly laid out for them: they like to discuss their feelings and every aspect of their relationships obsessively. It takes all the mystery away, but it was exactly what I was looking for. If they liked you and you liked them that was enough. No complicated bullshit, none of the baggage our women carry, you know, all the hang-ups, conditioning and shit that has been bred into them for centuries. It wasn't love I was after, you understand, it was a sort of oblivion, and I got that in full measure. I screwed my brains out. I was from the land of the Kama Sutra after all, and if I didn't know all the sixty-four positions in the manual, I made them up, and the women certainly seemed satisfied with what I had to offer. And I had a secret weapon that every woman I fancied seemed to find irresistible ... Do you know what an acrostic poem is?'

'No.'

'Never mind, give me a woman's name, any woman's name.'

'Meher,' I said.

'Someone you fancy?' he asked with a smile.

'Uh, no ...' I stammered in confusion.

'Hey, take it easy, da, didn't mean to pry, OK ...' He cast around for a twig and scratched something out on the dirt of the path:

> Mellifluous tone spells my dooM
> Eyes of flame in a flawless facE
> Her beauty is bracing and fresH
> Enchanted I slide into her gazE
> Realize I can't ever escape heR

The whole poem took him less than five minutes to write, with all the elisions and substitutions he had to make to get the letters to line up exactly. When he had finished, he said, 'That's probably the worst poem I've ever written and I've written some pretty awful ones, I can tell you. But if you give it to Meher, whoever she is, it doesn't matter if she's never read a book in her life, let alone poetry, it'll win her over. It didn't fail me once when it came to ensnaring women, and I ranged far and wide. You see how the letters of her name align on both sides of the poem, well even the most stand-offish beauty is guaranteed to melt in seconds when she thinks that she has not only driven you to verse but to a poem that you've created especially for her, no abstract one-size-fits-all rubbish. Believe me, it worked better than presents or flowers or chocolate, which was just as well because I didn't have any money.'

He laughed and said, 'Within months I was a bona fide slut. I read in a magazine there's a formula to know if you're one or not: you take your age, subtract fifteen from it, multiply the result by five, and if you've slept with more people than that, then you're officially a slut.'

He paused, pulled out a joint and lit it. 'Sure you won't have a drag?' he asked. 'Last chance.' I refused, and he shrugged.

'You know what, after all that, after a couple of years of non-stop fucking, I discovered it wasn't working – I still hadn't been able to let go of Maya. I realized then what I needed was to give myself to a woman and for her to really give herself to me, not just sexually, that would be too basic. What I needed was essentially to fall in love again, even temporarily, that was the only antidote.'

He took another deep drag, held it and let the smoke filter slowly through his nostrils, then said, 'There's tons of stuff that's been written about love but do you really know how it works until it happens to you? I'm asking this rhetorically, da, I'm not trying to excavate your romantic life. The point I'm trying to make is that all the theories we have about love are bullshit – it's got to happen to you for you to know what it's all about. I had had that with Maya, I now needed to find it again. I had encountered infatuation, plain animal lust, women who thought they were in love with me, women I thought were special, women I'd misread, women who had misread me, but I hadn't found the person who would give herself to me in exactly the same way and with the same degree of intensity with which I was prepared to give myself to her.'

He put out his joint, thought a bit, then said, 'The sort of con-nection I'm talking about, the special moment when two people make contact in a way that overrules the information hard-wired into their genes, is unmistakable. It can happen very early in a relationship or in the middle or after a long time, but you recognize it immediately – it's something to do with the eyes, with the mind, with the space inside the heart, that empty space that you can only show another person when you're ready to make yourself wholly vulnerable, know what I mean?'

It wasn't really a question he was asking me, he was interrogating himself, but for a moment I thought wistfully about the lack of romance in my life. I could see why women were drawn to Noah, there was an essential weightlessness about him, an air of unpre-dictability, recklessness, intelligence, worldliness, depth and wisdom that was very compelling. I wondered what it would be like to be him. It was only a momentary fancy – the pragmatic side of my character soon kicked in – and I thought it was a good thing I was nothing like him, otherwise I too would end up having to use a gravestone for a dining table.

While I was thinking these thoughts, Noah's narrative had advanced. He was telling me how he had finally found what he was looking for two months before he was due to leave the States. College was over, and a friend and he had decided to drive along the West Coast, a leisurely journey through a part of America neither had seen, taking in the sights and unwinding before they got on with the business of their lives. One day, in Oregon, they came to a small coastal town that advertised itself as 'The Whale Watching Capital of the World'. Finding rooms in a small B & B, they had bought tickets on one of the boats that took the whale-watchers out. There were a dozen customers on the pier early the next morning. Soon after they boarded the vessel, Noah and his friend were drawn to a busty blonde who managed to look inviting despite the decidedly unsexy orange life jacket she had on. They took it in turns trying to impress her, and when it was clear that she preferred his friend, Noah had shut out the woman and concentrated on the experience of being in a small boat on the sea.

'Americans use the word "awesome" indiscriminately to the extent that it has lost all its meaning, but I have never forgotten our first sight of the whales: it was truly awesome.'

They were not too far out to sea when the captain spotted their quarry – it was still possible to look back and see the scribble of the shoreline through the light morning mist – but out in front of the boat there was nothing but the limitless ocean, stretching to the very end of the world. What had appeared to be wisps of smoke now resolved itself into spume issuing from the blow-holes of whales, six of them, who drifted immense and grave through the green water. They paid not the slightest attention to the boats – for others had come up now – circling them and Noah had allowed himself to be taken over by the grandeur of it all. A light rain began to fall, and the woman next to him had exclaimed in annoyance as her spectacles fogged over. Momentarily distracted, Noah had turned irritably to see who was interrupting his contemplation of the whales and had looked into eyes the colour of a mist-whipped Nilgiri sky, grey-blue eyes he wouldn't have noticed if the spectacles hadn't come off, but eyes he would never forget now that he had looked into them.

'I told you didn't I that you can recognize the moment a woman is willing to give herself to you absolutely, right. Well I saw it that day and I knew everything was going to be fine. When there's only physical attraction, there is a sort of electric brightness to the eyes you're looking into, but when it's something more, it's as if they are lit from within by lamps or candles, the look is softer. I forgot about the whales and the ocean and was granted a vision of her that was so clear, so intense, that I could see every tiny detail, every pore of her skin, each strand of her eyebrows, the fall of her hair, the fine plane of her nose, the imperfections in her skin, everything about her bathed in the kind of luminescence that makes even the plainest of women beautiful.

'It wasn't that this woman needed that sort of alchemy to make her attractive, da, she was stunning, in a delicate sort of way – masses of ash-blonde hair, those amazing eyes, a smile made memorable by the endearing crookedness of her teeth. In any other circumstance I would have wanted to hurry her into bed, but I didn't feel the least inclination to play things that way, it didn't even cross my mind to write her an acrostic poem. But I wanted to see her again, and we made a date to meet that evening.'

They had gone to a small bar, crowded with locals and tourists, and had made a space for themselves in a corner, where they had talked without ceasing through that long evening, oblivious to the noise and confusion, telling each other their stories with the kind of intimacy usually reserved for long, deep associations. 'We took turns getting the drinks from the bar, and I remember once when it was her turn, she could barely get her small perfect hands around the necks of the four bottles she was carrying and she exclaimed, "I wish I had a few more arms."' He smiled at the memory, banal, everyday, and I knew he could see it as clearly as when it had first happened.

As the shabby table in front of them grew cluttered with bottles of Stella Artois beer that he had continued to order because Iva was from Europe, Croatia to be precise, their stories grew ever more intimate – he told her about Maya; she told him that she had never really been in love although she had left a boyfriend, sort of, back in Zagreb; he told her about the death of his mother; and she told him about the loss in an accident of a beloved aunt, the relation she was closest to, after her parents split up; he told her about his great passion, modern European poetry; and she told him about her addiction to skiing, the dangers associated with it that made her feel more alive.

As the night wore on, their conversation held them fast in its net. When they parted well after midnight with just a chaste kiss, promising to meet again the next day, he had never felt closer to any woman since Maya had been taken away from him. The next morning he was up early, clear-headed despite the long hours of drinking the night before, smoking a cigarette on the tiny balcony of his room and looking out to where the sea lay grey and unmoving as petrified stone, when he saw a flash of yellow out of the corner of his eye. Even before the young woman on the pier came within hailing distance, he knew it was Iva. He was about to call out to her, but decided not to, she was so beautiful and poised and connected to her lonely private self that to disturb her would be somehow to violate her solitude. He watched her pass, her flounced yellow frock furling and unfurling around her slim body, and he knew that it was an image that he would carry around with him for the rest of his life.

That night, when they walked to her hotel, their bodies touching with every step they took, he knew he wasn't wrong about his feelings of the previous day. When he eventually slipped off her dress, her body shone golden in the diffused light from the bedside lamp. He gazed at it for a long time, then bent over and traced its perfection with his lips, memorizing every inch. Their love-making was slow and unhurried, and unlike any of his encounters during the previous two years. And when they finally parted the next morning he was free of Maya and no longer needed to sleep with every woman he was attracted to.

'So what happened to Iva?' I asked.

'Oh, we hung out for a couple of magical weeks – I was even inspired to write a poem called "Whalesmorning" – and then we went our separate ways. You must understand that although this special connection I'm talking about supersedes pretty much every other bond, it doesn't mean you need to continue with the person who inspires it for ever. It's only that you will remember her for the rest of your days: she sort of seeps all the way into the marrow of your bones, not just your heart and mind.'

After his American sojourn, he had returned to India, and found a job as an editor with a small alternative publishing house in Bombay called Well Found Books which specialized in publishing poetry and obscure novels in translation. It was funded by an elderly Gujarati industrialist who had always wanted to be a published poet; when he found no takers for his verse, he had started his own publishing house instead. His tiny handful of employees accepted that the publishing of their employer's execrable verse was a small price to pay for the opportunity to publish other excellent poets. 'I didn't mind the job at first, da, it gave me the chance to publish the kind of poetry I liked. You know, guys who were trying to do stuff that took its inspiration from the modern European masters, whose work I adored because of its razor-clean rhyme structure and unsentimentality.'

Noah hadn't lasted very long in Bombay. After two years he could take his boss's pedestrian verse no longer, and as his own efforts to fashion the perfect poem had come to nothing, he had quit his job and returned to the Nilgiris. He had only intended to stay in Meham until he had worked out what he might do next with his life, but ten years later he was still here, and I remember thinking, not a little smugly, that the very quality that was so magnetic about him, his refusal to conform or fully engage with the world, could also prove to be a considerable disadvantage when it came to making your way through life. You could drift while others frantically tried to carve out a niche for themselves, but you couldn't drift for ever, and there would come a time when you simply stagnated without any real aim or ambition to keep you moving. As I thought about Noah in this way, I couldn't help feeling superior to him, because I had a job, I had convictions, I had a mission. I was trying to dilute his mystery, make him ordinary so I could pigeonhole him, I can see that now, and I would feel foolish in just a few days when I would have to revise all my assumptions about him. But I can't really blame myself; anyone else in my place would have done the same, for it is not easy to truly have the measure of those who live aslant to the rest of us.

8

The legacy of martyrs

Later that evening, as we sat drinking tea in a shack just outside town, Noah had a brainwave. He thought we might stop at the house of the chief disciple of the custodian of the shrine. Ravi Menon had been a history professor at Trivandrum University, and had moved to Meham upon his retirement five years earlier. He had been a devotee for over thirty years and could tell me everything I might want to know about the antecedents of the shrine and the dispute in which it was embroiled.

'He's over sixty-five but he still visits the shrine twice a week,' Noah said to me as he parked the scooter at the bottom of a tall stone revetment on top of which the professor's house was situated.

'Won't he mind us just barging in on him like this?' I asked as we walked up a steep flight of steps.

'Come on, da, this is Meham; we're all very informal around here. The professor's wife is an invalid so he doesn't go anywhere except to the shrine, and then he pays a nurse to look after her.'

Professor Menon lived in a small neat house that resembled a railway carriage – oblong, with four rooms running one into the other in a straight line. When we knocked on the front door, it was opened almost immediately by a short man with white hair and thick black-framed spectacles. Seeing it was Noah, a smile appeared on his face.

'Welcome, welcome, haven't seen you in a long time, thambi,' he said, and then, gesturing to me, said, 'Who is your friend?'

'He's from Bombay, sir. A journalist. He wanted to talk to you about the shrine, hope you don't mind?'

'Of course not, come on in. I'll get some tea.'

The room was very clean, although the furniture was cheap – wickerwork armchairs and coffee table, a threadbare rug on the floor and in the corner a small dining table covered with a plastic tablecloth.

'Ra-a-a-vi, who is it?' asked a shrill voice from within the house, 'Is it Dr Gopinath?'

'Be back with you in a moment,' the professor said, wrapping his dhoti more firmly around his waist and leaving to attend to his wife. A smell of antiseptic and urine hung over the room. It wasn't immediately noticeable, but it was unmistakable, the smell of a small-town hospital ward without adequate ventilation.

Professor Menon returned with two cups of tea, and when I told him I worked for *The Indian Secularist* he said, to my delight, that he knew the magazine – his university had subscribed to it. He said he admired it and Mr Sorabjee. We talked a bit about the Bombay riots, and the convulsions the country was still going through following the demolition of the Babri Masjid. I told him about my employer's book and the argument he was constructing, and the professor agreed that it was necessary and timely.

He then began to tell me about the troubles Meham was facing. He said the state hadn't had much trouble with sectarianism for quite some time because it had been ruled by a succession of leaders who hadn't been inclined that way; it had helped that a few of them had been atheists. What we were seeing now was part of the fundamentalists' agenda to sow new fields beyond the Hindi heartland and Gujarat with their poisonous seeds. In the 1980s one of their newsletters published a list of around forty shrines, masjids and other places of worship in Tamil Nadu that it claimed had originally belonged to Hindus. The Shrine of the Blessed Martyr, he said, was one of them.

He had heard of it while he was still teaching in Trivandrum, and when his wife had fallen ill and become paralyzed, he had come here, as he'd heard the custodian of the shrine could heal the sick. She hadn't been cured as he had hoped, but he had been impressed by the custodian, Brother Ahimas, and over time he had become one of his most ardent supporters.

No one knew exactly when the shrine had been established, the Professor said, all that people could agree on was that it had come into being many centuries previously during a time of much strife in the lowlands, with all sorts of caste wars going on. To make things even more interesting, there were numerous foreign missionaries in the mix trying hard to convert as many of the locals as they could. One could barely travel a few miles in any direction without bumping into one of them – Jesuits, French Capuchins, English Protestants, Lutherans, Americans, Belgians – and some of them even grew to be quite well known, people like Francis Xavier and Robert de Nobili. One of the most famous was a Jesuit called John de Britto, who became one of South India's first martyrs; he had such a hold upon his disciples that the ruler of the kingdom in which he lived, the Raja of Ramnad, decided to do away with him. To make absolutely sure the future saint – he was canonized a few centuries after his death – wasn't going to rise inconveniently from the dead, the raja had him tortured, beheaded and impaled upon a stake. As an extra precaution he had his arms and legs cut off as well. This didn't stop a cult forming around the martyr, and several shrines dedicated to him were soon established.

About 200 years ago, or maybe 300 (it all depended on who you talked to, the Professor said; that was the thing about myth, it was like plasticine, you could mould it into any shape you wanted to), a wandering Christian mystic called Gnanasundaram, a disciple of de Britto, came up into the mountains and decided to pray and meditate on the Tower of God. His only possession of any value was a piece of wood from the stake on which the saint had been martyred which the fakir had fashioned into a crude cross. One day, a tribal elder who was suffering from leprosy came to the holy man for help and was cured. News of the miracle spread, and soon there was a steady stream of pilgrims making their way to Meham, where a shrine was put up by devotees of the holy man. The pilgrimage was a hazardous undertaking back then – the area was teeming with tigers, leopards and all manner of poisonous snakes and insects – but that did not seem to deter the faithful or the desperate. The mystic turned no one away from the shrine, no matter what their religion was, because the faith he propounded was a curious mixture of non-denominational

Christianity, Hinduism and mystical Islam. Then he offended one of the local headmen – an occupational hazard for mystics and holy men, it seemed to me – and was beheaded. According to legend, no sooner did his head touch the ground than it was transformed into a mound of jasmine flowers. As the holy man's body dematerialized, the chief who had cut his head off repented, and the cult of the Blessed Martyr of Meham was born.

For hundreds of years thereafter there was peace, but then, during the time of the British, the first signs of trouble emerged. In the 1920s an obscure Hindu sect from the plains petitioned the British collector of the district to demand the return of the martyr's shrine to Hindus because it rightfully belonged to the followers of Lord Shiva. Needless to say the petition astonished devotees of the shrine. According to the sect, the Tower of God was shaped like a lingam, and this was physical proof that the place was holy to the lord of creation and destruction. A shrine to Lord Shiva had once existed on the spot, the sect claimed, but it had been demolished in the eighteenth century by a general of the Mysore Sultan, Hyder Ali. This was the spot the mystic Gnanasundaram had apparently chosen to set up his shrine, and as the Muslims weren't as opposed to Christians as they were to Hindus they had encouraged him to do so. There was obviously no proof of any of this, the professor said, but the beauty of myth and supposition was that there was no need for proof – your myth was as good as mine, and all that mattered was whether your voice was loud enough to drown out mine. The British collector dismissed the sect's petition, but in an act of monumental stupidity, or perhaps as a result of the prevailing policy to keep people from different religious communities at each other's throats, he allowed the sect to build a temple to Lord Shiva a few hundred feet below the shrine. Since then, every few decades the Hindus would demand retribution and the Christians would resist just as fervently. Through all this, ordinary devotees – Hindus, Muslims, Christians and Buddhists in their hundreds – had continued to visit the shrine and pray at the cross blessed by the martyr. Some people had even claimed that they had seen the cross bleed on days holy to Gnanasundaram, such as his Feast Day, but the Professor thought that was just another example of the myths that had sprouted around the shrine.

The most serious threat had come in recent times. When the Babri Masjid was demolished, just as scores of holy places elsewhere in the country were besieged, so Meham's shrine was also targeted. A group of hooligans, most of them loafers and petty criminals from around the district led by a local MLA, had marched on the shrine a week after the destruction in Ayodhya, but the tough-minded inspector in charge of the Meham police station had denied them entry. He was transferred soon after by the government, whose sympathies clearly lay with the fundamentalists, but the nationwide outrage at the wave of violence unleashed by Ayodhya and the prevailing mood in Meham, which was against the shrine being taken over, forced the government to change its stance. A permanent police picket to safe-guard the shrine was duly installed.

But just a few weeks ago, on the first anniversary of the Babri Masjid demolition, a better-planned attack had almost succeeded. It had been announced with a great fanfare by the Kadavul Katchi, a right-wing political organization headquartered in Coimbatore that had links to national parties, and this time the agitation was led by Rajan, the Bombayite I had been hearing so much about. Rajan was a bit of an insider because he had lived in Meham during his youth. The professor said he would have succeeded in occupying the shrine if it had not been for the weather. 'It had rained heavily for three days before the attack,' Professor Menon said, 'and there was a steady drizzle on the chosen day, so it would have been suicide for anyone to try and climb the last 108 steps to the shrine.'

'There are 108 steps?'

'Yes, thambi, the saint's Hindu devotees made sure there were precisely 108; it's an auspicious number. Another reason, by the way, for the fundamentalists to say it's actually a Hindu temple, although it is one of the few claims that can actually be refuted as the steps were carved by the owner of a stone quarry when he was cured of leukaemia after praying at the shrine. In rainy weather the steps are so slippery that until the district authorities took steps to prevent people from making the ascent, pilgrims would die regularly.'

There was something that didn't make sense to me, and I asked the professor why Rajan had chosen to telegraph his intentions ahead of the attack, when it would have been so much easier for him to march in unannounced with a few supporters disguised as pilgrims.

'Wouldn't it have been very difficult to dislodge him after that, especially if he could actually provide some proof to back his claims that it was a Hindu shrine?'

'He wouldn't do that,' the professor said. 'It would do him no good to take it over quietly; he needs the publicity, he wants to get people worked up. For him the question of whether that piece of rock is Hindu, Christian or animist is not about religion, it's a means to an end, and that end is Rajan's rise to power. He dons the garb of a religious fanatic because it is useful to him, not because he is any more religious than the next man. No, Rajan is as secular as any secular person you know, and uses religion in a purely secular way to achieve his goal. And so if he were to take over the shrine he would have to do so in a blaze of publicity. That is why he pressed ahead with the attack on the sixth of December, knowing there would be people watching. And when he retreated, vowing to take back the shrine for Hindus everywhere, he ensured he would have an even bigger audience the next time he tried. He had one reporter present a few weeks ago, next time he'll have eight.'

'So is he going to wait a year before he tries again?' I asked.

'No, he said in an interview with a Tamil newspaper that he was going to stage a dharna on Republic Day, asking for the shrine to be handed back,' the professor said.

'That's less than a month away,' I said.

'Precisely. That's why I am worried. Brother Ahimas is so unworldly that he thinks we shouldn't take any extra precautions, but I am really glad you're here to write about it, thambi, we need all the help we can get.'

Noah dropped me off at the foot of my hill, and as I trudged up to the house I was filled with misgivings. Until I had met Professor Menon, I had thought about the shrine solely in terms of the story I was going to write about it – Mr Sorabjee's instructions had been explicit – but that evening as I mulled over everything I had heard I wondered if there might not be a way in which I could help while doing the research and interviews for my article. I wasn't sure how effective I would be but I decided I'd try and set up a meeting with Rajan both to interview him for my story and to ascertain his real intentions regarding the shrine. I would also try, as unobtrusively as possible, to see what precautions were being taken to ensure the situation did not explode out of control. That would mean talking to the collector in Ooty, the inspector of the Meham police station, and prominent local citizens like Brigadier Sharma. I wrote up my notes, made my preparations for the visit to the Tower of God the next day, and then, just before going to bed, I picked up Mr Sorabjee's manuscript, as I had the previous two nights.

SHAHENSHAH AKBAR

Emperor of Faith

Elephants in musth are very dangerous. This is a condition that affects male elephants during the breeding season from about twenty-one to eighty years of age. An elephant in musth displays several symptoms – the temporal glands, located between the eye and the ear, become engorged and start discharging a strong-smelling brown fluid and the animal dribbles urine constantly. It becomes extremely aggressive, charging anything that moves without provocation; it is sensitive to the slightest noise, and even its mahout cannot approach it safely. For this reason, domestic elephants in musth are usually securely chained to trees to prevent them from damaging themselves or those who tend to them.

I am over eighty now, but when I was young I felt the urge to push life to the limits, something I am sure you will be familiar with. A friend and I would get on my motorbike and drive up and down Marine Drive as fast as we could in an attempt to impress the girls from Wilson College. It was the most reckless stunt we could think of. I am sure young people today would find it tame but I am inclined to think that even the most daring of you wouldn't attempt what Emperor Akbar did as a youth – he rode great musth-maddened war elephants, including those that had recently killed men, for sport. It was typical of the man. He thrived on challenges and the adrenalin rush of activities that put him in physical danger. To the consternation of his generals, he was always at the forefront of the various battles he fought, lopping off heads to join the towers of severed body parts the Mughals left on the field of battle. It was a custom handed down from their forebears, the Mongols, the tribes that the world had come to fear when they were ruled by the legendary Genghis Khan.

Akbar (1542-1605) was fourteen years old when he became emperor of Hindustan, the third to accede to the Mughal throne after his father Humayun and grandfather Babur. Unlike his predecessors, Akbar was the first Mughal truly to call the country his homeland, and he devoted all his energies and attention to what had hitherto just been a possession. The empire he inherited was by no means secure because the emperor's hold on many of his territories, especially in the farthest reaches of the subcontinent, depended entirely on the goodwill and fealty of the powerful amirs and his relatives, who controlled various important kingdoms. But Akbar proved to be a strong and decisive ruler, and he soon brought the state under his control.

Nothing in Akbar's early upbringing gave any hint of his revolutionary thinking about faith and spirituality. His father and grandfather had been aesthetes who took an interest in religion as men of culture were expected to do, but Akbar displayed no such inclination when he was young. He preferred to hunt and learn the art of combat, both of which he soon excelled at. Few men could match the emperor's physical feats of endurance and his marksmanship was spoken of with awe. But as he grew older, his passion for the arts of war and sex and his physical prowess began to decline and he became increasingly preoccupied with the welfare of his subjects and the duties of a ruler. Although the Mughal empire was the richest in the world at this time (by contrast, the total revenue of the king of England was only about one seventeenth that of Akbar's) it was a land of stark inequalities. The emperor, his princes, amirs and noblemen were prodigiously wealthy but there was also widespread poverty and famine in the land. Exercised by this, Akbar began to devote a lot of his time and resources to improving the lives of his people; a natural corollary of this shift in the emperor's priorities was a growing interest in the variety of faiths that his subjects followed, for Hindustan was already home to many religions. Akbar had Hindu wives but this was not unusual – like other emperors of the time, he had entered into marriage alliances with princesses belonging to vassal kingdoms – but what marked him out from his predecessors and other Muslim rulers was the unusual interest he took in Hindu theology, festivals and rites. This incensed the orthodox Muslim clergy, but he didn't pay them much heed and continued with his heretical ways; he was after all God's chosen representative on the planet.

In time, Akbar began engaging with holy men from every faith, and even convened regular meetings at a centre of religion and philosophy he'd set up called the Ibadat Khana. Initially, the holy men who debated the intricacies of faith at the Ibadat Khana were drawn from the various sects of Islam, but soon the Emperor opened up the forum to learned men of every religion: Hindus, Parsis, Jains and Jesuits. The Ibadat Khana, according to historians, was a tower from which walkways radiated to platforms embedded in an outer structure that encircled the core. The emperor sat in the middle of the inner tower while the wise men were placed all around him. Once everyone was settled the discourses on the true meaning of faith would begin. The sea of rhetoric would ebb and flow, controlled by the man at the centre, a man who would in time confound the Gods themselves with his thinking about faith. But that lay in the future.

In 1579 Emperor Akbar was at the height of his power, ruling an empire larger than any that had existed before or since in the subcontinent. He was not yet forty years old. For some time now, as we have seen, he had been annoying the orthodox Muslim ulema, who were technically in charge of all religious matters, but he angered them still further by formally making known his respect for all faiths. He celebrated Diwali, wore Hindu caste marks on his forehead, participated in Parsi and Jain rites and proclaimed that all religions were equally true.

And then, in his thirty-seventh year, he took the enormous step of promulgating a syncretic faith for his land of a thousand faiths, a religion that cobbled together the best of all the religions and attempted to do away with divisions based on faith. He called the new religion Din Ilahi or Divine Faith. He did not give up Islam, nor did he require any of his subjects to give up their beliefs. 'No man should be interfered with on account of his religion,' he said, 'and anyone should be allowed to go over to any religion . . .' Din Ilahi would be an additional faith that people could subscribe to. But even though he was the most powerful man in the land, literally with the power of life and death over his people, Akbar's Din Ilahi was a doomed enterprise because few of his subjects, non-Muslim or orthodox Muslim, could see themselves switching to a new faith or adding it to their own religion, especially as it was centred on a man, no matter that he was their emperor. However, for a brief instant, the country had been led by someone who genuinely believed in coming up with a faith or philosophy that would include all its people.

Akbar's vision, though short-lived, should be an inspiration to us all in this moment of crisis. We cannot do without religion but it cannot be left in the hands of small-minded men who will use it to advance their own petty ends. What we need is a man of God who is also a ruler of men, who can release faith from the squalid prison it has been locked into by the fundamentalists and, through his own example, show us how it can bring us together, not divide us. Our need is for an Emperor of Faith.

9

The Tower of God

Noah and I had arranged to meet at ten so that we could be at the shrine a little after noon, when Professor Menon was expecting us. He had told us Brother Ahimas would be free then and had invited us to stay on for lunch. I had intended to set off from Cypress Manor a little later than I would have normally done in order to give Noah an extra half-hour for any extra-curricular activities he might have planned, but just as I was closing the gates behind me, I heard an engine labouring up the hill. Within minutes the priest's scooter came into sight. Noah pressed the horn in welcome and it gave a weak chirp. He looked slightly less scruffy than usual having swapped his lungi and old T-shirt for jeans and a T-shirt with a faded picture of Jimi Hendrix printed on it. When I complimented him on his appearance, he laughed and said, 'I had to freshen up or your neighbours would have set their dogs on me. First time I've come up this hill in years, so I thought I'd break out my favourite T-shirt featuring Shri Hendrix.'

'My room-mate's a fan ...'

'And you're not? Come on, da, he just happened to be the greatest guitarist who ever walked the earth.'

I confessed that I didn't know too much about rock, whereupon he leaned over, almost toppling the scooter, grabbed hold of me, and said sternly, 'OK, you've got to make me a promise. When you go back to Bombay, I want you to listen to your room-mate's Hendrix tapes ...'

I laughed and said I'd do as he suggested. It took a little manoeuvring to turn the scooter around, and as he did so he told me a story about Hendrix. 'You know, the guy was re-imagining the way the guitar was played, taking it places that hadn't even been thought of let alone tried before, so on his first visit to England, all the great guitar gods of the time, Clapton, Keith Richards, Pete Townshend, the Led Zep guy, you know fuckers of that calibre, trooped over to the club where he was playing to check him out. During the intermission Richards went to the loo to take a leak, and the guy in the stall next to him asked what the superstars who were all bunched up next to the stage thought of the show.

"Oh, it's very wet up there . . ." Richards said.

"Wet?"

"Yeah, from all the tears of envy that are being shed . . ."'

The scooter's front wheel had got stuck at an angle, and Noah was wrestling with it. 'That's the only way to be, man, so far ahead of the pack that you basically make the rules . . . Otherwise you're fucked, you either have to conform or find a cave, drop out of sight . . . Here, help me with this scooter, da, I want to be out of here before someone tells the Brigadier and his cohorts that I'm trespassing on his hill.'

I thought of the distinguished-looking man he had avoided in the market, and I wondered again why the elite of Meham disliked him so much. They were probably old-fashioned and conservative, and would be offended by Noah's dress sense and manner, but surely that and his stealing the occasional fuchsia were not sufficient to unleash the guard dogs? He had told me quite a bit about himself, but would he really tell me if he had done something terrible?

We finally managed to get the scooter pointing in the right direction and I climbed on behind him with some trepidation, remembering the terrifying ride of the day before; then I thought of Mr Sorabjee riding his motorbike full tilt down Marine Drive and sheepishly told myself to relax. In any event, I needn't have worried because this time Noah drove sensibly, even sedately.

⁓ℰℋ⁓

It was a brilliant day, and we rode under the same sort of hard blue sky I had remarked on when I had first arrived in the Nilgiris. We took a different route this time, skirting the town. About a kilometre short of our destination the road descended gently towards a hairpin bend, beyond which lay the Valley of God, as Noah mockingly called it. He switched off the engine, and we began coasting downhill.

As we came around the bend, the great rift opened up before us. The first time I had seen it, it had inspired awe – the tremendous mountains, the whirling mist and cloud – but even on a clear, sunny day it was no less dramatic. Row upon row of granite peaks, marched up to the precipice, and then tumbled over to the plains many thousand feet below. At the very edge the Tower of God was outlined against the sky.

'It's quite a spectacle,' I said.

'That it is, ready to climb it?'

'Absolutely,' I replied.

'Hope you have a head for heights,' he remarked as he parked the scooter. From the road we descended to a plateau on which there was an observation tower, with glassed-in windows, urinals off to one side and a few shops. This was the point from which anyone who wished to climb the Tower of God would need to set off. In addition to the facilities for tourists and pilgrims, there was the police picket that Professor Menon had told us about. The three policemen on duty seemed bored, and after giving us a cursory glance went back to playing cards. The mist that had filled the valley the previous day had hidden all this from view.

'How long do you think the police will stay?' I asked as we approached the shops.

'I guess they'll be here for a while, not that these clowns could stop anyone.' Noah smiled, waved to the policemen, and we walked on. I saw militant slogans daubed on the surrounding rocks and even on the observation tower in praise of Lord Shiva and demanding the return of the shrine to him. Unlike similar establishments surrounding places of pilgrimage, the stalls here were free of gaudy pictures of gods and goddesses, cheap statues and devotional bric-a-brac. I remarked on this and Noah said, 'That was the collector's idea. He laid down orders prohibiting the sale of religious artefacts until further notice so, ironically, the shrine, which has been secular for hundreds of years, is even more secular today. Come on, da, let's have some secular tea,' he said with a laugh; 'we have quite a climb ahead of us.'

Finishing our tea, we were lounging around chatting when Noah happened to look up. Fists of cloud were beginning to uncurl in the sky, and he got up. 'If we're going to get to the shrine, we'd better start right away. The steps leading to the Tower will be impassable if it starts to drizzle.' He explained that it would take us at least an hour to get to the summit, the Tower was farther away than it looked. First, we would have to climb down from where we were sitting to level ground, then we would need to trek through a stretch of jungle that would get us to the Shiva temple, and it was only after that the climb up the Tower proper would begin.

After paying for our tea, we walked down a steep flight of steps to the path that led to the Tower. We crossed a bridge that spanned a clear mountain stream and then the path began to rise. On either side there were broad-leaved plants with white, bell-shaped flowers. I was reaching out to pluck one when Noah snapped, 'Don't, they're poisonous.' I drew back hastily, and after that we walked in silence until we reached a windswept ridge spined with a few hardy trees. Beyond lay a stretch of open land, and then the path led into what looked like impenetrable forest. The brightness of the day had dimmed considerably and a grey mist had begun to sift through the trees.

Within minutes of entering the forest I became jumpy. It was difficult to see the path in the gloom, and I remembered Professor Menon's tales from the previous evening about the wild animals that early pilgrims had had to avoid. Common sense told me that there was no threat but I had never been in a forest before, which I suppose accounted for my nerves. As we walked further into the woods, the light grew murkier. Everywhere around us there were furtive rustlings and chitterings, as if an array of unseen creatures was watching our progress and telegraphing it ahead to some nameless horror which lay in wait. I was telling myself to stop being so jittery when a terrifying cry erupted from the gloom. I almost tripped and fell, and frantically asked Noah what it was. His reply was a laugh. 'Nothing to be worried about in these woods my friend,' he said. 'The creature that made that noise won't eat you – it's a smallish bird called a scimitar babbler. It's very shy, very rare, you'll be lucky to see one.'

'So, no wild animals here?'

'If you'd lived a hundred years ago, maybe. Now the only nuisance is marauding monkeys, all spoiled rotten by the pilgrims and pujaris at the Shiva temple.'

As if in response to Noah's remark, there was a crashing in the trees and a rhesus monkey appeared on a nearby branch. He regarded us with bright-eyed interest. 'Don't do anything, don't make any threatening moves. When he realizes you don't have any food for him he'll leave you alone.'

Presently the forest began to thin, and we came to a clearing in which the temple to Shiva stood. It was a modest building, with none of the elaborate carvings of gods and demons or gopurams that adorned most Tamil temples, but the mist and the great forest that surrounded it imbued it with an air of grandeur and holiness that no human hand could have created. Involuntarily I bowed and put my hands together in a respectful namaskaram, almost expecting this gesture of devotion to be accepted by an enormous multi-armed figure stalking out of the gloom, a weapon in every hand and a rudraksh mala around his neck. But no such apparition emerged, and the only sign of life about the place was an old woman weaving marigold garlands in a stone quadrangle in front of the temple. She would pick up the flowers from a large basket that glowed orange in the poor light and skilfully thread them on to a string she held in her other hand. She looked up, but her eyes milky with cataracts didn't appear to see us. Noah greeted the old woman politely, and we passed on, leaving the temple behind.

In a short while we'd reached the base of the Tower of God, which, up close, looked even more impressive than it had appeared from the road. Steps were cut into it, and for the safety of pilgrims and visitors there was a guard rail, two strips of braided steel wire threaded through spikes hammered into the living rock.

Rubbish littered our passage – food wrappers, tins and bottles, broken chappals – and we had to pick our way carefully through the junk until we reached the steps. The profusion of rubbish was the one thing I had seen thus far that was common to other places of worship I had visited but I realized that nowhere on the approach to the Tower of God or the Shiva temple had I encountered the clotted masses of people – devotees, and those who preyed on them, freelance priests and other peddlers of salvation, hawkers, thieves and pick-pockets, and most of all the rows of beggars, screaming at the faithful and God to give them alms, salvation and a cure for the various afflictions they suffered from – who infested the other temples. Even as I thought this, I knew why they were missing: it was simply too cold for the poor and the ill-clothed to visit Meham in the winter; in the summer the scene would be altogether different. The forest and the tower of stone would be submerged in a noisy surge of humanity, which, in its urge to supplicate God, wiped out the very silence that was at the heart of the divine mystery. But perhaps that was only the way I saw it; others probably needed crowds of like-minded people to reinforce their own faith and maybe God himself needed the masses as much as he needed to walk alone.

I was about to set foot on the lowest step when Noah stopped me. He told me to be very careful, to test my footing on each step before moving on to the next; if I found myself slipping, I was to grab the rail. Apparently, it had only been installed quite recently, when three pilgrims had fallen to their deaths. 'Not that it was something that had never happened before. Every so often an old or infirm pilgrim would disappear, but nobody minded much, it was considered auspicious to die while you were climbing the Tower of God – granted you instant nirvana. But these three were a bunch of bloody NRIs from Vancouver or New Jersey, or one of those places, and there was an outcry, reports in the media and talk of suing someone, anyone, so the district administration had to do something.'

They had also become a lot stricter about enforcing the policy of not letting anyone on to the Tower of God during bad weather. Even now we had to proceed carefully, as some of the steps, especially those in shadow, retained some moisture from the rain of a few days earlier. Once I nearly slipped on a patch of moss, but regained my balance in an instant, without needing to clutch at the guard rail, which seemed dangerously flimsy to me. We emerged from the mist into brilliant sunshine, and no longer had to worry about our footing but I found myself in trouble for an altogether different reason. Although we had climbed just over half the 108 steps, my thighs, unaccustomed to the steep gradient, were screaming in agony. I said to Noah that I would have to rest, so we sat down on the steps. 'Don't look down,' Noah said, 'if you are not used to heights.'

The rest did me some good, but the pain returned almost immediately when we resumed climbing. Noah seemed as fresh as ever, so I grimly ignored the pain, planting one foot after the other, counting each step, determined to hang on because I knew that if we stopped again I would be able to climb no further. 101, 102, 103, 104, 105 ... and to my surprise we were on level ground. I had got the count wrong and relief had come sooner than I had expected. We were on a ledge that was cemented over; there were a couple of benches for pilgrims to rest on and a tall earthenware pitcher of water covered by an aluminium saucer on which there was a long-handled dipper. I eased my aching body on to one of the benches and watched as Noah drank some water. It was cold on the exposed ledge, but I was sweating from my exertions. I sat there for a while letting the breeze dry me off, then drank some water and, feeling quite refreshed, was ready for the final stage of the climb. It had taken us slightly over an hour to get to this point and I wondered at the fortitude of some of the more decrepit pilgrims who attempted the journey. From where we sat a concrete walkway sloped upward to the shrine and its outbuildings, but Noah wanted to take me along a different route. He explained that the benches and the walkway were new, and that a few years ago the final approach to the shrine wound around the contours of the rock formation. He suggested we follow the old route, it was much more scenic; besides, there was something he wanted to show me. We took a narrow path that followed the curve of the Tower and led us into a field of blue so intense that it seemed as though a patch of sky had fallen and draped itself over the hard grey stone. This part of the monolith was partially sheltered from the wind and had been taken over by long ropes of morning glory that hung over the precipice, blazing with flowers. As I took in the scene I saw in my mind's eye the old gardener feeding the flowers into the fire and telling me the only way to get rid of morning glory was to burn it. Some things, I thought, had no place in civilized homes and gardens, they were simply too overpowering and needed the quiet, wild places of the world in order to flourish.

A single strand of rail along which the vines had twined themselves was all that stood between us and the drop; when I realized this, I stepped back hastily. Noah said, 'That was wise. It's a good thing you don't have vertigo.'

The path wound around the rock and eventually led into the courtyard of the shrine. Here another surprise awaited me – the air had a subtle fragrance to it. At first I couldn't place it, and then I saw where it was coming from. In the middle of the courtyard was a trellis embedded into the concrete almost entirely covered by a luxuriant jasmine creeper spattered with tiny white flowers. At the base of the structure thick ropes of jasmine were heaped, most of them brown and faded. Noah explained that offerings to the saint took the form of jasmine garlands, in keeping with the legend of his death and miraculous transformation. The scent of old flowers accompanied us into the shrine.

Freshly lime-washed, it glowed bone-white in the high clear light. There was no furniture of any kind within – no pews, no table and no altar. There was a small raised platform where an altar would normally have been, and on it, mounted in a block of granite, was the miraculous cross behind an iron railing on which pilgrims had twisted prayer ribbons and attached handwritten messages.

'Ah, here's the professor,' Noah said from behind me, and I turned to see our host of the evening before, dressed in a blue sweater and white trousers. He greeted us warmly and suggested we go for lunch. As we walked out of the shrine, I was surprised at how large the summit of the Tower of God actually was. It must easily have been a couple of hundred metres across, and contained besides the shrine itself a low building towards which we were heading and another narrow two-storeyed building, which housed the living quarters of the custodian and others who stayed here.

As we approached the dining hall, I noticed vast cauldrons being washed in one corner of the courtyard. I asked Professor Menon whether many pilgrims visited the shrine and whether they were all fed. He said this was not the pilgrim season, it was too cold, but they were preparing for the saint's Feast Day, which fell on 5 January. They were expecting at least a hundred visitors then, especially if the weather held up. My mind flashed back to the conversation we'd had the previous evening, about when Rajan would try to enter the shrine. Something told me he wouldn't make his attempt during Republic Day – he wouldn't cool his heels in Meham for three weeks, would he? But if he made his move during Feast Day, there would be media in attendance, even if it comprised only local stringers, and there would be enough people to witness his triumph. And he would need to triumph this time; it wouldn't help his cause if, having thrown down the gauntlet, he was to fail again.

'Will you be able to attend the festival?' the professor was asking.

'I certainly intend to,' I said grimly. I told them my suspicions and the professor nodded. 'Yes, of course, it makes sense, I should have thought of that.'

'But why not take over the shrine in the spring, at Easter or one of the other major Christian festivals when there will be thousands more people from all over the country?' Noah asked.

The professor thought for a moment, then said, 'I think it would be much more difficult. You've seen the crush of pilgrims who arrive for Easter service at the shrine, not to mention the thousands of tourists who come hoping to see the cross start to bleed. It would be too tough to control. Rajan would prefer to deal with a more manageable crowd. No, I think Vijay is right, it will probably be Feast Day.'

'Should we tell Brother Ahimas?'

'I don't see why not, but I doubt he'll want to do anything. We'll just have to alert the police and the collector.'

~·~

Brother Ahimas was just the way I had imagined him to be. He was a man of medium height with long flowing white hair, an untrimmed beard and dark eyes that fairly shone with compassion. He unsettled me. His direct, open gaze and the saintliness he projected made me feel uncomfortably aware of myself. He greeted Noah affectionately, and then turned to me. Noah introduced me as a friend of his from Bombay, whereupon, unprompted, I launched into a hurried explanation of how I had ended up in Meham: the riots in Bombay, the attack, the aftermath, my work at the magazine, the assignment

I was on. All through my nervous chatter, Brother Ahimas kept his disconcerting gaze fixed on me. When I eventually ran out of things to say, he remarked gently, 'You have endured much at a very young age, thambi, but by God's grace you have survived. Come, let's have lunch, we can talk some more.' He took my arm and led the way to the lunch hall, followed by Menon and Noah.

There were three people eating in the big room. Brother Ahimas greeted them, walked over to a corner, settled down on a mat and invited us to sit. Volunteers served us a meal of sambhar, avial and rice on banana leaves. The custodian said grace and we began to eat. The food was simple but it was well prepared, and I quickly finished what was on my leaf and accepted another helping before I realized that none of the others had finished. I waited somewhat awkwardly for them to catch up with me, and wondered who might broach the subject of Rajan. When it became clear that Noah and the professor were not going to bring it up, I decided to plunge in. 'Aiyah, I think the shrine is in great danger; the people who attacked it earlier this month are going to try again on Feast Day. They might try to pass themselves off as pilgrims,' I said, adding as much detail as I could. The custodian heard me out in silence, and then said, 'Thambi, the shrine has been under attack many times in the past, but it still stands. For as long as it is God's will, no harm will come to it, and if God wills otherwise, it is only bricks and stone that will be destroyed.'

'But aiyah, what of those who make the pilgrimage? This shrine must be defended for their sake, don't you think?'

'It is said, thambi, that when the saint first came here, it was a wild and inhospitable place, but he didn't mind, he had been led here by God. In his time there was no building, no shrine; his message was spoken under the Nilgiri skies, and no matter what happens I have no doubt that the saint's message will live on.'

I couldn't argue with that sentiment, and as neither Professor Menon nor Noah seemed inclined to say anything, it seemed pointless to continue. 'Come now, you must eat, your food is growing cold,' the custodian said gently. I finished hurriedly, and we went out into the mild afternoon sun. For an old man, Brother Ahimas was very fit. He walked briskly to the outer edge of the Tower of God, where a low ridge provided a natural barrier. All around us the mountains padded away into the distance, an army of giants turned to stone. Under the luminous plane of the sky, the forests that clothed their lower slopes glowed green, and it was easy to imagine that we were looking at a wilderness untouched by man and consecrated by God. Far below us, dimly glimpsed through the haze, we could see a line of greenery that marked the passage of a river.

Why was it, I wondered unhappily, that even the earth's paradises were not spared from destruction? Was this God's own hand at work, tearing apart the perfection he had created? It made no sense at all.

'You're lucky, my friends,' Brother Ahimas said. 'This place is usually wreathed in cloud, but it's been an exceptionally clear day. I usually say my prayers here at dawn, and this morning I understood, as if for the first time, that we are truly blessed to live in this holy land. Long before the rest of the world emerged from the darkness of ignorance and apostasy, when other races were still worshipping the Gods of war and vengeance, the great sages and rishis of Hinduism understood that they were false Gods, and the only true God to be found within every one of us was the God of compassion.' He paused for a while, gazing out over the mountains. My mind went back to Mr Sorabjee's manuscript and the story in it about Emperor Akbar's debating hall of faith, the Ibadat Khana, and I thought Brother Ahimas would have fitted right in with the other religious savants who adorned it. He broke the silence. 'We have been able to find God in fire, water, air and stone, so why is it that we don't seem to be able to find Him in our hearts? The monuments we raise up in His name grow grander and grander but when will we realize that they have no value in His eyes if we fill them with hate and violence?'

He put his hand on my shoulder, looked me in the eye and said, 'That you have found a purpose after the trauma you have suffered is something we should be thankful for. But do not worry about this shrine. Nothing can destroy the handiwork of God.' He took his hand off my shoulder, made the sign of the cross over us and left.

When he had disappeared from view, I asked Menon if there was anything he could add to the details that he had given us the previous evening of how the shrine might be defended in the event of attack. 'It is possible to defend it, if you're wholly committed to the effort,' he said. 'If the attackers make it up the steps, there are only two approaches and they can be easily guarded. The only problem is that Brother Ahimas will not allow any form of active defence. He says the saint was an apostle of peace, and any violence will desecrate his memory. The last time, about a dozen youths, Christians, Hindus and Muslims, arrived at the shrine with a variety of weapons but Brother Ahimas sent them away. Fortunately, as you know, the weather saved the day, and soon after the town elders organized a peace march and calmed the people, so Rajan couldn't do any real damage, but if he is planning a sneak attack, then we will have a problem.'

'The more I think of it, the more convinced I am that he will make his move on Feast Day,' I said.

'Yes, we will need to be extra vigilant,' the professor said.

'I've said this to Vijay before but I'll say it again,' Noah said. 'I'm aware I'm the lone dissenting voice here but Rajan is too smart to want to alienate the people of this town. The shrine is part of their daily lives, they wouldn't want it to be destroyed. I think he might try to give us a scare, but I don't think he'll do anything drastic.'

I thought of the poor muddy streets of Meham, the aimless young men who stood around on its street corners, and their faces merged with the faces of the thugs who had tried to destroy Bombay and I knew Noah was wrong. He didn't know what people like Rajan were capable of, he didn't know how susceptible people with nothing else in their lives could be to the allure of religious feuding.

'We thought Bombay could not be destroyed, and that's what a lot of people thought about the Babri Masjid. But there's no telling what people can do when they are caught up in a religious frenzy,' I said.

'I agree with Vijay,' Professor Menon added sombrely. 'We should take every precaution we can.' He told us he would phone the police and the collector, and quietly arrange to have some of the town's young men patrol the approaches to the shrine.

It was time to go, I had to attend the New Year's Eve celebration at the club with Brigadier Sharma. I told Professor Menon that I would spread the word there about Rajan's intended plans so we could muster as much support as possible.

10

Fuchsia wars

The true gardener, Noah once said to me, sees the world very differently from the rest of us. Where you or I might remark upon the beauty of a rose or be captivated by the riotous colour of a bed of geraniums, the gardener will focus on a mottled leaf that might be the first sign of disease, or pick up a clod of earth and crumble it in his fingers to gauge its porosity and alkaline content, or read the clouds or the behaviour of birds and other strange portents which are incomprehensible to non-gardeners. I had never so much as uprooted a weed, so the mysterious world of the gardener was, I suspected, forever shut to me. The gentlemen gardeners of the Fuchsia Club of Meham seemed, at first glance, to be as ignorant of gardening as I was, but they didn't let that bother them.

The club's claim to be the oldest continuously active association in the Nilgiris was not belied by the age of its members. They all appeared to be over seventy; the Indian cabinet seemed positively sprightly by comparison. But neither their advanced years nor the fact that they had never dirtied their hands with topsoil prevented them from making vigorous contributions to the club's last meeting of the year.

⁓᷋ᜃ᷍⁓

As soon as I got home from the shrine I had hurriedly bathed and changed, and it was just as well that I did, for at a quarter to seven a midnight-blue Mercedes, buffed and polished until it shone, with a uniformed chauffeur behind the wheel, pulled into the driveway.

The Brigadier got out to shake hands, and I was immediately conscious of how underdressed I was in my grey trousers and sweater. In contrast, the Brigadier could have stepped from the pages of a magazine aimed at the Distinguished Older Gentleman: grey flannels, blinding white shirt, crested blazer, regimental tie and well-shined black shoes. Everything about him exuded wealth. Noah had told me the Brigadier's wife's family were prominent Delhi industrialists. He must have barely met the army's height requirement, but his erect carriage, fierce, upswept, almost cartoonish moustache and direct gaze more than made up for his lack of inches. He took in my attire and frowned for a moment, then said, 'Umm, you'll need a tie, but we can fix that quite easily, old boy.' He sized me up a little longer, and then bellowed, 'Karunakaran.'

The chauffeur, who seemed to be ex-army as well, stiffened to attention.

'Tie lao. Jaldi,' the Brigadier growled and, to my astonishment, the chauffeur opened the boot of the car and brought out a portable tie rack on which three ties were draped.

'Always be prepared is my motto,' the Brigadier said smugly. 'I fancied that you might not know the rules of the club, old chap, so here we are.' He drew out a silvery grey patterned tie, shook his head, and finally decided on a plain red tie that he thought would go with my beige sweater. Before I could react, he had folded out my collar, slung the tie around my neck, knotted it expertly, bent my collar back into place, and then stepped back to examine his handiwork. He pronounced himself satisfied and we set off.

On the way to the club, he told me about the genesis of the FCM. Noah had already told me a bit about it, but I wasn't about to say that I knew anything – I wanted to avoid the inevitable question about my informant – so I let the Brigadier hold forth.

❧

About twenty years ago, while he was serving in the army, he had been posted to the Nilgiris as a member of the directing staff at the Defence Services Staff College in Wellington. He had attended the college as a young student officer several years earlier, and both he and his wife had been enchanted by the place. During his second sojourn in the Nilgiris his wife had succumbed to the allure of gardening, the favoured pastime of senior army wives and other upper-class women in the district. In the course of one of her periodic forays to the Sims Park Nursery, which offered the widest selection of plants, she had noticed a small shrub with vividly coloured flowers and had immediately bought it. The gardener who was showing her around didn't know what the plant was, so he had taken her to his superior, who had identified it. The Brigadier winked at me, and said with a bray of laughter, 'The poor man didn't know to pronounce it, he called it a Fuck-sia.' I smiled along with him, and he continued his story.

The lone bush had flourished in the Brigadier's garden, but all his efforts to procure other specimens had failed. The nursery didn't know how it had come to be included in its shipment of plants and so didn't know how to order it, and none of the Brigadier's contacts could get any more for him. Meanwhile, the exotically named De Groot's Happiness was the envy of every gardener in the district.

When he retired from the armed forces, he and his wife had decided to settle down in the Nilgiris, rather than return to Bhopal, his home town. They had bought a house in Meham, and transported the treasures of their garden, a number of fuchsias among them (for the efforts of the Brigadier and about a dozen other equally determined gardeners had succeeded in procuring a few more varieties of the plant from other hill stations in India) to their new home. It was around then that the Brigadier had taken over the gardening club at Meham, an association affiliated to the Meham Club, which comprised a score of elderly gentlemen who used it as a pretext to get away from their wives and families for one afternoon every month. Gardening played a very small part in their deliberations, it was more a time for gossip, good food and vast amounts of rum. After the Brigadier arrived, all that had changed. Determined to make the best of his retirement – he had seen too many of his fellow officers drop dead or go to seed when they were discharged with a pension – he poured all his energy and enthusiasm into the gardening club. He did not let his lack of experience with spade and pruning knife deter him; there would always be proper gardeners who could be relied upon to actually sow the seeds, water the plants and stamp out the weeds; what was necessary was to make the gardens of Meham the best in the district, and that needed strategy, organization and a firm, decisive leader.

The objective of every fanatical gardener in the Nilgiris was to win first prize in one or another category at the annual Flower Show that was held in Ooty. There were prizes awarded for Garden of the Year, Outstanding Large Private Garden, Outstanding Medium Private Garden, Outstanding Small Private Garden, Outstanding Rose Garden and numerous others besides, and to the elite nothing mattered more than to come first in their area of specialization. It was accepted that Garden of the Year and Outstanding Large Garden would go to establishments like the Defence Services Staff College in Wellington or Chettinad House in Ooty, which had armies of gardeners to primp, polish and tweak every blade of grass and every petal, so the competition was most intense at the medium garden level, especially for the S.A. Dorai Ever Rolling Cup. None of the gardens in Meham had ever won or even been placed among the finalists in the category and the Brigadier was determined to change that. He bullied, harangued, threatened and cajoled his fellow members to shake off their sloth and get to work, and within a couple of years Meham's gardens began to win prizes, especially the Brigadier's own garden, which won top honours in three of the five years it was entered in the competition. Then the Brigadier's wife, Neeti, who was the person who executed her husband's plans, died, and the Brigadier lost all interest in his garden, until his daughter, a fashion designer in Delhi, visited him one winter and exclaimed over the beauty of a fuchsia shrub. It had once been the hub of an exquisite arrangement of flower beds shaped like a wheel, but now there was nothing but weeds. Anxious about her father's health, his daughter nagged him to take an interest in the garden again. Deep within the Brigadier's gloom a memory glowed of his wife's excitement when she had first glimpsed the fuchsia. It was the first time he had thought about the garden in the two years since her death. When his daughter returned to Delhi, he sent word to his old accomplice, the flower thief called Arumugam, to say he was back in business.

The Brigadier had always been an obsessive man, but beneath his obsessiveness lay a methodical mind, which was why he had been such a good soldier and officer, and latterly a gardener. As he grew obsessed with fuchsias, he renamed the Gardeners' Club of Meham the Fuchsia Club of Meham, successfully petitioned the authorities who ran the Flower Show to institute a prize for Best Fuchsia Garden and aggressively set about making his garden the finest in the district.

In this, Arumugam was a key ally. He had become a flower thief quite by chance. As with many other subsistence farmers in the district, when the small plot of land he farmed was sold to pay off a debt to a local moneylender, he had had to find some way to feed his wife and seven children. He found temporary employment as a gardener at one of the big hotels in Coonoor. One day, a fat woman decked out in an expensive sari had tottered up to him in her high heels and asked him to give her a cutting from a rose bush he was pruning. Without thinking, he had said five rupees as he handed over the twig. She beat him down to two rupees, but a career was born. When he was laid off from the hotel, he went into the business of stealing and selling plants full time. He had a phenomenal memory and a natural ability to identify hundreds of species and sub-species. All he had to do was look at a garden once to know exactly which plants flowered where and how valuable they might be to the intensively competitive gardeners of the district. He played no favourites; he stole from everybody and sold to everybody. A friendly, diminutive man, he had been arrested so many times by the police that he was no longer confined to a jail cell when he was caught but allowed to hang around with the policemen.

After the death of the Brigadier's wife Arumugam no longer took the bus to Meham, but when the Brigadier began to obsess over fuchsias, he was once again summoned to the big bungalow on top of Tiger Hill. There weren't too many varieties of the shrub to be had and they were well guarded, but Arumugam was resourceful: he was friends with a vaidyan in Meham bazaar who would mix him potions that could put a Rajapalaiyam hound to sleep, he knew which servants to bribe, and he was careful not to get caught with the stolen goods in his possession. He was no longer arrested nearly as frequently, and the Brigadier's fuchsia garden flourished. It took top honours in its category five years in a row and a visiting gardener from a fuchsia club in Somerset, to which the FCM was affiliated, pronounced it among the finest he had ever seen.

Our car had come to a stop behind a long line of cars and buses and trucks, seemingly every wheeled vehicle in town, and the Brigadier ordered the driver to find out what was causing the traffic jam. 'These municipal authorities are useless. Give me the army any day, we knew how to get things done,' he said grumpily. The driver returned to say that there had been a landslide further up the road, and there was room for only one vehicle to proceed at a time.

'If I was in charge I'd get a bulldozer to clear it away, put fifty jawans on the job, three shifts. How the hell does this country think it's going to get anywhere if nobody will take any responsibility? The bloody contractor who was hired to do the job is probably being paid by the hour, or isn't being paid enough or has another more lucrative job somewhere else, or hasn't been paid a big enough bribe. I'm sick of all this. I wish I had permission to shoot anyone who was incompetent or a moron or both, I'd solve both the population problem and the country's inefficient ways at one and the same time.' The Brigadier ranted in a mixture of Hindi and English, clearly in order to include both the driver and myself, but as his anger began to subside, he switched back to English, and then he fell silent, gathering his thoughts. I thought now would be the time to talk to him about Rajan and his proposed assault on the shrine. The previous evening, when Noah had dropped me off, I had told him about my invitation to the annual general meeting of the FCM, and he had said, 'I don't much care for them, as you know, and I especially don't like the Brigadier, but he and his group are very influential in this little dung heap, so you should try and persuade them to help. But on no account should you mention my name, even hint at the fact that you know me, especially to the Brigadier, because you'll then be damned in his eyes for ever.'

I was about to interrupt the Brigadier, who had begun prattling on about his fuchsias, when I realized with dismay that the car was turning into the gates of the club. Had I missed my opportunity?

Perhaps not, because it might be even more useful to place the matter before the whole group. As the car pulled to a stop, I said hastily to the Brigadier, 'Sir, there is a matter I want to discuss with you and the other members of the club. Could I have a few minutes after the meeting?'

'Of course, old boy, of course.'

We walked up a flight of steps, past a file of silently bowing retainers dressed in white, green and gold, and through chilly rooms with high ceilings, in which fires were just being lit, infiltrating life into the dead glass eyes of the stuffed heads of tiger, gaur, sambhar and leopard that sprouted from every wall. In the dining room the tables were set with spotless white napkins and cutlery, the library's shadowed light and winged armchairs needed only a corpse to complete a scene from an Agatha Christie novel, and in the billiard room perfectly arranged billiard balls awaited the drunken onslaught of partygoers with inexpertly wielded cues. In an hour the place would be jumping, the rooms filled with light, noise and a press of bodies, but for now we had it to ourselves. The meeting was being held in the bar area, the Brigadier said, because the private room in which they traditionally met was being renovated. As with the other rooms in the club, the bar was deserted except for a couple of white-jacketed and white-gloved bearers, and the barman who stood behind the long counter that ran along the far wall.

We were the last to arrive. The other members of the FCM sat around a rectangular table. The Brigadier took his place at the head of the table, waved me to an empty seat to the left of him, and made the introductions. To his right was a man with a face that was entirely hairless, except for two tufts that escaped like steam from his ears. He was introduced as Venkateswaran, a retired forestry official. Beside him sat the man whom Noah had evaded at the butcher's shop. Dr Das, I learned, had been a very senior official at BARC, the atomic research institute in Bombay, and even in retirement the importance of his job remained sculpted on his face. Next to him was a small man with quick deft movements, the local GP called

Kuruvilla, and beside me was the last member of the group, Kathirvel, a wealthy building contractor. There was an empty chair next to Kathirvel which prompted the Brigadier to make a rather tasteless joke. The absent member, Mr Lal, a tea planter in his nineties, was critically ill. Fixing me with an alarmingly conspiratorial eye, the Brigadier said in a loud whisper, 'People have been saying for years that Lal is about to sleep in heaven. The only problem is he keeps going halfway and coming back.' He laughed uproariously at this, but I noticed I was the only one joining in, so I suppressed any further signs of mirth for fear of giving offence.

Although the FCM was only a private association of gardeners, the Brigadier ran its annual meeting as though it were the board meeting of some large conglomerate. He was a director on the board of a few companies in Madras and Delhi and thought, no doubt, that his cronies in Meham could do with some business discipline. The Chair was duly elected, apologies accepted, and then we got on to the agenda proper. I had received a poor photocopy of the single sheet of paper entitled 'Agenda' and this is how it read:

1) Election of the Chair
2) Apologies
3) Minutes of the previous meeting
4) Petition to the Collector
5) De Groot's Happiness
6) Jack Stanway
7) Hidden Treasure
8) Brian M. Cox
9) Forfar's Pride
10) Wally Yendell
11) Any Other Business

As there weren't enough copies of the minutes to go round, I shared with the building contractor. He had a heavy cold and smelled of onions and Vicks VapoRub so I tried to keep as far from him as possible. As with any meeting, some of the participants were more active than others – the Brigadier and the doctor dominated the proceedings with the forestry officer chipping in from time to time

148

on technical points. The nuclear scientist seemed profoundly bored by everything and didn't say a word. There being no dissenting voices, the minutes were swiftly passed, and the next items on the agenda were taken up. The Brigadier held forth at length on the attempts of the club to get the press office of the Flower Show in Ooty to include a picture of the year's prize-winning fuchsia garden with the press release handed out to the media. For reasons that weren't quite clear to me, this had not yet happened, although talks on the matter had been initiated more than two years previously. The Brigadier proposed that a delegation visit the authorities before the details of the current year's show were finalized.

'We should, it's only right,' the nuclear scientist said vehemently, and then, just as suddenly, he subsided into the somnolence he had displayed since the beginning of the meeting. The Brigadier instructed the forestry official, who was recording the minutes, to note that a three-person delegation comprising the Brigadier, the building con-tractor and the forestry official would visit Ooty within the next fortnight. The group then began to discuss passionately items 5–10 on the agenda, varieties of fuchsia that the club was trying to develop with varying degrees of success. The nuclear scientist spoke for only the second time that evening about his attempts to get the Brian M. Cox variety to thrive in his garden, which seemed to be going rather well. The others around the table had less success to report, and none of them seemed to be able to get the hottest fuchshia in all the Nilgiris, the Wally Yendell, to sprout in their gardens; the Brigadier had passed around seeds and advice from the affiliated club in Somerset but all the members reported that they had failed to propa-gate the flower.

'Our climate is much like the climate of the plant's native habitat in Peru and Colombia. If our friends in England, where the conditions are much less conducive to the proper growth of fuchsias, can breed these plants, why can't we?' the Brigadier said irritably to the gathering. A flower bloomed in my mind, its pink petals gorgeously flounced and crinkled like a ballerina's tutu, and I wondered how these gentlemen would react if they knew that the fuchsia they coveted grew in solitary splendour in the lee of a cemetery wall? I listened to the Brigadier ranting on for a while but grew bored and, shutting out his voice, I began to look around surreptitiously.

The meeting had been going on for nearly an hour, and in this time the room had begun to fill up. Five large card tables had been installed and on four of them games were in full swing. Dotted across the wooden floor were clumps of sofas, and most of these were occupied by large men and women, the men in suits and the women in heavy formal saris, sipping drinks and gossiping as they waited for the dining hall to open. From the neighbouring billiard room came the sharp crack of balls.

A tall young woman, beautiful in a way that dimmed the lamps in the room, walked in and every man present felt a momentary pang that she was not his. Trying hard not to stare, I took in her shoulder-length hair that matched the black sari she wore, the feline eyes, the straight plane of her nose that would look imperious when she grew old, the complexion of ivory and cream and the perfectly made-up face. Her gaze passed over me and the others in the room, made the slightest gesture of acknowledgement to someone outside my direct line of vision, and then she was gone, leaving a long afterglow in my mind. I wondered who she was; she seemed to belong in a sophis-ticated city setting, not in the Meham Club bar on New Year's Eve. I heard my name being mentioned, and dragged myself reluctantly back to the meeting. The Brigadier was saying, 'If we don't have any other business, gentlemen, then I'd like to invite Vijay, my young friend from Bombay, to say a few words.'

As the members focused their attention on me I became acutely conscious of the laboured breathing of the building contractor and the hairless dome of the forestry official. I could feel my confidence ebbing away, so there was nothing for it but to jump right in: 'I have been told that a week from now a Hindu extremist is planning to attack the Shrine of the Blessed Martyr.'

If I had been expecting a dramatic reaction to my announcement, I was disappointed. The nuclear scientist, Das, looked at me severely and said, 'Young man, where on earth have you got this information from?'

'From Brother Ahimas, or rather his people, sir,' I said. 'You know there was a demonstration earlier this month—'

The Brigadier cut in. 'You don't have to teach us about this town, old chap. But there is nothing to worry about; this is Meham in the Nilgiris. It has the lowest record of violence in the country. This is not Ayodhya, this is not Gujarat, this is not Bombay . . . I am a good Hindu, and I am quite happy to live with a Shiva temple and a Christian shrine side by side, and I believe the majority of Hindus here feel the same way. Even if this group is going to take out a morcha, as you say, all there will be is a small group of people marching, some slogans, some banners. Bas. And if it rains, not even that.'

'Sir,' I remonstrated, 'I would agree with you if it weren't for the man leading them. He is believed to have participated in the Bombay riots.' I realized I was deliberately embellishing the facts as I knew them, for I had no proof that Rajan was involved in the Bombay riots, nor that he was planning to attack the shrine on Feast Day, but I had to pique the interest of this group somehow.

'What is he? A professional mercenary? In Meham? Impossible,' the doctor said with a vehement shake of his head.

'But the custodian and others at the shrine are very afraid. They feel there will be violence . . .'

'They should go to the police or the collector; nothing for us to worry about here.'

I gave it one last try. Professor Menon's fear had been real. 'In that case, could you talk to the inspector and the collector? I'm sure they will listen to you. This man Rajan is supposed to have a lot of influence.'

'Did you say Rajan, D.P. Rajan?' the Brigadier asked, leaning forward.

'Yes sir, Rajan, I'm not sure about the initials, but he's—'

'Oh, I know Rajan, there's nothing to worry about. He's a businessman visiting us from Bombay, in the sari business. I think he already has a shop here, but he's thinking of setting up another one, also one in Ooty. Met him at the club recently.'

'Pleasant young man, respectful, polite, not at all what I expected from a Bombayite . . .' the doctor chimed in.

'And what might that be, Kuruvilla?' Das asked in his sonorous voice. 'Do we Bombay people have two heads or maybe a tail?'

There was laughter at this sally, and the Brigadier began to speak, edging into his closing remarks. Realizing that this was perhaps my last opportunity, I cut him off, gesturing with my hands to show that I meant no disrespect.

'Please, sir, give me a couple of days and I'll prove to you that I'm not being alarmist. This could become Meham's greatest tragedy, and if we don't prevent it, we will only have ourselves to blame. Sir, Meham might be the most peaceful place in the whole country, but it's also a poor town. I've heard that unemployment has been high ever since the tea business collapsed, and I'm sure there are plenty of things mischief-makers can exploit: land disputes, old debts, other simmering hostilities that just need a spark to ignite them. Think of the trail of havoc that was set off by the breaking down of a centuries-old mosque in a town that none of us had even heard of ...'

Still nobody reacted and the Brigadier stepped smoothly into the silence.

'Well, that was most fascinating. I will look into my young friend's concerns personally and take whatever action is necessary. And now, if there is no other business, I hereby adjourn this meeting. Gentlemen, we have some serious drinking to do to bring in 1994.'

He signalled to a passing bearer, and drinks were ordered. As the others rose to head towards the increasingly noisy celebrators at the bar, he gestured to me to remain seated.

'You are a young man, Vijay, and when you have seen enough of life as I have, you will realize that often things have a way of working themselves out, even if they seem at first sight to be potentially very dangerous. Now I don't know how reliable your information is, but I want you to make thorough inquiries and I will do everything I can to help including introducing you to Rajan, who might be here tonight. He's a nice chap and I think you'll find your worries are groundless.' The bearer materialized at his elbow with the drinks and the Brigadier helped himself, gave me mine, then said to me, 'I don't hold with all this fundamentalist nonsense myself. Religion is for the puja room and the mandir, and that's it. I was an army man for nearly forty years and there was never any of this trouble in all the years I was in active service. You probably weren't born when the '71 conflict took place but I was present at the surrender of the

Pakistani Army in Dacca and I can tell you that if anyone wanted to know whether India was secular or not, they just had to take a look at the officers commanding the Indian Army. The chief was a Parsi, the great Sam Maneckshaw, who lives nearby in Coonoor, the officer orchestrating the surrender was a Sikh, his second-in-command was a Jew, and his field commander was a Hindu – all this in stark contrast to the Pakistani Army. This fundamentalist goondagiri will blow over, I tell you, old boy ... nothing but politics. They should let the army run the country, then there will be discipline, none of this bakwas ... How's your drink?'

'Its fine, sir.'

'Oh come on, Papa, stop boring this young man,' a voice said behind me, and even before I clambered to my feet, I knew who it was – the precisely pitched, convent-bred accent could have belonged to only one woman in the room.

'Vijay, I'd like you to meet my daughter Maya,' the Brigadier said. Thrown into confusion by the name the Brigadier had mentioned, I turned to shake her hand, barely managing to maintain my composure. Her gaze was cool, containing within it just a hint of amusement. 'Vijay's from Bombay,' the Brigadier said, 'and Maya is visiting me as she does every year at this time. Unfortunately her husband Rahul couldn't come down – business, you know – you city folk lead such hectic lives, even holidays aren't exempt any more.' Just then I became aware of a sharp pain, and looking down I found a small boy kicking me ferociously on the shin. Maya noticed what was going on, and said, 'Sanjay, stop it, or you'll be sent home with the ayah this instant.' The little monster paid not the slightest attention to his mother, and continued to kick me as I tried to manoeuvre out of range. His mother cuffed him, and he promptly burst into tears, whereupon, throwing an exasperated glance at her father and me and muttering, 'Nice to meet you, Vijay,' she headed off, pushing her wailing brat ahead of her. The Brigadier smiled indulgently at the antics of his grandson. 'You mustn't mind him, he's got far too much energy for any of us to be able to cope, but Maya does a good job. Pity she's leaving tomorrow, otherwise I would have had you over to the house to meet her. Come along now, let me introduce you to someone your own age, enough of this old fogey.'

Drinks in hand we walked over to the bar, which was lined with earnest tipplers. The barman, his forehead shiny with sweat, scuttled crab-wise from one end to the other, pressing drinks into outstretched palms. The crowd at the bar was exclusively male, overweight and elderly for the most part, although here and there I could see a younger man nodding dutifully as he was harangued by some old bore. The room had grown exceptionally noisy and it was difficult to make oneself heard. This did not seem to bother the Brigadier, who merely raised his voice a couple of decibels as he greeted every man seated at the bar with thunderous enthusiasm. We made slow progress. I nodded politely every time a new name was cast my way, but I was having a hard time concentrating because suddenly things were falling into place – the Brigadier's intense dislike of Noah, so he was the enraged father who had tried to have him expelled from school . . . I could see why Noah had fallen for her, she must have been just as beautiful as a teenager. Did she remember her one-time boyfriend, did she think about him every time she visited Meham or was her husband her antidote just as Iva had been Noah's? And what about Noah, surely his informants would tell him every time Maya came to town, did he not want to try to get in touch with her?

I was jostled out of these thoughts by the Brigadier's baritone in my ear. 'Here we are, old chap,' he said, and I noticed we had arrived at the far end of the bar, around which a group of young planters was lounging. 'Take good care of my young friend from Bombay,' the Brigadier said somewhat imperiously to one of them. 'He must leave with a good impression of our renowned Meham hospitality. OK, Kamath?' He nudged the planter jovially almost causing him to spill his drink.

Kamath was a man in his thirties with a goatee and a serious air about him. When the Brigadier was out of earshot, he whispered to me, 'Old fool thinks he's still a big shot. It isn't a problem, though, he is easy enough to handle.' And then he said worriedly, 'You're not a friend of his, are you?' I said I wasn't, and he relaxed. 'So what brings you here?' When I told him I was on holiday he said, 'Best place in the world to holiday. But after two weeks, you need to get the hell out, otherwise you'll go mad. Just joking, of course.' He nodded to himself and said, 'So who's been showing you around, not the Brigadier, I hope?'

One of the things I had learned as a journalist was never to give away too much information about yourself to people when you first met them, and although Kamath seemed harmless, I didn't mention Noah or any of the other people I had met in Meham. Not that it mattered, for Kamath didn't seem to want to know too much about me; he was a talker, and whatever reserve he might have possessed had been eliminated by the rum and Coke he was drinking at a rapid clip. Within a few minutes of our meeting he had finished the drink he was holding and had taken a large gulp of the replacement. He seemed to be able to hold his drink well, I didn't notice any obvious waywardness of speech or manner, except that he was adamant that I quickly finish my whisky and soda and start another. 'Only way to bring in the New Year is to be totally pissed, man. If you start with a hangover so bad that you feel like killing yourself, there's no place to go but up.' The whisky was starting to give me a pleasant buzz and a deeper appreciation of every banal comment Kamath made. I took a hefty swig from my glass and he looked approving. He knocked back what was left of his drink, and while he tried to attract the attention of the bartender carried on talking, about himself, his wife Lalitha – a pleasant-looking woman with an oval face and big dark eyes, who sat chattering animatedly with a group of women some distance away – their two young children and the tough times the tea industry was going through. He wanted desperately to get out of Meham, he said; he would like to go to Bombay or Delhi, perhaps even America, but who would take a thirty-two-year-old planter with no qualifications besides a BA and the ability to tell the quality of a batch of tea by swirling its brew around in his mouth?

'I envy you, man, living in Bombay and all. What do you do?'

I told him I was a journalist, and he nodded. He ordered another rum and Coke from the harassed bartender, and raised his eyebrows when I declined to follow suit. I quickly explained that I was taking it slowly, I wasn't much of a drinker and couldn't keep up with him. He looked very pleased to hear this. 'That's OK, man,' he said magnanimously.

The alcohol was beginning to make me feel light-headed, but it had also begun to wash away my apprehensions about Rajan and his designs on the Shrine of the Blessed Martyr. The noise and the laughter swelled around me and I felt the last remaining knots of tension dissolve in my head. I looked around for Maya but it was difficult to spot anyone in the crowded room.

'Have you seen the sights, man? Have you been to the Tower of God?' Kamath bellowed into my ear.

'Yes,' I said happily, 'I climbed those hundred and eight steps and felt every last one of them. Unlike Noah—'

'Did you say Noah? The charasi?' Kamath enquired. 'I haven't heard any gossip about him in years. What's he up to?' He seemed genuinely interested in what I had to say for the first time since I had met him. I was beginning to answer his question when I realized with a rather fuzzy sense of dismay that the liquor wasn't helping me be discreet. However, it didn't seem so important any more, and I said airily, 'Oh, not a whole lot. But he's a good guy, I've spent quite a lot of time with him.'

'Really, and the Brigadier knows this?'

I sobered up a little at the note of incredulity in his voice, Noah's warning loud inside my head. 'No, he doesn't,' I said. 'Please do me a favour, don't tell him, he might take it amiss.'

'No, I won't, don't worry, yaar.' He looked at me conspiratorially. 'But what a guy that charasi is, man, he's done quite a good job of lying low. For years nobody in Meham's so-called high society could talk of anything but him, not that there's a whole lot to talk about in this dump, but his talent for scandalous behaviour would have got him noticed anywhere ... Oh shit, here I go again, insulting one of your friends.'

'No, really, it's OK. I must admit he's quite eccentric, living in a graveyard and all ...'

'He lives in a cemetery, huh, that's pretty weird ... even by Noah's standards.'

'Yes, it is quite unusual,' I murmured.

'Look, don't get me wrong, I've always kind of liked him,' Kamath said. 'Come on, let's get some fresh air, and I'll tell you all about him.' He drained his drink, waited for me to do the same and we pushed our way through the crowd in the direction of the door.

Outside Kamath wandered off into the dark and I could hear him pissing into one of the flower beds.

'One of my New Year's Eve rituals,' he said. 'I try to puke or pee into the bed of phlox the club committee insists on growing right in front of the entrance. Prissy little flowers, they absolutely deserve to be pissed on.' Then settling himself comfortably on the steps, where I joined him, he told me about Noah. Apparently, they had been at St Jerome's at the same time, although Noah was three years his senior. Much of what Kamath told me I already knew, and so I prompted him to tell me about Maya. I told him I'd just met her.

'Quite a knockout, you should have seen her when we were at school. Fuck, she was amazing. Noah was a pretty cool guy too back then, so you could see why they would get together. But things became messy quite soon. It was rumoured that he had got her pregnant, and although there was no evidence for this, we assumed the worst – you know how it is when you're in school, everyone fantasizes like mad. But of course what made things really bad for Noah was the fact that her father was Brigadier Sharma. He might seem harmless now, but he was a real terror back then. Maya was pulled out of school and sent to live with her grandparents in Delhi, while Noah only managed to avoid being expelled because his father grovelled before the authorities.'

'But surely the Brigadier wouldn't have it in for Noah for so long, just because he went out with his daughter in school?'

'No, it gets worse. After Maya left, Noah went to pieces, man. He started hanging out with the local rowdies, began to miss classes, do drugs – basically he went crazy. I'm surprised he didn't kill anybody, he was so volatile that he kept getting into fights all the time. I remember once in the market near the bus stop he got into an argument with a guy twice his size, a bus conductor who had caught him travelling without a ticket. A bunch of us from school were there, it was a half-day, and we were basically loafing around. We saw what was going on, so we gathered around to watch the fun. The conductor was getting really angry, he was threatening to drag Noah off to the police station, really screaming at him. I'll never forget what Noah did that day, man. He was smoking a cigarette, and just as the conductor began to yell at him again, he took the lit cigarette out of his mouth and threw it down the man's throat. It stopped the bugger cold, he began gagging and clutching at his throat, and Noah just strolled out of there. He was quite something.'

'Is that why the Brigadier can't stand him? Did he get into a fight with him?'

'No, sorry, I was digressing a bit. See, Maya had a brother, Karan, who was a couple of years senior to me, and he absolutely idolized Noah, wanted to be just like him. When his hero started doing drugs and shit, he took the same route, only Noah escaped while Karan was really fucked. I don't know exactly what happened, but he was taken out of school and sent to Delhi as well. A few months later we heard that he had committed suicide or died of a drug overdose, nobody was quite sure which, but the Brigadier blamed Noah for everything. He had him arrested on charges of drug running, and although nothing could be proved and Noah was released, the school authorities couldn't take it any more and he was expelled. This time even his father couldn't save him. After he was thrown out, he'd be spotted hanging around the market with the local riff-raff, then his father retired to his home town in the plains, somewhere near Nagercoil, and Noah went with him.'

I was tempted to question Kamath's last statement. I'd believed the elderly priest was Noah's father, but this was apparently not the case. Yet there were so many other places where my informant's story didn't mesh with Noah's that I thought I'd just let him continue, see where his narrative led. The Brigadier had been transferred a few months later, Kamath said, and peace returned to Meham; then, a couple of years after he had disappeared, it was rumoured that Noah was back in town. Apparently he had tried his hand at various things in the plains, but nothing had worked out and he had decided to return to the place he knew best.

He had found work as a salesman in a grocery shop in the bazaar. It was the last permanent job he'd had. After less than a year he had quit or been told to go, and had begun to live by his wits. It was said that he was part of a gang that stole cars in towns in the Tamil Nadu plains, drove them up to Meham, repainted them, changed the number plates, filed off the registration numbers and sold them through second-hand car dealers in Karnataka. When the gang was rounded up by the police Noah was arrested but all charges were dropped, presumably because he was only loosely connected with the gang, and nothing could be proved against him. Then he had found temporary employment as a gardener in one of the big hotels. Perhaps that was how he had met Arumugam, I thought.

'That might have led to a sort of career, except that the Brigadier retired from the army and decided to settle down in Meham. Nobody here has the guts to take on the Brigadier, you know, so Noah was let go from even that measly job, and after that he just dropped out of sight. People said that he was making a living as a flower thief, stealing and selling exotic plants – you know how cut-throat the competition is around here.'

'I've heard that the flower thief was actually a chap called Arumugam,' I said.

'I bet Noah told you that,' Kamath said with a short, not unkind laugh. 'As far as the world was concerned, Arumugam was the thief, but he was just the fall guy; he was a stupid labourer who couldn't even grow a potato, let alone spirit delicate plants out of well-guarded gardens. No, the way I've heard it, Noah would do the job, give Arumugam a hefty cut and let him be arrested by the police because apparently he had sworn he would never get arrested again after his encounters with the cops, and he never was ... After that I lost in touch with local gossip. I went to college in Madras ...'

When Kamath returned he had lost sight of Noah, in fact he thought he'd left town – someone had told him he was working for an insurance company in Coimbatore.

'No, he told me he's been living in the cemetery for the last ten years ...'

'Wow really? It's amazing he's kept out of sight for so long. I must say I did hear a rumour a while back that he had been employed by a local church as some sort of caretaker, but it was one of those random pieces of information ... So that's where he's been all this time. It's astonishing when you come to think of it, all that frenzy and commotion in his youth, and now the peace of the graveyard. It almost seems appropriate, Noah was always original in his approach to life.'

Kamath's story and the chilly night air were beginning to clear my head. Feeling vaguely disloyal as I did so, I asked him if he knew whether Noah had studied in America.

'America. Come on, you're joking,' Kamath said, shaking his head vigorously. 'To the best of my knowledge, he has never left Tamil Nadu.'

'Are you sure? Maybe when you were in Madras ...' I asked, trying to be casual.

'Look, I don't live with him so I don't know *everything* about him. But I would certainly have known if he'd left town. Even when I was in college, during vacations I'd catch up with everything I'd missed. Meham is a small town, and in a place like this everyone knows everybody else's business.'

But he hadn't known Noah was living in St Andrew's Cemetery; it could be that he didn't know quite as much as he pretended to. I knew I was probably grasping at straws, but I was hoping against hope that not everything Noah had told me was a lie. Feeling increasingly discouraged, I asked him whether he knew if Noah had ever worked for a publishing house in Bombay, whether he had written poetry. Unexpectedly Kamath said he wouldn't be surprised if Noah had published poetry. Apparently in school when he wasn't being punished for some misdemeanour or other or wasn't on the sports field, he was always carrying a book around with him or was holed up in the library. 'There was a rumour doing the rounds that he went there so frequently because the librarian, Miss Welk, a fairly attractive woman in her fifties, would allow you to kiss her for a rupee, but I think that was just the perverted imagination of 400 boys in their early teens. No, Noah was always a great reader, and if memory serves me correctly he even won a couple of prizes for poetry recitation at the annual school fete. He wasn't a fool by any means.'

Kamath lapsed into silence for a moment or two, then said thoughtfully, 'He was a strange fellow, was Noah. Such a huge bundle of contradictions, you know, fearless when it came to challenging authority, obviously intelligent, always up to something, and with the sort of negative charisma that made every girl want him and every boy envy him. But even back then I knew that he would crash and burn. I'm surprised he's still alive ...'

I nodded, and Kamath said, 'Living in a cemetery, huh, doesn't surprise me really. He's the sort of guy who'd think it's pretty cool to hang out with ghosts.'

❧❀❧

We saw the lights of a car turning into the drive. Kamath exclaimed with surprise and peered at his watch. 'It's half-past eleven, somebody's making a pretty late appearance; Meham must really be catching up with the times if you can go party-hopping here on New Year's Eve.'

The car, a white Ambassador, drew up under the portico, and a man stepped out. We couldn't see him clearly until the car pulled away, but as he came forward into the light, Kamath shot to his feet with a fervent, 'Welcome, welcome, sir. I had heard you were back in Meham, but I didn't know you were coming to the club tonight. I could have picked you up.'

The man he was fawning over was trim and compactly built. Although I would later learn that he was in his mid-forties, he looked much younger. He had clear intelligent eyes, an unlined, clean-shaven face, a full head of hair parted neatly in the middle, and a smile that was quite disarming. Seemingly impervious to the Meham chill and club rules, he was dressed in a well-cut cream safari suit, with an obviously expensive shawl slung around his shoulders. He chatted easily with Kamath in an accent that I couldn't place but found oddly familiar. The mystery was explained soon enough, for Kamath who seemed to have momentarily forgotten I existed, turned to me and said, 'Vijay, I would like you to meet Mr Rajan, one of Meham's great men. Sir, this is Vijay from Bombay; he is visiting us for the holidays.'

I was taken aback, I hadn't expected to meet the man who was looming so large in my mind. The last traces of alcohol in my system were dispelled by the shock of the encounter. Through my agitation I saw that Rajan had put out his hand. I shook it mechanically, and willed myself to register what he was saying.

'Are you enjoying yourself in Meham, Vijay?' he asked in Bombay-accented English. 'They say we have the third-best climate in the world, after Kotagiri and ... and ...'

'Somewhere in northern California, sir,' Kamath said with a fawning laugh.

'Thank you, Kamath,' Rajan said, and added something in Kannada at which Kamath clucked and fluttered and cackled. Turning to me, he asked where I was from, and when I said K— he immediately switched to Tamil. If his dexterity with languages was meant to impress, it did; it was an effortless performance. He asked me where I lived in Bombay, and when he learned it was Colaba, he said we should meet when we both returned to the city – he owned a shop on Colaba Causeway and was there at least twice a week. An overweight man in an ill-fitting suit lumbered up, and Rajan asked him in Hindi whether he had found a good spot to park, at which his companion said irritably that he'd double-parked – there was no space to be had anywhere along the driveway.

'I could have my driver move my car,' Kamath offered eagerly. Rajan said he shouldn't bother, he was only going to be at the club for a short while to wish his friends the very best for the New Year before going on to the Ooty Club to greet his friends there, but Kamath insisted and he gave in graciously. The overweight man was introduced to us as Mr Mansukhani, the friend Rajan stayed with when he visited Meham. Kamath rushed off to find his driver, followed by Mansukhani, and I was left with the man I had been demonizing ever since I had first heard of him. Although I tried to steel myself against his easy charm, Rajan had the knack of breaking through people's defences, and I soon found myself conversing with him about Bombay, shaking my head ruefully about the myriad annoyances of the city but agreeing with him that there was no place on earth quite like it. The other two returned, and Rajan was preparing to walk into the club when it struck me that here was the perfect opportunity to fix an appointment.

'Sir, Mr Rajan, I would very much like to have a meeting with you.'

'Sure, bhai, sure, let me give you my card. Give me a call when you are in Mumbai.'

As he was fishing around in his trousers for his wallet, I blurted out, 'No, here in Meham. I am doing an article for a Bombay paper, and I would like to interview you.'

'*Times of India?*' he asked and I nodded, comforting myself with the thought that it was not a total fabrication; I had once published a short piece in the newspaper. Rajan conferred quickly with his friend and then said with a smile, 'No problem, bhai. Tomorrow morning, eleven o'clock. At this address in the market.' He scribbled something on the card he was holding out. 'Give me a call in the morning and Mansukhani will give you directions on how to get there.' He shook hands with Kamath and me, as did his friend, and then he was gone, walking rapidly and confidently into the club.

'Hey, man, that sounds great. Can I come with you to the interview?' Kamath asked.

'He might clam up, you know. It's always best to do interviews one on one, I've discovered; you're able to draw your subjects out more.'

Kamath looked dubious. 'But he's a public figure, he must be used to having people around all the time.'

This was true, but I couldn't have Kamath around; I wanted to get Rajan to open up, especially with regard to his designs on the shrine, and that would be next to impossible with others around. I said that in my experience even the most experienced politicians were more forthright if they were interviewed on their own. Fortunately Kamath seemed not to want to argue the point, for had he asked me the names of famous politicians I had interviewed I would have been unable to give him a single one.

'He's a great man, you're in for a treat. When you know there are people like him from Meham, it makes you proud to have grown up here.' He went silent for a bit, then added, 'And so humble, so friendly, despite everything he's achieved. He's a crorepati, could buy up all those bastards in the club and still have enough money left over to hang the Kohinoor around the neck of that actress he's sleeping with. And to think he started with nothing. Right here, man.'

'He began his career at the Meham Club?' I asked in some surprise.

'No, no.' Kamath laughed. 'But he might as well have, his origins were no less lowly than if he had been a marker at the tennis courts. I was just a kid then, but my mother told me that he worked briefly as a salesman in a sari shop in Upper Meham, I think his uncle owned it. Then he got a job in Corporation Bank, as a Class IV employee. He was sacked from there, ran away to Bombay, and that's where the legend begins.'

Rajan had arrived in Bombay without a paisa to his name, and made his way to Matunga, the stronghold of Tamil immigrants to the city. Obtaining a loan from a moneylender, he paid twenty rupees to the local dada for a four-foot by four-foot space on the pavement from which he hawked handkerchiefs, children's clothes and cheap trinkets. Within a couple of years he owned three or four handcarts that sold pav bhaji, omelettes and sev puri on Chowpatty Beach and in the mid-town office areas, and after that there was no stopping him. He was soon one of the richest pheriwallahs in Bombay. By the time he was thirty-five, he had made his first crore of rupees, and owned shops and apartments in Matunga, Colaba and Dadar. He became active in the community, built a hall where weddings and festivals could be celebrated, started a school for street kids ('I've heard the one thing he has always regretted is his lack of education. He is supposed to speak six or seven languages fluently – if he'd had the opportunity, he would have earned a triple PhD from Harvard,' Kamath said enthusiastically, 'and so he has always tried to help underprivileged kids.') and generally grew to be a man of influence in the area. 'Soon enough, the politicians came calling, he became involved in municipal politics, then state politics, and they say he's very close to the BJP and the Sena.'

'I know. I've heard he was involved in the Bombay riots.'

'Be careful, my friend, with your allegations,' Kamath said. 'If you don't know anything about Rajan, you shouldn't be perpetuating the lies people spread about him.' I was about to retort but held my peace, I still needed to know as much as Kamath could tell me about the man.

'Why is he leading the agitation against the Meham shrine?' I asked.

'Because it is a Hindu temple,' Kamath snapped irritably. 'It is time we Hindus showed the minorities their place. They should realize that it is because of us Hindus that they are able to live peacefully and prosper in this country. Do you think if people like us emigrated to a Christian country like Britain or the US and tried to create trouble there, we would be tolerated? No chance, man, we'd be kicked out and told never to come back.'

I was angry now, but my anger was mixed with sadness. What had this country come to, if educated middle-class people like Kamath could harbour such sentiments? Would he think differently if he had read a book like Mr Sorabjee's during his formative years or was that mere wishful thinking? Controlling my emotions, I said, 'This is not America, Kamath. The people who are being attacked are not newcomers or immigrants, they have lived here for centuries just like you and I. They put their faith in the constitution, in the law—'

'Nonsense,' he said. 'But forget it, yaar, this is too boring, let's go in and have another drink. It's nearly time to bring in the New Year.'

'Fine,' I said. 'But you still haven't told me why Rajan is leading the agitation against the shrine. I'll need some background for my interview tomorrow.'

'Well, he's man of some influence here, you know. He owns shops and is said to have made a substantial contribution to one of the hospitals. People respect him, and that is why the Kadavul Katchi roped him in to help.' He began to talk about the political scene in Tamil Nadu, and compare it to the politics of his native Karnataka. Realizing that I was not going to get any more useful information from him, I suggested we go back inside as he had proposed.

We couldn't get further than the entrance to the bar for the place was now heaving. Everyone in the club had crammed into the room as the midnight hour approached and there wasn't space for even the waiters to circulate. A group of teenagers began to count down the hour, and at the stroke of midnight a large pile of fireworks stacked on the tennis court was set alight. I could hear the Brigadier's baritone boom out, '*Should auld acquaintance be forgot. And never brought to mind ...*'

Three score voices joined in, singing lustily and tunelessly. Beside me Kamath was singing too, caught up in the immediacy of the moment. I left him and the other members of the club to their revels and wandered out into the crisp, cold night. The stars were raining down from the heavens and rising up to meet them was the sound of church bells calling the faithful to midnight mass. I walked to the very edge of the property and looked towards the Tower of God but the dark was too absolute for me to see anything.

～●❧～

I got home at half past one in the morning. Although it had been a long day, I found it difficult to drop off. There had been so much incident and revelation that had come my way that I found it hard to absorb it all: the very real fears of Menon, the stories about Noah, my meetings with Maya and Rajan. I could feel myself being swept headlong into the lives and affairs of people I had barely met, and there was no question but that I was struggling to maintain my composure and balance. I longed to go to someone for advice, Mr Sorabjee, even my father if it came to that, but I knew that I would be told not to get involved. Yet how could I not? By nature I am level-headed and pragmatic, but when something has been brewing in me for a while I can be impetuous. It was so when I made up my mind to leave K—, and that was why I had decided to try to cover the riot in Bombay. In Meham all the things that could be expected to get me going were present in full measure; if anything they were more pronounced than ever before in my life. I still hadn't fully emerged from the trauma of the attack on me in Bombay, I was haunted by the destruction I had witnessed in the wake of the riots and explosions, and I was convinced that something like that should never be allowed to take place again. How then could I sit by and watch as Rajan and his cohorts attacked people like Professor Menon and Brother Ahimas? Even as I felt myself getting pulled into the situation, I was aware of how ill-equipped I was to deal with it.

I would have liked to have talked to Noah, but after my meeting with Kamath I wasn't sure I could bank on someone who appeared to be generally untrustworthy. I would need a much more reliable ally if I was looking to take on Rajan. As I thought about my impending interview with him I grew nervous, for it was clear that I was up against a formidable adversary. Finally, more to distract myself than anything else, I picked up Mr Sorabjee's manuscript although I suppose I also had the vague notion that I might find some information in it that might come in useful if I was to get into

166

a debate with Rajan the following day. It struck me as I began reading that it was a clear indication of how slender my resources were that all I could come up with for my encounter with Rajan was a book written for teenagers, but I consoled myself with the thought that at least I had Mr Sorabjee speaking into my ear.

MAHATMA GANDHI
Emperor of Truth

Every city, small town, and village (for all I know) in this country has a Mahatma Gandhi Road or Salai or Chowk. His statues are crammed into hundreds of public squares, his visage adorns currency, shop fronts and a variety of consumer brands, and we all religiously take 2 October off to celebrate the day of his birth. But pigeons desecrate his bust with their shit, the streets that bear his name fill with rubbish, and the empty homilies chanted in his name make a mockery of the legacy he bequeathed to our nation.

The Mahatma may be the most famous Indian who ever lived, but although more has been written about him and by him – there are a hundred volumes of his *Collected Works* – his message has been forgotten, and I doubt that anyone under the age of twenty-five really knows what he stood for. So, who was this man, what did he stand for, and why is it important that his message be heeded in these ungodly times?

The other emperors I have written about, Ashoka and Akbar, were men of their time, but their greatness lay in being ahead of their time. However, Gandhi was perhaps the only one who truly transcended time, his message was not only for the age he lived in, but for all time to come. In my eyes, he is the greatest of the three because, unlike the others, he was not born to greatness; he did not inherit an empire, he had no armies to command, treasuries to fund his campaigns

167

or the power of life or death over his subjects. He hadn't killed another human being or living thing in combat or sport and, importantly, he held no title when he was at his most powerful. Yet millions were ready to be brutally injured or to die at his command, he defeated the strongest empire of his time, and kings and presidents and heads of state came calling on him.

What made him such a force to reckon with? I intend to skim over his great civil, social and political strategies, they have been covered in exhaustive detail elsewhere. Nor do I intend to discuss his eccentricities, or his contentious economic theories and ideas of governance, this is not the forum to debate them. Instead, after sketching the man in the simplest of terms, I would like to let him speak himself on the subject that is at the core of this book.

The Mahatma returned to India from South Africa just before he turned forty-six, having spent almost half his life outside the country, first in England, where he had studied to become a barrister, and then in South Africa, where he had gone to work as a lawyer. The trials and triumphs of his formative years, the temptations of the flesh and spirit, the early attempts to formulate and implement a political strategy, his identification with the poorest of the poor, all these are well known, as are the staggeringly ingenious tactics that brought the British to a standstill: the satyagraha in Champaran in 1917, the agitations in Ahmedabad and Kheda in 1918, against the Rowlatt Act in 1919, the Non-Cooperation Movement of 1920-2, the Dandi March of 1930 and the Quit India Movement of 1942.

But it isn't because of these achievements that he fits into my pantheon of emperors. The reason I include him is because he was unambiguous about the need for

India to be a tolerant, non-sectarian, multi-faceted and harmoniously plural society. Writing in his book *Hind Swaraj* he stated, 'In reality, there are as many religions as there are individuals, but those who are conscious of the spirit of nationality do not interfere with one another's religion ... In no part of the world are one nationality and one religion synonymous terms; nor has it ever been so in India.'

And towards the end of his life he said, 'Right from childhood I have been taught that in Ramrajya or the kingdom of God no person can be unworthy just because he follows a different religion.' He repeated this in January 1948, weeks before he was shot and killed by a Hindu fanatic precisely because he held such beliefs: 'When I was young I never even read the newspapers. I could read English with difficulty and my Gujarati was not satisfactory. I have had the dream ever since then [of] Hindus, Sikhs, Parsis, Christians, and Muslims [living] in amity not only in Rajkot but in the whole of India.' The crucial thing to note about him was that even while he expressed these sentiments for the country and its people he never gave up being a believing Hindu (just as Ashoka continued to be a Buddhist and Akbar remained a Muslim while proclaiming the virtues of secularism) and never thought of India as anything but a deeply religious land. Therein lay his genius - articulating his strategies for winning freedom and maintaining the secularism of the nation through the medium of his faith. If he hadn't been a pious Hindu, the nation and the world would never have heard of satyagraha (truth force) and ahimsa (non-violence); believing the latter was Hinduism's greatest contribution to the world, he used it brilliantly as a weapon. He wrote in *Harijan*, 'The hardest metal yields to heat. Even so must the hardest heart melt before a sufficiency of the heat of non-violence. And there is no limit to the capacity of non-violence to generate heat.' And he saw his mission as 'to convert every Indian whether he is Hindu, Muslim or any other, even Englishmen and finally the world to non-violence for regulating mutual relations whether political, economic, social or religious'.

Even more than ahimsa, Gandhi worshipped the truth. According to his grandson and biographer Rajmohan Gandhi, 'His truth had four meanings: truth as the Universe's reality (the sat or satya of Hindu thought), truth about facts, truth to a view or resolve, and the truth of the voice within.' He wielded truth, love and non-violence as weapons, and showed India and the world how these could be more effective than mere guns or steel. Today, those who would rule us are using lies, hate and violence to achieve their ends. Would that another Gandhi rise amidst us, we have never had more need of someone of his strength and sagacity, a man of God who saw his God for what he truly was: 'God is Life, Truth, Light. He is Love. He is the Supreme Good.'

And there the manuscript ended. It had concluded rather abruptly; I would point that out to Mr Sorabjee, I thought, and switched off the light. Lying in the dark, I worried again about my interview with Rajan tomorrow. I felt I was no match for him, I even thought I should duck it, and then my stubborn nature reasserted itself: I would go through with it, do the best I could. If I was going to help the people who depended on me, if I wanted to be worthy of my father, Mr Sorabjee and my own ambition to be someone who had done something with his life, then there was no way I could give up. The decision taken I began to relax and presently sleep claimed me.

I I

The rioter

Mr Khanna's driver hadn't yet returned from his holiday, but the butler had managed to arrange a taxi to take me to town, and I set off for my meeting with about an hour to spare. My resolve of the previous night was considerably less sturdy, for I still had little idea of how to tackle Rajan.

I was dropped off just outside the bus stop, where a long line of black and yellow Ambassador taxis, fat and ungainly as bumblebees, were parked by the side of the road. As I got out, I realized I had no idea where Nilgiri Cloth Stores, the location at which I had arranged to meet Rajan, actually was. I had written down some directions when I had talked to Mansukhani on the phone, but I had been expecting to pass them on to Mr Khanna's driver and when he hadn't turned up, it had put a crimp in my plans. My taxi driver didn't know, so I asked one of the others for help. Within minutes I was surrounded by a gesticulating scrum shouting directions at me. Eventually, they arrived at some sort of consensus, and armed with their coordinates I set off to find the shop. I plunged into a side alley as I had been instructed, and within minutes I was lost. The further I penetrated the maze of badly lit streets, the less certain I was of ever reaching my destination. I entered a narrow lane with wooden doorways set into discoloured walls. A small boy squatted over an open gutter, relieving himself. I passed him, my steps dragging, and saw that at the far end of the alley a rectangle of sharp, white light seemed to indicate the end of the maze. I directed my steps towards the opening, and found myself on a street that was busy with people and traffic. As I looked up and down the street, I saw the queue of black and yellow taxis not too far away. I had evidently been going round in circles for nearly an hour. It was time to give up and go home, I thought wearily but not without a sense of relief, for now I wouldn't have to confront Rajan. Best to leave the whole business alone, as Mr Sorabjee had enjoined me to, enjoy my holiday, or maybe just alert the police to my suspicions and write an article for the magazine when I returned to Bombay.

As I was thinking these thoughts, I had been walking away from the taxi rank, which I had adopted as a sort of landmark, and now I found myself climbing a flight of chipped and broken stone steps that I remembered Rajan's friend had told me to look out for. At the top of the steps was a pharmacy, and next to it was a tin board on which was painted in red, 'Nilgiri Cloth Stores'. Outside the shop were two men dressed in crisp white shirts and veshtis, the uniform of political workers in this part of the country. So he was still here. There's still time to go home, I thought. I paused on the steps, undecided, but then I was swept by a vision of the assault on me in Bombay. I hadn't thought of it for months, but it came back to me now clear in every detail. I was paralyzed with terror for a couple of moments but instead of making me retreat it only served to make me more determined – no, I couldn't just stand passively by and let events take their course.

As I approached the sari shop, Rajan's cohorts glanced at me incuriously, the dark glasses they wore lending a faint air of menace to their presence. I asked them whether Rajan was in, saying I had an appointment to see him, and the heavyset one nodded and gestured for me to go in. Within the long rectangular room, the walls rippled like coloured water in the dim light of candles. The setting could have been lifted from a fantasy, the insubstantial walls of shimmering silk, the hunched figures that emerged from the gloom, the air of mystery that pervaded the place, but the reality was more prosaic – there had been a power cut.

Rajan and his friend Mansukhani sat behind a glass counter on the far side of the room. Beside them was the brightest source of illumination around, an emergency lantern that glowed white in the dark. A shop assistant materialized at my side, but Rajan had already spotted me and waved me over. As I approached the two men, I began apologizing for being late, but Rajan cut me short, 'Arre, bhai, this is Meham, no hurry, no worry – you should simply enjoy. It's not like Mumbai, tension everywhere, no time for anything. But if I had to live here I would die. Of boredom.' He laughed, the sound loud in the quiet confines of the shop, and I laughed dutifully along with him. His hulking friend didn't even smile. An old-fashioned rotary telephone on the counter, with a lock embedded into the dial, began to ring insistently. Rajan's friend picked up the receiver, listened in silence to the caller for a minute or two, then spat a couple of words in Hindi into the phone and hung up. He leaned over and whispered something into Rajan's ear. A frown briefly wrinkled the latter's forehead, then his expression relaxed and he said to me, 'What will you have to drink? Chai? Pepsi?'

I began demurring but he brushed my protestations aside and told his friend to order us some tea and the delicious pakoras that the hotel across the street made daily. Mansukhani bellowed instructions across the room to one of the shop assistants then the two men settled back into their seats and waited for me to begin. For a few agonizing moments I had nothing to say to them, all the questions I had rehearsed for the interview had evaporated from my mind. This wasn't a wholly unusual occurrence, there had been moments in the past when a combination of nerves and excitement had made interviews go awry, but this was different. Rajan sensed my confusion and stepped into the breach.

'Have you seen the sights, bhai? Coonoor, Ooty, you should see the Botanical Gardens, Doddabetta ...'

When I didn't answer immediately, he added, 'Mansukhani can organize a taxi for you.'

I forced myself to speak and said a friend had taken me around. He nodded and said in Hindi, 'Achcha, achcha, this place is so beautiful, not like the hill stations in the north, Nainital, Mussoorie, all ruined, ugly buildings everywhere, the forests cut down ...' I would never have taken Rajan for an environmentalist, and grew even more confused in my sense of him.

'You should have come last year, my friend, when the kurinji was flowering. You know the kurinji?'

I nodded. Noah had told me that in the years when the kurinji

173

flowered the peaks of the district seemed to emerge from lakes of blue, which was how the Nilgiris or Blue Mountains had got their name.

'It was fantastic. Everywhere you looked the place was covered with flowers, especially towards Mukurti. Now you'll have to wait twelve years for it to flower again.'

As he rambled on about the sights of the Nilgiris, my mind finally settled down, and the questions I had formulated began to come back. I had thought I would start by asking about his early years in Bombay, just to get him talking, then move on to the riots, where I hoped to trap him into some sort of admission that he had been involved, before steering him around to the agitation he was about to lead on the Shrine of the Blessed Martyr. If I could pin him down, uncover his plans, I could give the Brigadier and the authorities something to work with. It would not be easy, but I would have to try. Just as I was about to begin, the tea and pakoras arrived. Rajan urged me to try one; I almost scalded my tongue, it was so hot, and he smiled kindly at me, and all at once I was as comfortable as I was ever going to be. I opened my notebook, and said, 'Sir, please tell me briefly about your early years in Bombay.'

His account fitted almost exactly with Kamath's: the arrival in the city without money or contacts, the passage to Matunga, the early years as a pheriwallah, the growing prosperity. There were some facts he added to the ones I already knew: he had served a term as a municipal corporator and, besides his charity work in the Tamil community in Mumbai, he was thinking of setting up a school in Coimbatore for underprivileged children. 'By God's grace I have made money—'

'They say you're a crorepati, a wealthy man,' I interjected, but he continued smoothly on, pausing only to smile modestly.

'I have tasted political power as a corporator, and now my only desire is to serve the people. I started with nothing—'

I didn't know how long I had and I was getting a politician's patter, so it was time to speed things up a little. I interrupted him.

'Sir, is it true that you were involved in the killing of Muslims in the Bombay riots?'

Something moved, far back, in the cool impersonal gaze that Rajan had fixed on me. I had got through to him, I thought exultantly, but any advantage I might have secured was taken away immediately as Mansukhani blundered in.

'Lies, bloody lies,' he blustered, 'Mind, Mr Mumbai journalist, what you say about Rajan sir. How dare you—'

Any discomfiture Rajan might have felt was gone, and he moved in calmly to defuse the tension. He put a restraining hand on Mansukhani's shoulder, murmured, 'Friends ... friends,' and then resumed the conversation in an unflustered tone.

'I am a small man who is trying in his own way to do something. People will always make up stories, try to put me down, people who are envious, people who for their own reasons might think I have done them some harm, people who have nothing to do but create mischief ...'

The lights came on, startling us all.

'Sir, I have been told that on the ninth of January you were part of a Hindu mob which set fire to a Muslim man in Dharavi, while shouting slogans that this would be the fate of all Muslims in Bombay to avenge the murder of a Hindu family in Radhabai Chawl.'

I had made up the story on the spur of the moment, substituting Rajan for the thug who had been accused of the crime and whom I had interviewed for my magazine during our coverage of the riots, but to my amazement Rajan didn't deny the allegation immediately. Wasn't his hesitation proof of his involvement, I thought, if not in Dharavi, then somewhere else? He let the silence build for a few moments, and then said calmly, 'Do you know, Mr Vijay (it was the first time he had addressed me formally this morning), that I personally distributed food to scores of Muslims who were affected by the riots and the bomb blasts. Muslims work in my factory, they work in my shops; I have my hair cut by a Muslim barber. How can you accuse me of harming them?'

I could have told him about the many suspected killers I had interviewed, others who had been asked to appear before a commission of inquiry, who all said much the same thing, who talked in public about their Muslim friends, lovers, colleagues, but who in private admitted that that hadn't prevented them from murdering other Muslims.

'There are many people who are accused of murdering Muslims who say the same thing,' I said.

'So you are accusing me ...'

'No, sir, all I am saying is that you are known to be close to the Shiv Sena, who were accused of systematically targeting and killing Muslims during the riots, and that your name has also come up in that connection.'

'It is true that I am close to the Sena, but that does not mean I killed Muslims.'

'But do you think it was right to target the Muslims in Mumbai and elsewhere in the country? They have done no wrong ...'

Mansukhani, who had been restraining himself, could hold back no longer.

'All Muslims should be sent back to Pakistan where they belong ...'

'So should you. Isn't your ancestral homeland, Sindh, in Pakistan?'

He gave a strangled yelp. I thought I'd gone too far, I was sure to be thrown out now, but Rajan was quick to intervene. He spoke to Mansukhani, and the big man got up and left, but not before throwing me a murderous look.

'My question, sir, is why do people like you, and the parties you belong to, target Muslims, Christians, other minorities? That is not the spirit of Hinduism?'

'Does the spirit of Christianity allow you to kill people from another faith? Or the spirit of Islam? We Hindus have suffered at the hands of brutal rulers from these religions – do you not find that reprehensible?'

'Of course I do, sir, any sane person would, but all that was a long time ago. The people belonging to those faiths are not responsible for what their ancestors did; that is an unreasonable argument.'

He said calmly, 'I don't dispute that ...' and then before I could put my next question to him, he asked me an unexpected one. 'Are you a patriot, Vijay bhai?'

It was a question that I would have mocked in years past, it seemed such an antiquated and simple-minded way of describing oneself, but since the attack and the subsequent year at *The Indian Secularist*, my idea of myself had changed. And as my concern for my country and countrymen had grown, questions such as the one Rajan posed no longer seemed irrelevant. Rajan mistook my silence.

'I see you are hesitating,' he said, 'and that is part of the problem with today's youth. If we don't feel passionately about our country, then how will it ever achieve the greatness that is written into its destiny? That is the difference between you and me, Vijay bhai.'

'I may not call myself a patriot, sir, but I feel very deeply about my country. In fact that's why I feel proud to be working for ...' I hadn't been sure that my ploy of passing myself off as a *Times of India* journalist would work with someone as astute as Rajan, but it seemed to have done the trick, and it would be silly if I gave myself away now. Indeed, it was quite possible that our interview would be abruptly terminated if Rajan came to know that I worked for Mr Sorabjee's magazine. Or perhaps not, you never knew with people like him, but it seemed sensible not to take the risk.

He didn't seem to notice my slip, and continued with a smile, 'Ah, you young people. You think patriotism is an old-fashioned word, but I don't mind so long as you are committed to this country. Speaking for myself, I am proud to call myself a patriot. When I was around your age we were at war with Pakistan, and I wasted no time in applying to join the army. At that moment all thought of my future vanished from my head. All I wanted to do was fight for my country and if death was to be my reward, so be it. I was turned down because I failed my medical. I had a heart murmur, they said, but I would have given anything to have been sent to the border. I would die for my country, Vijay bhai, the integrity of Bharat is well worth dying for.'

'So why are you trying to destroy it from within?' I asked.

The smile faded, and the impassivity settled back into his eyes.

'I don't understand the question.'

'I think you do, sir. You have not denied your links with right-wing Hindu parties, and you don't seem unduly perturbed by the barbaric murders of our fellow countrymen who just happen to be Muslim, Christian or Sikh. You claim to be a patriot who is prepared to die for his country, but you do not seem to mind killing your own. That is not being a patriot in my eyes; I would prefer to think of people who think and act like that as traitors. They and anyone who associates with them are the enemy within, not the poor luckless souls they target. You should know by now that people who are trying to lead their meagre lives as best they can have no option but to fight when they are cornered. You know that the bomb blasts in Bombay would never have taken place if the riots hadn't happened. Don't you see that if you continue in this vein, you will have a hundred Kashmirs, a million Bombays, everywhere in the country?'

'So you are a patriot after all. I like your spirit, bhai.'

Rajan's reaction astonished me. I had expected him to be annoyed with me, or at the very least defensive, but he did not seem in the least put out.

'We need more young people like you, Vijay bhai, passionate if a little misguided. But you are quite right, if the minorities are targetted, there will in all likelihood be further casualties as and when they fight back. But I don't agree with you that India will be finished; we will have enough people and resources to rebuild the country once peace is restored. But we must not shrink from our task because the only way to make this nation mighty is by removing things that weaken it. You look surprised, my young friend. Don't be. I will prove to you why it is possible to be a patriot and one who craves a strong Hindu nation at one and the same time. But first put away your notebook and pen because I know who you are and what you are doing here. You do not work for the *Times of India*, you are employed by *The Indian Secularist*. I know of Mr Sorabjee, I think he's a good man, but he will eventually pass on without having achieved any measure of success. He and people like him are largely irrelevant in today's India. They had a small role in leading the country's battle for independence, but today's challenges are different. The country is poised for greatness, and the only way it will achieve this is if we are resolute and move forward in a united fashion. And that will only happen if the majority leads the way; no nation is strong that has its people pulling in all different directions. If the majority community is powerful and determined, the minorities will automatically fall into line, and then we can all coexist peacefully.'

'That is a complete fantasy, sir. No country which targets its own people has ever prospered, and you need only to look to history to see how wrong you are. Most fundamentalist regimes have fallen sooner or later, after creating fear and mistrust, and ruining their countries—'

'Why look to history alone, bhai, shouldn't we look at our present situation as well? We have spent so long pandering to the minorities that we have neglected the majority community; it has been weakened, and that is why we don't rule the world.'

I was about to remonstrate but he gestured to indicate that I wasn't to interrupt him just yet. 'Let me tell you a story, Vijay bhai, about an ordinary man, an inoffensive, hard-working man, the sort of person we will need to support and strengthen if we are to secure the future of this country. A man who went about his business for thirty-three years without saying an unkind word about or to anyone, who followed the dictates of his caste and religion faithfully, who was never late for work, who fulfilled all his duties as a householder. A good man, you might say, slightly dull but a man you would want at your back if you had to fight your way out of trouble. He must have had hopes and dreams when he was young – all of us, no matter how wretched our place on earth, can dream if only for a few precious moments.

'This man's dream ended when he was eighteen and his father died. He was suddenly responsible, as the eldest son, for seven siblings and his widowed mother. To be an eldest son is in many ways the worst possible thing that can happen to you in a country like ours. Vijay bhai, are you an eldest son? Yes, I can tell you are, I am one too, and I am sure you know exactly what I mean when I say it is a terrible thing to be an eldest son. Everyone bemoans the plight of women in our country, and I admit that the lot of women is deplorable, but I mean something different when I talk of how hard it is to be a first-born boy. I'm sure you understand, Vijay bhai, I can see you nodding, because I'm talking about the weight of expectations placed on you by your parents, your family. All through your childhood and youth you have been spoiled and exalted, even if you come from a poverty-stricken background, and then suddenly you're an adult, and you are magically expected to turn into a mighty banyan tree under which your family can shelter for generations to come. It doesn't happen that way, does it now? Think then of the frustration and self-loathing that it engenders in those who are placed in such a situation. But they are the lucky ones, Vijay bhai, the ones who can afford to indulge in self-loathing and whine about their bad karma. There are others who simply have to lock up their dreams in a cheap trunk and quietly get on with the business of surviving and providing for their families, with no accolades or praise or gratitude. That is what the man in my story had to do, Vijay bhai. He may have been a moderately bright student, or a dullard or a genius, no one ever knew, but I was told once that his only dream had been to earn a college degree – it was a badge of honour for men of his caste – but that didn't happen because he had to go to work the day after his father was cremated. I suppose he was granted some small measure of luck, in that he found a job, a very small job, in a mill in Coimbatore, first as a storekeeper, then for thirty-two years as a clerk in the proprietor's office. It was a thankless job, I'm sure, but it was a job his entire family was grateful for.

'I have said that he was a deeply devout man, but I haven't told you just how devout he was. Every day he would bathe early in the morning, before anyone else in the house had even woken up, and bare-chested in his wet dhoti he would perform his devotions to Lord Shiva in a corner of his tiny house that had been converted into a puja room. He would stand motionless, chanting his prayers. He was a frail man and it would have broken your heart to see his concave, almost hairless chest, everything about him was so thin and weak, yet he was determined to serve his Lord, his family. He was a man who did his dharma no matter what.

'One day, three weeks before he was due to complete his thirty-third year with the mill, he was called into the proprietor's office and told that he should not come to work the next day. He thought there was some festive occasion or perhaps a death in the proprietor's family, as a result of which the mill would be closed for the day. He didn't ask any questions, that was not his nature; he did what was asked of him, he never questioned anything, never, and I think that was his undoing. As he was leaving, the proprietor, a fat man who paraded around in a gold-bordered veshti and angavastram with rings on every finger, told him to pick up that week's wages from the payroll office. A festival then, he thought. But when he met the accountant, he was told that the mill was being sold; it had been in the red for years and was now teetering on the edge of bankruptcy.

'I wish he had shouted then, showed some vestige of manliness, stormed into the owner's office, spat in his face, asked him whether all that he was worth after thirty-three years of service – sorry, thirty-two years, eleven months and a week of service – was eighty-two rupees, one week's wages. Even the mill workers were better off, the union managed to get them some sort of settlement, but he was white-collar, a clerk, he had always been proud of that, and it gave him no protection when it mattered. When he returned to his house that day, he took his eldest son aside and told him that should anything happen to him, it was his dharma to look after the family, and most important to repay the 70,000 rupees he still owed to moneylenders and various family members, money he had borrowed for the dowry and marriage expenses of his daughters. He had never been a demonstrative man, and so, even in his moment of crisis, he didn't break down or show any form of emotion that might have been construed as a cry for help.

'For the next two years his family watched as his dignity was eroded day by day, by the creditors who came calling, the various small-time merchants and shopkeepers who treated him like dirt just because they paid him a pittance to do their accounts for them, the members of the extended family who cut him off. He put up with it all, he would do whatever was necessary to provide for his family. He wouldn't let his boys stop their schooling, he was determined that they should have the education he never had, and even though there was no money, the minimal fees were paid at the government school the boys attended, and textbooks were bought. His daily devotion continued, his faith in his Lord did not diminish one bit.

'But when a man is down on his luck, nobody, not even God, has much time to spare for him. The daily jobs began to peter out and finally there wasn't enough money to buy textbooks for the new school year. When the boys stopped going to school and the father finally had no work to do, their two-room house in a street where the open gutters flowed with shit grew too small for them all to be together. The boys began to roam the streets. The younger one, who was eleven, began to run with a gang of pickpockets and street urchins, but the older one tried to find work, so that at least some money found its way home. But it was never enough, and finally the man who owned the miserable house told them that if they didn't pay the rent, they would have to leave. He was a compassionate man and they were given a month to find the money. But of course there was no miracle forthcoming, although the man's faith in his Lord was unwavering. He had reached a stage now where I think he might even have taken a job as a sweeper or scavenger, which as you know would have been worse than death for someone of his caste, but even there the competition was too intense. So he did the only thing he could do – he died. There would be one less mouth to feed, and his wife could throw herself on the mercy of her relatives.

'He was only fifty-three when his heart gave out on him. As he was washed and readied for cremation, his eldest boy, now nineteen, found that his father's malnourished body was so light he could lift it without any effort whatsoever. Many years later, his mother told him that in the desperate years to keep the boys in school his father had reduced his intake of food to one small bowl of kanji a day.'

Mansukhani came up in his ponderous, flat-footed way, and told Rajan that it was time to go to his next meeting, but he was waved away.

'I hope I'm not boring you, Vijay bhai. Let me assure you there is a point to this story and one that should answer some of your questions about me and why I do what I do.' His mesmerizing eyes were fixed on me, there was no sign of any emotion on his face, and it wasn't as though he were asking my permission to tell the story; it was what he intended to do, and there was no doubt in his mind that I would listen for as long as he wished.

'It is not an uncommon story and not even an especially grim one. There are millions of stories that are worse in this country of ours – our hundreds of millions of Gods are greedy for sacrificial victims – but this story had a very powerful impact on me because, as must have become obvious by now, that man was my father. I was the nineteen-year-old boy who lit his pyre, and every decision I have taken in my life has been informed by his struggle to do his dharma, to be unwavering in his devotion to his Lord.'

'In what way?' I asked. 'I can understand your determination to succeed, but I do not understand your hatred of Muslims and

Christians, your condoning of the deaths of thousands at the hands of bloodthirsty mobs, the spreading of hatred and divisiveness among the various communities.'

'I am not a criminal or a murderer,' he said, 'and I do not condone the killing of anybody, but I did applaud when that so-called masjid was torn down. I support every movement to recover the lost glories of Hinduism in Hindustan. And I'll tell you how that relates to my father. In him I saw the silent, voiceless, powerless face of the majority, the 800 million who have silently borne the depredations of the invading Muslims and Christians, and I will tell you right now that if he had been alive in December 1992 my father would have rejoiced in the breaking of the structure. Do you know why? I don't think he had anything against Muslims or Christians beyond the prejudices and conditioning of his generation. No, he would have rejoiced because he would have participated vicariously in the victory of the God he had served all his life. That is the power we are about to unleash, the energy of the majority, the hundreds of millions without dreams or any means of rising above their dismal lives. And can you imagine the effect that torrent of energy will have on this country's fortunes? We could be the greatest superpower the world has ever known—'

'Or you could be burnt to a cinder. Can't you see that? Can't you see the trail of destruction that has ensued from the moment that mosque was brought down? You talk, Mr Rajan, of harnessing the power of the majority, but if you do that by trying to destroy millions of your countrymen, you will bring this country to its knees. You will not have Ram Rajya, you will have a war that lasts a thousand years instead.'

I was shaking by now. The spell Rajan had cast on me as he told me the story of his early years was broken, and I was enraged by what this man and others like him were trying to do. Mansukhani hurried up, but Rajan himself, cool and impassive as ever, gestured to his friend that he was all right.

'Calm yourself, Vijay bhai, it is pointless to get emotional; we are only talking among ourselves as friends.'

I fought to control my anger. I had come here with a purpose, and if I was going to have any chance of finding out his intentions regarding the shrine I would have to humour him, at least for a while.

'My friend,' Rajan said quietly, 'your emotions are understandable, but you do not appear to know your own history and the way this country works. From time immemorial, whether it was Ashoka or Raja Raja Chola or Akbar, whoever has shown strength and determination has brought this country to greatness. None of these mighty rulers came to power by peaceful negotiations alone, regretfully blood was spilt, but once their enemies were subdued, all Indians, regardless of their caste or religion, prospered. Imagine the heights to which this country could rise if for the first time the majority were to be empowered – not just a Hindu kingdom here or a Hindu kingdom there, but every Hindu everywhere one hundred per cent behind their leaders – the world would never have seen anything like it. But to bring us all together we need to win a few battles in the name of Hinduism. The breaking of the masjid was one, and there will have to be others because they serve to invigorate and encourage our co-religionists.'

Had Rajan just co-opted Ashoka and Akbar to his malign cause? I thought in disbelief. 'Sir, are you trying to rewrite history? I know that's what people like you do, but Ashoka and Akbar were the least communal of India's rulers—'

'I am not saying these great figures were communal, Vijay bhai, I am saying they brought Indian civilization to heights never dreamt of before, and that is what we are also trying to do. We are fighting a battle to win the heart and soul of Hindustan, a battle to make the Hindu era the greatest in the history of India. And the minorities will have nothing to fear once we have achieved our goals, Vijay bhai. After all we were all Hindus once. They will be treated well. It is the duty of the elder brother to take care of his younger brothers and sisters.'

Although his voice was no louder than it had been and his face exhibited no signs of great emotion, there was no mistaking the electric energy he exuded. Had I been susceptible to his point of view or even a doubter I would have been swept away by his charisma, no question about that, but what I felt beneath my anger was fear for the first time as I began to get a true sense of the man and his mission. Nothing but an all-out effort could stop him.

'Forgive me for not fully understanding, sir,' I said as calmly as I could, 'but is your agitation to take over the Shrine of the Blessed Martyr part of this war you are talking about? So far as I can tell Brother Ahimas and the devotees at the shrine haven't done the Hindu community any harm, people of all faiths worship there—'

'They destroyed a temple of Lord Shiva that stood on that spot,' Mansukhani said suddenly. I had been concentrating so intently on Rajan that I hadn't noticed the other man's presence.

'You don't have any proof ... and—'

I couldn't finish because Mansukhani interrupted again. 'Proof-shoof not necessary,' he said. 'The place is holy to Shiv-bhakts, and we know Ahimas is using foreign funds from Rome, from London, from all Christian countries to convert Hindus. He has a lot of money—'

'I have seen no evidence of this,' I said.

'They are very clever these Christians,' Mansukhani said. 'Not as violent as the Muslims, but they lie, they cheat and they will trick you, given the least opportunity.'

I ignored Mansukhani and tried to turn my attention back to Rajan, but the fat shopkeeper wasn't about to shut up. 'If I was him I wouldn't be so peaceful in my attempt to take over the Tower of God, not after what these Christians did to him. Do you know that when he had no money and had his mother and his brother and all his sisters to support, the bank manager of the Cooperative Bank in Meham, a low-caste Christian cur, had him dismissed from his job, just so he could give it to one of his Christian relatives?'

Rajan's composure cracked and he snapped at the big man, castigating him for interrupting. As Mansukhani cowered under the onslaught, all his bluster gone, my fear deepened, for if there was a personal element to Rajan's attack on the shrine, there was no point in hoping that he would ever give up. His tongue-lashing of the hapless Mansukhani was brief. He ordered him to inform the people he was scheduled to meet next that he would be half an hour late, and he told him that he wanted to speak to me alone. He then turned to me, his mask back in place.

'I have nothing against Brother Ahimas or Christians personally,' he said in his calm, unexcitable tone. 'All we intend to do on Republic Day is to stage a peaceful dharma outside the shrine, demanding that it be restored to us.'

'You mean Feast Day, don't you?' I cut in.

If I was hoping to surprise him into admitting his real intentions I was to be disappointed. Rajan simply ignored the interruption and carried on.

'We do not want violence, and if our Christian brothers and sisters comply with our demands, there will be no problem. We will respect their sentiments; we can look into rebuilding the shrine elsewhere, moving their miraculous cross. Anything is possible . . .'

'And if they don't give in to your peaceful demands, presumably you will force your way into the shrine. Didn't you just imply that you don't see any harm in blood being spilled in the great war being fought in the name of Hinduism?'

'I would never harm anyone myself.'

'What if the devotees resist?'

'We will worry about that when it happens,' he said smoothly.

'You will never succeed in taking over the shrine,' I said a little shrilly. 'The people of Meham will not allow it.'

'Vijay bhai,' he said imperturbably, 'you talk blithely of the people of Meham but have you talked to any of them? In the bazaar, on the estates, in the shops? That's the problem with you English-speaking pseudo-secularists, you are totally out of touch with everything. You know, one of the few things I remember from my childhood was a field trip that we once took with a teacher. We were studying zoology, and he took us to an uncultivated area a few miles from school that was dotted with acacia trees. He wandered around for a while then stopped at a particular tree and told us to look up. When we did, we thought the tree had started bearing jewelled fruit. And then one of the gems spread its wings and flew a short distance to another branch, and we realized they were beetles so beautiful that if they had been strung into a necklace it could only have been presented to a maharani. That night I told a few of my friends that we were going to get ourselves some of the beetles, so at the weekend a gang of us walked to the acacia forest and plundered a crop. We put them in old Bournvita bottles with holes punched in the tops to enable the insects to breathe, and we put a few branches from the trees into the jars as food. For two days we were as rich as princes, but then the beetles began to die. Taken out of their natural habitat, they died slow agonizing deaths, leaving only their glittering green and gold wings behind. You people are like those golden beetles, Vijay bhai; you might glitter and preen for a while, but this is not your natural habitat, and soon you will all die out. That is why it doesn't matter what you write or say or think because you are not truly Indian, just like those beetles that died you are living on borrowed time.'

'If we're living on borrowed time, then so are you,' I said grimly. 'You are not the first to try to impose your vision of fundamentalism on the people, and you won't be the last. The people will spurn you when they realize you have nothing substantial to offer except hate and lies. As I recall you talked about Ashoka and Akbar, but perhaps you don't realize why people still revere them today, or perhaps you do know, but would rather not face up to the facts, Mr Rajan. I have just been reading about them, and the truth is that people still love them for their all-encompassing vision for this country and its people. If you don't have that, you might be successful in the short term but it will never last.'

'You have us all wrong, Vijay bhai; we are not interested in short-term gains. We don't care if people reject us today, we're prepared to fight for a thousand years, two thousand, until we win this battle. Unlike you, we are of this soil, we are the majority and our brothers and sisters will eventually see the light. We can be patient, we have the numbers and resources on our side. Think about it; if you don't believe me, that's OK, talk to the common people and see what they think.'

Mansukhani returned, and this time Rajan got up to go. He apologized for not being able to spend any more time with me, shook hands and walked out. I followed, hearing that calm, unflustered voice in my head and the poison it dripped. I was sick with discouragement, afraid that Rajan was right. So what if he was stopped this time? I thought, as I made my way to the taxi rank. As he had proclaimed, the fundamentalists had the time, the people and the wherewithal eventually to win the war. But even as I thought that I remembered Mr Sorabjee's determination to keep fighting as the

187

darkness descended on Bombay – no, the struggle must go on.

Just before I got into a taxi, I paused to take a look at the scene around me. A bus had just pulled in and was disgorging its passengers – office workers, shopkeepers, farmers – who merged with the groups of people clogging the streets of the town. There were too many people here, I thought, too many people who had nothing to do, who could explode into violence at a moment's notice. A small altercation broke out between some of the passengers at the bus stop – two men were arguing fiercely about something – and as I watched them my mind went back to something I had witnessed in Bombay. The packed local train I was in was slowing to a stop at a suburban station when a middle-aged man, a clerk by the look of him, balding with his remaining hair neatly oiled and combed over his shiny scalp, accused a burly man who was standing next to him of picking his pocket. The big man, who could have silenced his accuser with a stare, chose instead to try to make a run for it. In an instant the crowd was upon him, attacking him with a venom that I still remember. Twenty or thirty men, all of them dwarfed by their victim, went at him with a fury born of long years of being over-looked, ignored, bullied and frustrated in their tiny, tiny lives. They slapped the cowering giant with their open palms, they beat him with their chappals and their worn, shiny briefcases, pulled at his hair, kicked him as he crouched down, burying his face in his hands, and all I could think of as the train pulled away was that if he had only opened his mouth and roared at them, they would have scattered and run. But perhaps he was simply bewildered by the unexpected savagery of the attack. Rajan had talked about the revenge of the dispossessed and I did not disbelieve him – their fury lay just beneath the surface, and if it was properly channelled, as professional agitators were capable of doing, it could become a truly destructive force.

When I got back to Cypress Manor, I telephoned the Brigadier, as he had told me to, and gave him a detailed account of my meeting. He promised to make his own enquiries and invited me to tea the next evening. I then called Professor Menon. I caught him just in time as he was leaving for the shrine. He intended to spend the next few days there along with six young men who had volunteered to defend the shrine if it came under attack (Brother Ahimas had been told that they would be helping with the Feast Day preparations). He said he had tried to telephone the collector but had failed to reach him. He had also missed the inspector of the Meham police station, who had been out on a case.

I volunteered my services to try and meet the officials and also asked if I could be included among the shrine's defenders, but Menon thought I would be more useful if I kept to my role as a reporter. There was a slim hope, he said, that Rajan wouldn't resort to any extreme action in the presence of a Bombay journalist as I might file a negative report about him. We left it at that, and I said I'd see him on the fifth.

12

The solitude of emperors

The entrance to the Brigadier's property was only half a kilometre away from Cypress Manor so I decided to walk to my appointment. The journey was uphill all the way, but it was cool, and it wasn't strenuous walking on the well-metalled road cut into the hillside. Every so often I would pass a gate opening on to a driveway, but the houses here stood in such large forested grounds that there was not a building to be seen from the road, let alone another human being. It was said that the higher a person lived on Tiger Hill, the more important he was, and certainly if anyone doubted that the Brigadier was the overlord of Meham, the site of his residence would have ended their argument, for the road stopped at a tall iron gate at the summit. A uniformed guard at the gatehouse would not let me pass, he was obviously unused to visitors arriving on foot, but after he had telephoned through to the house, he allowed me in reluctantly. For half a kilometre, I walked through forest, soaring eucalyptus and jacaranda trees and a mix of conifers and other species. There was birdsong, and once a small greyish-brown animal that stood about a foot high scurried into the undergrowth. The road crested a small rise, and abruptly the forest gave way to a smooth lawn that unrolled all the way down to the enormous bungalow that stood at the centre of the property. Brightly coloured flower beds encircled the house like a necklace, its clasp provided by two enormous monkey puzzle trees that grew in front of the building. Everywhere I looked vivid splashes of colour and imposing trees punctuated the green swell of the lawns. An army of gardeners, tiny figures in that immensity of space, toiled diligently in the strong afternoon light, nipping, pruning, weeding, heightening the perfection of the garden. It was easy to see why the Brigadier had won so many prizes at the Flower Show.

As I neared the house, I saw an ancient Fiat parked by a hedge and wondered who the visitor might be. A uniformed bearer showed me into a small study, asked if I would like some tea, then left unobtrusively. I was glad of the opportunity to collect my thoughts because I had spent most of the night in fruitless pursuit of a workable plan to stop Rajan. The more I reviewed my encounter with him, the more worried I became; the calm uninflected way in which he had talked about leading the demonstration, the fervent dedication to his cause ... who could stand up to that combination? I wasn't convinced the Brigadier would be able to deal with Rajan, but of all the available options, he certainly seemed to be the best. He knew everybody of consequence in the district, and if he could persuade enough powerful people to rally round, then Rajan might be forced to abandon his plans or at least postpone them until we were better prepared.

The bearer entered in the noiseless way of the well-trained servant and told me the Brigadier would see me now. I was ushered into a cavernous living room with bay windows that overlooked the garden. The walls were covered with army memorabilia and here and there a trophy animal's head peered mournfully out. The paintings were ordinary but on every available surface – the mantelpiece, the coffee table, the peg tables, an enormous rosewood chest that stood against one wall – there were vases filled with a dazzling array of flowers which scattered notes of light and perfume throughout the room. The flowers must be the work of the housekeeper, I thought. There was no sign of her now but the Brigadier and Dr Kuruvilla were having coffee in a nest of sofas by one of the windows. Upon seeing me, the Brigadier beckoned me over with a cheery 'Hello old chap, good of you to come' and, having instructed the bearer to get a fresh pot of coffee, announced that he and the doctor had just concluded their weekly chess match. 'I should have taken both his bishops when I had the chance, I'd have won for sure, but he has the luck of the devil when he plays black.'

'No luck, my friend, just skill,' the doctor said equably.

'Then how do you account for the fact that I almost always beat you when you're playing white?'

'Not true,' the doctor said brusquely, and the Brigadier gave vent to one of his booming laughs.

Then, ignoring my presence, they began to discuss an infestation of spider mites that was threatening their beloved fuchsias. Eventually, the Brigadier glanced my way. 'You must be growing impatient, my dear boy, but don't fret, I have some good news for you.'

'Good news? What good news?' the doctor asked.

'Oh, Vijay here has been worried that there might be trouble at the shrine. Remember, he brought it up at the meeting.'

'Yes, so should we be worrying or not?' the doctor asked impatiently.

'Don't mind my friend here,' the Brigadier said with a wink. 'He might not have a soothing bedside manner but he's a good physician.'

The doctor didn't appear to be too pleased by this description of himself but said nothing. The Brigadier then told us he had gone to see Rajan the previous evening after I had telephoned him. He hadn't found him at the shop but had eventually tracked him down at a leper colony that had grown up by the river that flowed below town.

'Such an inspirational young man,' the Brigadier said, 'so dedicated to helping the poor. Volunteers from town distribute clothes and money to the lepers, and he funds it all. He was telling me about the charity work he does in Bombay and Coimbatore. You know as a people we don't do enough charity – all we seem to do when we have money is build temples or go on pilgrimages. We could learn from the Americans, now there's a country that has developed philanthropy to a fine art. And just imagine, if each of us who could adopted just one family below the poverty line, then we'd be a poor country no longer.'

The doctor cut in sharply, tugging at his little goatee, 'You're digressing again, Mohan.'

'So I am, so I am,' the Brigadier said unperturbed. 'But then again, perhaps I'm not. You see, I'm beginning to be convinced that this young man, Rajan, poses no threat to the shrine.'

I was about to interrupt, but he signalled me to be quiet.

'As I said to you a couple of days ago, I have met him on several occasions and I am amazed that even after all the troubles he's had, he holds no bitterness towards anyone. He is determined to give something back to society, instead of just enjoying his money. Men like him should be held up as an example to our people; we don't need to look outside our country to find examples of those who have risen from the bottom of the heap . . .'

He reached for his coffee, and I said agitatedly, 'Sir, that isn't at all the way he came across to me. I think he is very good at hiding his true motives and I believe he wants to destroy the shrine, not just as part of his fundamentalist agenda but for personal reasons as well. Do you know that the bank manager who dismissed him on trumped-up charges was a Christian, and he thinks by taking over a Christian place of worship—'

'I would hardly call the shrine a Christian place of worship,' the doctor put in drily. 'Every church in the district hates Brother Ahimas's guts for allowing unbelievers in, not obeying the rules and regulations of any normal church, let alone the Church of South India . . .'

'Listen, young man,' the Brigadier said patronizingly, 'I think we can safely discard the notion that he is going to all this trouble just to get back at some slight that happened twenty-five years ago, but let us assume that he wants to take over the shrine for political reasons. Why here in Meham? Surely he could have found something in Bombay?'

I repeated what Menon had told me: 'The extremists want to expand their territory and this state has hardly seen any communal violence—'

'That's a bit of a stretch,' the doctor said grumpily. 'Even if he occupies the shrine, it's hardly going to inflame passions in the whole state.'

'Sir, you have no idea how quickly these things can spread. Some obscure incident in Bihar or rural Karnataka, and the whole country is up in arms within a couple of days.'

'I suppose it's because of journalists like you,' the doctor said impolitely.

'I don't think anything like that is going to happen here,' the Brigadier interjected. 'If Rajan was really serious about taking over the shrine, why didn't he simply assemble an army of goondas, march on the Tower of God, occupy the shrine, chuck Ahimas, Menon and the rest of them over the precipice and proclaim the glories of Lord Shiva from the summit?'

'Because he's a superb politician, sir, not an ordinary street thug. He is building up to a terrific climax that will portray him as a great champion of Hindu interests. The 6 December attack was designed to fail, the bad weather simply made it look more plausible, and the next one will be carried out in the full glare of publicity, but this time he will make sure it's a success.'

I wondered whether I should talk about my theory of the attack being carried out on the saint's Feast Day instead of Republic Day but decided against it. I would first need to convince the Brigadier that the threat was real.

'What do you think, Doctor saab?' the Brigadier asked.

'Don't know, the young fellow may be on to something,' the doctor said, his hand worrying at his goatee again. 'But then again he could be overreacting. I do agree with you, Mohan, this chap Rajan seems to be all right. He wasn't here when I moved to the Nilgiris twenty years ago so I don't know about any of the scandals this young man is talking about, but when I met him he came across as a perfectly good sort.'

'What did he come to see you about?'

'Oh, an old medical condition, can't tell you what it is, I'm afraid.'

'Heart murmur,' I said, 'he said so himself.'

The doctor glared at me. 'Well, now that the cat's out of the bag, I suppose I can talk about it. It's not that serious, but I told him he shouldn't exert himself too much.'

As the two old men chatted on I could see that I was wasting my time here. Nobody felt Rajan was a threat besides me and Menon. And then as the doctor held forth on the various medical conditions afflicting the heart a solution presented itself to me. I was appalled that I could even think it – I should have suppressed it the moment I thought of it – instead I spoke it out aloud.

'Dr Kuruvilla, I have a question. Is there a way in which a drug could be administered to make someone's heart condition worse?' I asked.

'What?' both men said simultaneously.

'Only temporarily,' I said hastily. 'Until the crisis has passed.'

'Listen, young man,' the doctor said. 'As a doctor I am sworn to save lives, not take them. I will not listen to any more of this nonsense, do you hear?'

The doctor's sharp reaction sobered me up. What on earth was I doing? I wondered. Had I totally lost my mind? No, this had gone far enough. Perhaps my own paranoia and fear were pushing me to exaggerate the danger. I tried to view Rajan from a calmer perspective, and I saw how he could be perceived as a man dedicated to alleviating the woes of the people; and, if on the side, he worked in the cause of Hindus, led a demonstration to a shrine built on a site that was ostensibly holy to Hindus, how did one more demonstration in a country of a million demonstrations matter? A few hours of noise and tension, and then things would go on as before. But even as I thought this, at the back of my mind I could see myself interviewing the survivors and victims of communal violence, people who had been leading normal, boring lives, until, in an instant, things had swung out of control. I had interviewed the murderers too, and besides a few obvious goondas, the majority of them were ordinary men, fathers, sons, husbands, who were perfectly good neighbours and citizens until some politician or ambitious priest invoked the name of God. When I viewed Rajan through that prism, he didn't seem so harmless any more but how was I going to convince these men to adopt the same view?

I must have looked crestfallen because the Brigadier spoke up now, the patronizing tone absent from his voice. 'No need to look dejected, old boy, even though I think you might be overreacting. I didn't get to where I am today by not taking into account every eventuality. I think there will be only a harmless demonstration, but just in case things turn nasty I've made arrangements. A good soldier is always prepared, you know.'

'Arrangements?' I asked.

'Soon after I met Rajan, I went to see Inspector Shanmugam to enquire about the bandobast that had been arranged for the demonstration. He has about twenty-five constables, of whom there are only eighteen at the station at the moment – the rest are on leave or posted elsewhere – but he has promised to send at least a dozen men to guard the approaches to the shrine. And he even promised to unlock the armoury and equip the policemen with rifles, something that is only done when there is a real emergency. He said he would be present and would personally arrest Rajan if he behaved in a manner that threatened the shrine.

I was pleasantly surprised by the local inspector's stance – if he seemed a good man.

'And that's not all,' the Brigadier said, looking very pleased with himself. 'I phoned the collector and told him that he should be prepared to rush in reinforcements at short notice, should the situation get out of hand. Also, to be absolutely on the safe side, I phoned the brigadier of the Madras Regimental Centre in Wellington. I taught him at the Staff College, and he said he would be in touch with the collector and the general in Madras, in case there was any reason for the army to be called in.'

This seemed the moment to tell the Brigadier about my suspicions that Rajan would strike on Feast Day and not Republic Day. He nodded and said he would alert the people he had talked to. A thought occurred to me and I asked the Brigadier whether Rajan knew about the extra security that was being arranged.

'Of course he does, I told the inspector to inform him so there wouldn't be any nonsense.'

'I don't think he scares easily,' I said.

'Perhaps not when he is up against street thugs in Bombay, but he hasn't faced the army, has he now? I have seen the toughest bad-mashes, rioters and gangsters who have committed ten, twenty murders, quail when the army arrives on the scene of a riot. I remember in Lucknow—'

'My dear chap,' the doctor said abruptly, 'you can bore this young fellow, but I've got to get going.'

He shook hands with us and saw himself out. As his vehicle wheezed into life and rattled away, the Brigadier said with a smile, 'Kuruvilla is worth crores, yet you wouldn't think it to look at him. Drives around in that old bone-rattler, has no airs or graces. He's a good man. That's why I like this place: there are good people here, and everything is so peaceful, serene. I couldn't live in a big city, especially in the north, even if I was paid to.'

He paused to take a sip of his coffee. 'So, Vijay, are you enjoying yourself? This Rajan lafda is nothing, you'll see. I hope you've taken in enough of the beauties of this place. Notice you're not much of a plant fancier though.'

'I'm a city boy, sir. I haven't had much experience with plants, but I can see why they have their appeal.'

'Yes, yes, they are beautiful to look at no doubt, but only when you become a true gardener do you realize that they can become an obsession.'

'Yes, sir,' I said dutifully.

He must have noticed that I was still preoccupied, for he said, 'There's really no cause to worry, you know.'

'I'm sure you're right, sir, it's just that I've seen how much damage these fundamentalists can do, and those images never leave you. You wonder when it's going to happen next.'

'I think I understand what you're feeling. You know I find it odd that people should call a situation where people of the same nation turn against each other a civil war. Nothing civil about it, take the word of an old soldier. All death is horrible, but that's the worst. It's different when you're fighting for your country, facing a heavily armed enemy who could easily kill you if you don't get him first.'

Through the window that faced me I could see gigantic streaks of black and grey beginning to radiate across the fawn of the evening sky. The light had started to fade. A storm front was moving slowly up the valley and a faint hope stirred within me. There were still two and a half days to go to Feast Day, and if there were heavy showers, it might dampen the celebrations but it would also put paid to Rajan's plan. He would make another attempt, I had little doubt about that, but the whole point about keeping people like him in check was to keep trying to thwart them every time they tried.

'That's the only sort of situation where killing is permissible,' the Brigadier was saying. 'I'd be the last person to allow anything to happen here so don't worry, it's all taken care of. It looks like it might rain, would you like me to have you dropped back?'

'No, sir, it's only a short walk. I'll be fine.'

When I got home, the butler handed me a note scrawled on a piece of paper: 'I've found out something that I think you'll find very interesting. Come as soon as you can.' It wasn't signed but the butler told me Noah had sent it through one of the kitchen servants who lived near him. I didn't set off immediately as I hadn't yet got over the stories Kamath had told me about Noah – if he was so unreliable, why should I bother with him? Besides, I didn't want to get caught in the storm. In the end I did decide to go, the note sounded quite urgent, and I thought I shouldn't dismiss Noah outright. After all he was still an ally, perhaps the only one I had left if you discounted the defenders at the shrine, especially as the more I reviewed my meeting with the Brigadier, the less I was convinced that any real action was going to be taken to contain the threat. I could see he admired Rajan and the so-called arrangements he said he had made seemed merely to consist of reassurances from people he had spoken to on the telephone.

❦

The impending storm had hastened the onset of darkness, and by the time I was on the road great sweeps of night were suspended from the sky, tinctured by the last sun. Everywhere the landscape glowed red, and not for the first time I was struck by the beauty of the place. But it was a beauty that held no charm for me, as I wondered what the coming days would bring. I had done everything I could to help except make a round of the authorities, which I would do tomorrow. Once that was done, all I could do was hope that people like the Brigadier and Noah were right and that this place would never be a setting for sectarian violence.

As I neared the cemetery I was startled to hear a loud stream of abuse emanating from within it. I broke into a run, Kamath's stories about Noah's penchant for getting into fights running through my head. I hoped I would be of some use if he was indeed in a scuffle, I remembered how useless I had been when the rioters had set upon me in Bombay.

When I entered the cemetery I was confronted by an extraordinary sight. The last light of the day illuminated a lone tree before which

198

Noah stood, holding a large hammer. There was no one else about, and the abuse I heard coming from Noah, was, as far as I could tell, directed at the tree. Of medium height, it had slender, wand-like branches that grew in great profusion at the base of the trunk, gradually tapering off towards the crown. Pale green flowers spotted the foliage and in the dim light it seemed the tree was wreathed in green fire. Even as I watched, Noah placed a large nail against its trunk and swung the hammer violently, pounding it deep into the bark, cursing viciously all the while. Had he gone completely mad? What had the tree done to offend him?

Nervously I said, 'Everything all right, Noah?'

Noah broke off in mid-curse and said, 'Oh hello, Vijay, I didn't think you were coming.'

The transition from seeming rage to normality was so instantaneous and total that I began to doubt his sanity all the more.

'Sure, you're OK?' I said uncertainly.

He laughed. 'Oh this. Sorry, didn't mean to scare you, da, but I was trying a trick an old gardener once taught me. There's something wrong with this avocado tree. Year after year it flowers on schedule, birds and insects visit it so it's being pollinated all right, but for some reason it never fruits. The chap I mentioned this to told me that sometimes you needed to give a tree or a plant a little push to get it moving in the right direction. Scare it a bit, and you'll see the results, he said. I've tried it for a couple of years now' – I looked to where he was pointing and saw that the trunk of the tree was pierced by over a dozen evil-looking nails – 'but to no avail. Doesn't cost me a thing to persist, though ... So how did club night go?'

For a moment I didn't know what he was talking about – my visit to the club seemed already to belong to the distant past – and then all at once Maya's beautiful face came to me. I wondered if I should tell him that I had met her but decided against it. If his sources had told him she was here, as I was convinced they had, then the information would be superfluous, otherwise it would just create the sort of distraction that I was anxious to avoid. For similar reasons I decided against bringing up any of Kamath's revelations. From this point onward my main interest in Noah was as an ally, no matter how shaky, until the threat of Rajan was seen off.

'Hey, what are you thinking about? Did you meet a girl?' he asked, amusement in his voice. But I was in no mood for banter, so I said abruptly, 'Your note?'

'Oh, that. Well, I thought you would be interested to know you were right. I've heard from two independent sources that Rajan is planning to do something on the saint's Feast Day, only there are some aspects of his plan that don't make any sense at all.'

He had gone to Ooty that morning, he said, and while he was there he'd met an old acquaintance, a stringer for a Madras newspaper, who told him that he had received a call from Mansukhani, telling him to be present outside the shrine at noon on Feast Day, when there would be a big demonstration and Rajan would have a major announcement to make.

'I don't know why he bothered with all that eyewash about Republic Day ...' I said.

'Yes, it's curious that he has begun to broadcast his plans, but it gets even more intriguing. One of my friends at Meham police station told me that Rajan arrived at the station and was closeted with Shanmugam, the inspector, for over an hour. When he left, my friend learned – you know how it's impossible to keep things secret in a small-town police station – that Rajan had given the inspector one lakh in cash for himself, and another lakh to be shared between the policemen in the station; to further sweeten the bribe he promised to get the inspector's son into Presidency College. But here's where it gets really bizarre: the only thing he wanted the inspector to do was what he would have done anyway if he wasn't an ivory-skulled, corrupt little prick.'

'Don't seem to like the inspector much, do you?' I said.

'Oh, I guess he's no better or worse than anyone else, it's just that he arrested an old friend of mine – remember I told you about Arumugam, the flower thief – just because he had to fill some arrest quota for the month. Sure, Arumugam is a repeat offender, but he's so old now the only thing he could possibly steal is milk from his goat.'

Lies again, I thought. But I managed to control myself with the thought that in the light of the greater threat that loomed, Noah could be a liar, a thief, none of it mattered, I couldn't afford to lose him ...

'So here's the really weird thing,' Noah was saying. 'Rajan wanted Shanmugam to arrest him as soon as the demonstration got under way, even rough him up a little. I would have thought he'd want to evade arrest until he had breached the shrine.'

'True,' I said. 'You can see why he'd want to be beaten up or arrested, he'd become an instant martyr to the fundamentalist cause, but what good would that do if the shrine was left undisturbed? No, we're missing something. Perhaps we should go and see the inspector ourselves.'

'I doubt he'd tell us what Rajan was planning,' Noah responded, 'even if he knew, and I doubt he knows very much.'

'Then the only thing we can do is make sure security around the shrine is so tight that not even a cockroach can get in.'

'The police here certainly don't have enough manpower to achieve that, even if they were willing; only the army could do that.'

'So let's get the army,' I said. 'The Brigadier was telling me earlier today that for the army to get involved in civilian law and order, the head of the district administration would need to speak to the general in Madras—'

'And you're going to get all these high-powered people to jump to do your bidding on the basis of your piddling little suspicions? Come on, be realistic, da.'

'So would you rather do nothing?' I said irritably.

'There might be nothing we need to do. Rajan will have his little demonstration, get arrested, become a hero to the fundoos; the shrine will continue to flourish, Meham will revert to its sleepy everyday state, you will go back to Bombay, get laid, lose your youthful idealism, and life will go on . . .'

'But what if I'm right? You know Rajan, you know the man is not just talk. He wants to do this, not just for the sake of his brand of politics, but to settle a personal score.'

'You mean the tamasha at the bank?'

I nodded and said, 'The Brigadier didn't think the matter was so serious that it would have stayed with him all these years.'

'The Brigadier is an old fool with his head stuck so far up his arse that if it went any deeper he could see through his mouth. No, he doesn't know what he's talking about, and what's more, he didn't see what I did. That manager was a bastard, a conniving, slimy, casteist son of a bitch, even though he was some sort of Pentecostalist. He was one of the congregation that prayed ineffectually over my mum and I saw more of him than I liked at one time. Anyway, he wanted to get one of his jati into the bank, so he threw this poor bugger out, had him charged at the police station with theft. I think he might even have had to serve a little time before he disappeared to Bombay, but the whole thing stank, da, and when you're nineteen, twenty, every humiliation, every setback cuts deeper than anything that can happen to you in later life. I have no doubt Rajan remembers every minute of his shame as clearly as if it had happened to him yesterday. I could tell you what happened to me at that age without forgetting a single detail. If he could have taken it out on that bank manager, I'm sure he would have, except the fucker died of a heart attack about ten years ago. But the man was a great supporter of the shrine, made donations to it and prayed there all the time, hoping his sins would wash off, no doubt, so I think Rajan would get a lot of satisfaction if he did decide to take it over.'

'There, you've said it yourself,' I said quickly.

'I said *if*,' he said. 'All I think he's going to do is give everyone a good scare . . . and that will be that.'

'And if you are wrong, would you want any harm to come to Brother Ahimas, the professor, all those inoffensive pilgrims?'

'Listen, da, don't drag me into it, OK.'

'Even if your friends are affected . . .'

'You're not listening to me, Vijay.'

Oh, but I am, I thought to myself. I am listening to you and I wonder why you are determined not to get involved, no matter what. Is it because of something in your past that you haven't told me, or is it because this is the way you are? I thought about everything that he had said, everything that others had told me about him, and I still couldn't get an accurate fix on him. What is the key to your mystery, Noah? I wondered, but this was hardly the time to probe, so I changed tack.

'Look, if you don't want to get involved directly, maybe you could just help me with a couple of things . . .'

Mr Khanna's driver still hadn't returned, and I didn't want to be at the mercy of local taxi drivers as I criss-crossed the district, especially now there wasn't much time left. It would be good to have a local around, not only to help me get to the various officials I wanted to meet, but to lend weight to my arguments should that become necessary. Noah may not have been the perfect back-up but he was the only one I had. With these thoughts running through my head, I said to him, 'You're from here. I promised Menon I would call on the collector and the inspector, and it would be great if you could accompany me to see them.'

'What are you going to tell these people? That you suspect Rajan is about to do all sorts of awful things? Don't forget he's a bit of a hero in this town. And you don't want me with you, da; they will throw you out if they see my face.'

'Look, Noah, I'm a stranger here and we don't have much time. If you don't want to come in with me that's OK, but at least take me to their offices. You know your way around.'

'And what are you going to say to them that the Brigadier hasn't already said? Just trot out your suspicious? Don't forget nothing has actually happened so far besides that demonstration that fizzled out.'

'That's why the Rajans of the world always win – we wring our hands once something happens, we don't do anything beforehand. You saw all the pious proclamations after the Babri Masjid was destroyed. What if people had actually done something to prevent it from being destroyed?'

'Hey, you're the hero.'

'Noah, all I'm asking for is one day of your time, nothing more . . .'

There was a long pause, and then he said, 'You're one stubborn fucker, I'll give you that. I've got some work planned for tomorrow, so we'll go the day after, there's enough time. But let's agree here and now that that will be the end of it. I will take you to see these guys, nothing more.'

As I was leaving I pointed to the threatening sky and asked if he thought the weather might come to the rescue. He laughed and said, 'Don't bank on it. An acquaintance of mine, a retired weatherman who lives nearby, once said to me that you can always rely on the weather to let you down, it's the only thing that's more unreliable than humankind.'

I am no great believer in karma or predestination, shaped as I was in my early years by a father who was for the most part a rationalist and an empiricist. But as I think back to my time in Meham, I wonder if I had any choice at all in the way events unfolded. Take something as simple as my decision to read Mr Sorabjee's manuscript once more that evening. Why did I decide to do that? I had already read it once, and although I wanted to read it again in one go, to have a better sense of its narrative flow, I can't fully explain why I decided to reread it that very evening. I'm sure I could have found something else to read in Mr Khanna's study to pass the time if I had looked hard enough (he did not own a television, and the records that were stacked next to the old-fashioned Philips radiogram did not interest me) but after a cursory glance at the bookshelves, I picked up the envelope in which I had deposited Mr Sorabjee's manuscript, extracted the pages and began reading. When I came to the end of the chapter on Gandhi, I found I had missed something on my first pass – a concluding chapter that gave its name to the book and had somehow got stuck in the envelope.

THE SOLITUDE OF EMPERORS

We do not know what to do with one of our most precious resources, solitude, and so we fill it with clutter. Perhaps this is not entirely our fault, for it is within our deepest solitude that the bogeys that we are otherwise able to ignore and the cold fires of madness lurk. Solitude, true solitude, can drive us insane, so sensibly we turn our backs on it and pursue the superficial concerns of our daily lives. And perhaps that is how life is meant to be for the vast mass of us, the followers and wannabes who will never be. Perhaps that is what the one who created us proposed all along, it was never his intention that every one of us would amount to something or make a difference, if that were so it would disrupt the natural order of things, which would be intolerable. But those who are driven enough or bold enough or mad enough or exalted enough to look without flinching into the emptiness within will find in it insights vouchsafed only to the select few.

The great ones were not afraid of solitude. All leaders of men know that loneliness is a condition of their existence, but only the greatest of them are able to transcend mere isolation to find the solitude in which the worlds of the Gods and men intersect. It was here that the emperors discovered their most potent ideas, ideas that helped shape the moral imagination of nations in hitherto unheard-of ways, it was here that they encountered their destiny. But it wasn't easy, even for them, to go beyond the ordinary, to find that place where, though men, they became the equal of God. Nobody will ever know the true nature of the solitude of emperors and that is understandable for if it were easy to comprehend then it would no longer be extraordinary. But as the lives of the emperors have been endlessly fascinating to those who would know them, attempts have been made to probe the source of their genius, some more successful than others. I have drawn on all the accounts I have been able to find to present my own view of where and how the three men I have brought together in this narrative found the ideas that enabled them to transform the world they lived in.

With hindsight we can see that they were always destined to become supreme rulers of men, but even for them the greatness that lay within took long years of preparation to access. They filled their lives with study, struggle and dogged endeavour. They consulted with wise men, consorted with the great cultural experts of their time, immersed themselves in timeless scriptures and works of philosophy. They went to war, they dealt in peace. And even as they engaged with the affairs of men, deep inside they were preparing to walk with the Gods. And, one day, often without warning, they were ready to take the greatest decision of their lives.

Accounts of the life of the Emperor Ashoka, as well as his own edicts, tell us about the anguish he felt as he walked the battlefield in Kalinga, alone among the dead, the wounded and the vanquished. His exultation gave way to deep sorrow and it was in this state that he was granted the vision of what he must do next. All those years of war and anger, all those years of dipping into Buddhism, and now, in an instant, he was sure about the future.

Emperor Akbar's epiphany came during a great hunt that had been organized for him on the banks of the Jhelum River. A crack marksman, the thirty-six-year-old ruler and his party waited at a strategic point as the animals were driven towards them. At the point when the carnage should have begun, not a shot was fired, the emperor seemed to have fallen into a trance. When he finally came out of it, he ordered the hunt to be abandoned.

Some historians think he might have suffered an epileptic fit, but whatever the nature of the seizure, from that point onwards his interest in religion deepened and expanded. Hitherto his deliberations about God and faith had been largely limited to Islam, but now he opened up his meditations to include the ideas of holy men of all faiths. And in due course he took the ultimate step – of founding a faith that included them all. His journey to this moment of transformation had been long, and so when the time was right, he was ready.

The Mahatma's preparation for his moment of transformation was equally intense. Indeed, Gandhiji says himself that he had several moments of revelation, and all of these have been extensively discussed and documented so we shall only examine the most famous of them – when he was thrown out of his first-class railway carriage at Pietermaritzburg railway station on the way to Pretoria. By his own admission, Gandhi was a timid man up until that point. However he was gradually evolving, for every time he was faced with a crisis, either moral, spiritual or physical, it toughened him and imperceptibly helped change him into the man he would become.

Every one of these incidents in his early life – his visit to a brothel with a school friend in Gujarat, his unavailability when his father was dying, his refusal to copy at school, a small act of dissimulation that he confessed to his father about, his attempt to use his connections to the Raj's political agent in Kathiawad to obtain a favour for his brother that resulted in him being thrown out of the agent's office – all these along with his abiding interest in religion, including his interaction with various esoteric sects while still a student in England, prepared him for the day his thinking would irrevocably change course and he would experience the 'tremendous convulsion of the human spirit' (in the words of C.F. Andrews) that would reorder his priorities for ever.

Our examination of the turning point in his life need not detain us too long. He was travelling from Durban to Pretoria to represent a client in an important legal matter. At Pietermaritzburg he was thrown out of his compartment by a white railway official although he held a first-class ticket. The train left without him and Gandhi spent the night at the station, cold and miserable, wondering whether he should take the next ship to India or whether he should stand and fight. He decided to make a stand, and this is where in his deepest solitude he found the inspiration to do what he had to do. From that moment onward, in his words, 'The only tyrant I [would] accept in this world [was] the still voice within.'

The new emperor we await will need to combine the renunciation of Ashoka, the syncretic abilities of Akbar and the truth of Gandhi, but these qualities alone will not be enough. He will need to add something more to the mix, something that is uniquely his own, for the problems of our time are more complex than anything the world has seen before. I wish I could tell you, my young friends, what it is that you should be looking for in this new leader, what traits will set him apart from the pygmies who masquerade as our leaders today but in truth I do not know. All I know is that when he arrives in our midst he will have a vision so breathtakingly clear and innovative that it may not even be recognized immediately, something every genius ahead of his time has had to contend with.

The new emperor will come, just as surely as his predecessors walked the earth, but I did not set out to write this tract merely to suggest that we passively wait for his (or her) advent. No, a thousand times no. It is the duty of each one of us, the young and the young at heart, to find a way to make a difference even as we keep an eye out for the great one who will inevitably rise up among us to sweep away the forces of darkness.

I began this chapter by saying that most of us, especially the young, wilfully squander our most precious resource, solitude. But it doesn't need to be that way. There will always be those who are doomed to live their lives with about as much wisdom and meaning as dull-witted bandicoots, but I have no doubt that there are also many of you who would like to be different. And you can raise yourselves up by looking into the solitude that dwells within each of you to discover strength and direction just as the great ones did. Don't assume it will be easy to find – it will require discipline, courage and fortitude – but I am not suggesting you engage in years of penance and monastic rigour as the mighty sages and rishis did, your place is in the world and not out of it. Indeed, if anything, you will need to live more fully than most so that the space within your hearts and souls is enriched and vibrant.

I exhort you therefore to go out and mingle and learn. Inhale the genius of this country. Do not discount anything, the transcendent poetry of the Sufi and Bhakti poets, the architecture of Hampi and Fatehpur Sikri and Mount Abu, the teachings of Ramana Maharshi and the Shirdi Sai Baba. Let the plaintive wail of the shehnai fill your senses, the plangent notes of the sarod and the sitar slice through the dullness of your waking life. Watch rhododendrons moult on a Himalayan slope, surf the breakers at the point where three seas mingle in Kanyakumari, hunt in the Western Ghats with the hamadryad, the only snake on the planet that is fast and deadly enough to prey on other snakes, walk the shadowy forests of Arunachal with the clouded leopard, the least known great cat in the world. Celebrate the colours of Holi, the lights of Deepavali, the food of Ramzan and the gifts of Christmas. Eat meen moily in Cochin, kebabs in Lucknow, dhansak in Cumballa Hill and dhokla in Ahmedabad. No other place in the world can boast the width and depth of history, art, spirituality, food and music that this country has to offer, and it is all yours for the taking. And there is no call to limit yourself to this country; there is nothing to stop you from roaming more widely through the literature and music and art and philosophy and scripture of the West and the

East to feed the wellsprings of your creativity and quietude.

At the same time, do not neglect to absorb the poverty and violence and savagery and injustice of this country of extremes. Experience the despair of the coalminer in Dhanbad, where the very land is on fire, understand the hopelessness of the marginal cotton farmer in Andhra Pradesh, mourn with the widow of the Sikh garage owner who witnessed her husband being burnt alive in the Delhi riots of 1984. Let their pain become yours.

You might wonder why you should listen to this old Bombayite hectoring you so let me tell you a story, about how and why I decided to give up my comfortable life to dedicate myself to the work I have done for over twenty years now. In 1969 I had gone to Ahmedabad on a business trip when riots broke out, and I was stranded in my hotel. On the evening of the day after the riots had been 'brought under control' I was walking through one of the shopping districts when I came upon a narrow street where over a dozen people had been killed. The bodies had been taken away and policemen were lounging around, but something I saw that day led me to abandon my plans of a quiet retirement and start the magazine I edit to this day. At the far end of the lane was a heap of discarded footwear: cheap plastic chappals, rope sandals, badly torn and mended shoes. At first I didn't comprehend what I was looking at, and then it struck me – this pile of rubbish had belonged to the victims, who had discarded them in the hope that they would gain some extra speed and agility to save themselves. As I stood looking at the poignant memorial to those who had lost their lives, I saw with pitiless clarity that I could never hope to spend my remaining years sipping Blue Riband gin and tonic on the lawns of the Bombay Gym as I waited for the day I would make my last journey to the Towers of Silence. I had at some level always been concerned about sectarian violence and the direction the country was taking, but as I hadn't been affected by it personally I had seen no need to do anything about it beyond sending the occasional cheque to some rehabilitation effort or other. That day everything came together, and I knew exactly what I should do. I started *The Indian Secularist* a year later, and only wish I'd had my epiphany a few decades earlier.

And so, my young friends, I say to you: immerse yourself in the beauty and terror of this great country, enrich and deepen your hearts and your minds. Let every disappointment instruct you, let every triumph strengthen you. And all the while, even as you are part of the world, learn to walk alone. If you keep at it long enough, the day will come when you are able to look within yourself to find out what you need to do to answer those who seek to diminish our nation.

What we might be called upon to do might not change the lives of millions of people as the great emperors did, and as we hope our emperor in waiting will do, but we should do it anyway – every little bit helps. I'm sure all of you know the story of the squirrels that helped Rama cross the sea to do battle with Ravana; all you need to propel you forward is the courage, conviction, passion and energy that only people of your age and innocence are abundantly gifted with. In the battle you will need to fight, your religion does not matter; your caste does not matter; your position in society does not matter; do not worry if you are a misfit, or haven't been applauded as a 'winner' – some of the greatest heroes of all time were written off as no-hopers, charlatans and discards by myopic arbiters of society.

You should know that big decisions are hard to take. You will be tempted to do nothing when the time comes, or to pass the responsibility to someone else or to take advantage of the situation for your own benefit, but stepping up to do the right thing no matter how difficult is always the most rewarding course of action. It is something that you will remember with pride for the rest of your life.

There are a thousand causes you can potentially commit to in this country, but as the subject of this book is the misuse of religion I will limit my appeal to this area. I cannot tell you what you should do, you will find that out for yourself, but I can tell you that the only qualification you need is an unwavering commitment to tolerance, and the only commandment worth keeping is the one that maintains that men and women of every faith are equal in the eyes of God and this nation. An ancient commandment, a fundamental right and perhaps a naive and overly idealistic sentiment, but no less powerful for all that. You have no time to lose – the forces arrayed against you and yours are arming at a furious pace – and as you wait for your own champion to arrive, you must continue to fight in whatever way you can to restore sanity and decency to our nation, you emperors of the everyday.

This was extraordinary, I remember thinking; it was almost as though Mr Sorabjee was personally urging me to get involved, to do my best to help stop the impending tragedy. Feeling vindicated, I went to the study where the telephone was to call my employer. I wanted more than anything else to hear his calm, measured voice. I wanted to describe everything that had taken place until now and see if he had any advice for me, but to my chagrin the telephone was dead. The butler had warned me that this was a fairly regular occurrence, the phone lines often went down and it could take days for them to be fixed. Cursing my luck, I slammed the useless phone down on its receiver, went back to my bedroom and reread the last chapter. Its power was undiminished; it served to strengthen my resolve.

13

Seven steps to a tragedy

1. The storm I had been hoping for never materialized. It did rain all the next day but it was nothing more than a gentle easing down of moisture that barely wet the leaves. By nightfall the rain had stopped and the mist rolled in. If it stayed misty it would be helpful, but I remembered Noah telling me it was rare for the mist to last more than a couple of days, especially at the Tower of God where strong winds blew all year around. I wandered aimlessly around the house, reading the last chapter of Mr Sorabjee's book every so often until it was imprinted on my mind. I tried the phone regularly, but it remained stubbornly dead.

The taxi that had been hired before the phone went down arrived on time the following day, and I was at the bottom of the hill on which the cemetery was located by seven thirty, the time we had arranged to meet, but there was no sign of Noah. I didn't think it was wise for the car to attempt the deeply rutted road, so I instructed the driver to wait and set off on foot. It was still very dark, there was no sign of the sun, and I wished I had brought a torch with me. I hoped there were no snakes around, and then I remembered that they didn't like the cold. As I made my way up the hill, I was filled with foreboding about the next day as I thought about Rajan, the young boy growing up in this bleak environment. Had he already been dreaming of the violence he would wreak upon the world, or had that come later, a straightforward reaction to the injustice that had been meted out to him? And was he really a killer? I had charged him with murder during my interview and he hadn't denied it, but did that automatically make him guilty? I knew that even if he was involved in some way with the riots it was probably true that he hadn't killed anyone himself, merely orchestrated it. How evil did that make him?

❧❀

2. When I got to the cemetery I could hardly see my way to the gate because the mist pooled thickly, streaming between the trees and the great bulk of the church. None of the dogs was around, but where was Noah? Now that I knew he didn't live in the parsonage I wondered what he did in inclement weather. On one of my visits I had seen a disused gatehouse with part of the roof and a wall missing – perhaps I would find him there. I moved forward cautiously, calling out his name. There was no response but I spotted a weak glow in the direction of the peepul tree and decided to investigate that first.

I came out of the mist into the flickering light cast by a small fire and stopped short, arrested by what I saw. Noah squatted beside a patch of freshly turned earth, dressed only in a T-shirt and jeans despite the cold and the wet. His T-shirt was bloody. Next to him was the great bulk of Godless. At my approach the dog cocked its eyebrows at me but made no other movement or sound. His eyes shut, the headphones of a Walkman clamped to his ears and a lit joint in his hand, Noah seemed totally at ease. He took a long pull at the joint, slowly released the smoke, then suddenly began to sing loudly. The composition of the macabre scene altered in that instant.

I began backing slowly out of the light under the watchful gaze of Godless, my mind empty of everything but the thought that I should get out of the cemetery immediately. I was finally seeing Noah for what he was, a man who could commit murder. I had no idea who his victim was, but I wasn't waiting around to find out.

Godless's barking crashed into the space vacated by the tuneless melody of his master, Noah opened his eyes, lazily surveyed the scene, and said, 'Sorry, Vijay, had some business to take care of. We're in no hurry, right?'

214

His voice was relaxed. Wordlessly, I gestured at his bloody clothes, the rusty shovel that lay at his feet. He looked at me uncomprehendingly for a moment, then took the headphones off and said, 'I found one of Godless's bitches near the bridge a couple of hours ago – some lorry driver had run her over. Thought I'd give her a decent burial. Not one of his regulars, I've seen her around occasionally, but what the hell?'

I wondered what he had been doing wandering around in the early hours of the morning, but my relief at his explanation was so great I brushed the thought aside. It was a minor detail, perhaps Godless had led him to the corpse. I edged back into the light.

'Do you know the Tibetans believe dying people enter something they call a bardo state just before they pass on? That's when their *Book of the Dead* is read out to them, to prepare them for their journey,' Noah said. 'Poor bitch, all she's going to get is Roger Daltrey singing 'Behind Blue Eyes' and her unfaithful paramour standing watch. And the bugger had to be bribed to stay with bones ...' The big dog seemed to know Noah was talking about him, and his tail thumped on the ground.

'I thought you'd killed somebody,' I said.

'Not the first time I've felt like it, but hey I've become a pacifist in my old age, da.'

'We should get going, Noah,' I said, trying to get the day back on track.

'OK, give me a moment. Get lost, Godless, your vigil is over,' he said, batting the dog on the rump. The dog trotted off and Noah said to me, 'Do you like The Who?'

When I admitted I didn't know their music he said enthusiastically, 'Bloody great music to listen to when the mist rolls in. Or the Doors. It makes your melancholy so fucking deep, especially if you're smoking first-rate dope, that you come close to touching the void. One of these days I'll want to experience it so much that I'll get carried away and jump – falling, falling, falling into eternity ... Wouldn't that be a great way to go?'

'You don't really mean that, do you?'

'Course not. It takes great courage or great despair or the great stupidity of youth to be able to kill oneself, and I don't have any of those ... but look, I know you want to get going, so I'll stop blathering and go get changed.'

He walked off into the mist, and I sat down beside the fire, surrounded by the shadowed faces on the tombstones looking down on me like an attentive audience, all sorts of thoughts teeming in my head. I had brought the last chapter of Mr Sorabjee's book with me to pass on to Noah, hoping that he would be struck by what my mentor had to say. But would that do the trick with someone like him?

Noah returned, having swapped his bloody T-shirt for his favourite Jimi Hendrix one. He asked me whether we had an appointment to see the collector, and I admitted that we hadn't; I had been told just to turn up and take my chances. It was the sort of small-town behaviour I should have been anticipating. He shrugged and said, 'No hurry then,' and sat down beside me, lit the stove and put the kettle on. When the tea was made, we both sat in silence for a while watching the play of the fire on the mist. What a strange man he was, I thought, a man who would carry a stray dog for miles to give it a farewell, yet a man without faith.

As if reading my thoughts, he said to me, 'You must think I'm pretty weird, huh, hanging out in the cemetery and all?'

'Well, I have wondered ...'

'Listen, da, you'll be gone in a couple of days, and I doubt we'll ever see each other again, but you're an OK guy, Vijay, so I'm going to tell you something nobody knows about me. Just keep it to yourself is all I ask. As you know, my mother died when I was ten, and I've told you that screwed me up pretty badly, made me junk religion and all, but what I didn't tell you was that for many months I'd come and hang around in this cemetery, every opportunity I got. She's buried here and I would tend her grave, put fresh flowers on it, that kind of stuff. I would also talk to her as though she were still around, tell her my problems. She was always in my head, so it was easy to do. I read later that this is quite a common reaction when you lose a parent, especially when you're very young, but I didn't grow out of it. I kept coming back to the cemetery for as long as I lived here and gradually got used to hanging out with the dead – not just my mother, others too, they seemed to fit quite naturally into my scene. Later, I got friendly with some Todas, they're the original inhabitants of the Nilgiris, and they believe their dead make their home in a place just like ours until they are reborn. It's right here in the mountains and there's a constant criss-crossing of spirits and living people between their respective worlds so it all made a strange kind of sense. Anyhow, as I became more and more reclusive, it was convenient to chat to the people who were buried here – it was less taxing than having to deal with the living. It's not that crazy when you think about it, most religious traditions believe the dead hang around for a bit before they move on to the next life. Even scientists agree that we are basically recycled from people and things that existed centuries ago, and until that happens everything that has passed on decomposes into a sort of free-floating state, so who is to say that the dead don't exist here as naturally as you or I ...'

There didn't seem a whole lot to say to this latest revelation. I must be getting used to him, I thought, because I didn't even find it particularly crazy. Perhaps if I managed to persuade him to become more involved in the business of the shrine, he could enlist the services of the 'unrecycled' dead to scare Rajan off.

❧

3. We finally got to Ooty at half past one. The mist had thinned by the time we set out, but our progress was slow because visibility was still poor, especially on the hairpin bends where we couldn't see more than a foot ahead of us. To make matters worse, our taxi broke down just short of town, and we wasted over an hour while the driver sorted out the problem.

I was disappointed by Ooty. Charing Cross, the main intersection, was chaotic and dirty, and it set the tone for the rest of the place. The mist erased much of the grime and the squalor, but the town bore scant resemblance to the enchantment promised in the tourist brochures.

The collector's office was an old colonial building set on an elevation above the town. Groups of men loitered in the compound, the usual crowd of supplicants, hangers-on and minor functionaries that could be found around virtually every seat of government or bureaucracy in the country. We had formulated a rough and ready plan of action in the car – I would reprise my role as a *Times of India* reporter who was holidaying in the Nilgiris and had decided on the spur of the moment to write a story about the controversy surrounding the Tower of God.

At reception we were told that the collector was out touring the district but was expected back at around 3.30 in the afternoon. Noah was all for leaving but I insisted we stay. More than ever it seemed important to me to meet this powerful official, if only to impress on him the urgency of the situation; and if he heard it from a *Times of India* reporter perhaps he would have no option but to take it seriously. After we had waited for an hour in a crowded room that stank of unwashed bodies and wet wool, I suggested we have a coffee and return closer to the hour the collector was expected. We stopped at a roadside restaurant, and then wandered through the misty streets before returning to the collectorate. This time we were told the collector wasn't expected back at all that day, but when I began waving my journalistic credentials around I was told I could meet the ranking bureaucrat in the building.

After another half an hour of waiting in a small antechamber on hard folding chairs, I was summoned to an office which the electric tube-lights did little to brighten. A portable heater in which a single heating filament glowed was the only source of warmth. My interview with the official, whose precise rank I never found out, was brief. I asked him whether I could get a message to his superior about the trouble that was expected in Meham, but it was obvious within minutes that he didn't share my concern. He said that the Meham police station had already informed them about the demonstration and had made arrangements to ensure that everything went off peacefully. He said he would tell the collector about my visit but beyond that wasn't prepared to do anything. I left the office feeling dispirited and, collecting Noah from the waiting room, made my way out of the building. To my annoyance, he was whistling.

As we walked towards the taxi, I noticed a small knot of men bearing hand-lettered placards and shouting slogans protesting against a lockout of tea estate workers at an estate in Kotagiri. That might work, I thought, but when I suggested to Noah that we should think of organizing our own demonstration to counter Rajan's, he wasn't enthusiastic. When I pointed out that there had been a peace march the last time the shrine was besieged, he said, 'We'll never get permission from the authorities. And there's not a whole lot you can do to stop Rajan from inside a prison cell in Meham.'

'There doesn't seem to be a whole lot I'm doing outside,' I said. 'Who would we have to go and see?'

'The collector maybe, but as this is a local matter the inspector in charge of Meham police station could probably give permission.'

'Let's bring it up when we see him then,' I said.

'I think you're just wasting your time,' he replied.

'I'd like to try anyway.'

━❦❦━

4. On the way back to Meham, I asked the driver to make a detour to the Tower of God. Noah argued that we couldn't climb up to the shrine as well as get to the police station on time, but I brushed his objections aside. I had no clear plan in mind, all I wanted to do was check to see that everything was all right. When we got to the Tower, we could barely see it for the clouds but, to my dismay, the white shroud was beginning to disperse. It was very windy, and at this rate the approach to the shrine would be clear by nightfall. I asked Noah what he thought the chances were for bad weather the next day, and he shrugged and said it was always possible there would be rain.

As we weren't going to make the climb, there was still enough time for tea before we went to the police station. It was dark and gloomy in the tea stall, so we went back to the road and drank our tea sitting on the parapet. It seemed a good opportunity to give Noah the chapter from Mr Sorabjee's manuscript. We had only one more stop to make, and if I was going to convince him to accompany me to the shrine the next day – which was as far as I had got with my plan to stop Rajan – then I would need to do it this evening. I collected the chapter from the taxi and gave it to him.

As he read, I took in the scene in front of me: the evening light coiled inside the mist, the complete absence of noise, the great mountains looking oddly humble, their peaks lopped off by low-

219

hanging clouds. Yet, by this time tomorrow, people could be dead or badly injured, the shrine could have been taken over and the calm of this spot destroyed for ever. I thought of Menon and the other defenders huddled nervous and frightened within the misty precincts of the shrine, and I wondered, anger flaring through me, what Rajan was up to. Could anyone stop him? Were we doing enough?

Noah broke into my reverie. 'The old man writes pretty well, should have billions pounding the streets in no time.'

'He speaks from the heart,' I said stiffly. 'I find it inspiring.'

'Hey, no offence,' Noah said. 'Just joking, that's all.'

We sat in silence for a few minutes, and then I said, 'So what do you think?'

'About his argument, you mean?'

'Yes.'

'Well, can't quarrel with it, but I'm wondering how many people will take it to heart. People can be pretty apathetic, I don't need to tell you that.'

I told him then of Mr Sorabjee's comment after the bombs had gone off in Bombay – about his message being worth it, even if it got through to only one person – and Noah nodded.

'Does it speak to you?' I asked, trying to sound casual.

'Not me, my friend,' he said, sounding just as casual as I did. 'I belong to the ranks of the apathetic masses, I'm not like you.'

I looked down to conceal my disappointment and my glance fell on my watch. 'Damn, we should have started ten minutes ago, we're going to be late. Let's continue this conversation in the car.'

'You go ahead, there's a bus due about now. I'll take it, and we can talk later.'

5. The Meham police station was a small dun-coloured building tucked into a fold of the hillside directly above the bus stop. A blackboard hung on the veranda with numerous columns recording the number of crimes in the town – burglaries, petty theft, pick-pocketing, rape – over the past three years. I couldn't help noticing that there hadn't been a single murder in that time.

The building comprised four rooms, the largest of which was an area that opened off the veranda and was crammed with desks, uniformed constables and various people wandering about. A woman, dressed in a faded sari, her hands joined together in supplication, was entreating a constable seated at a desk to do something for her, but he seemed to be ignoring her. Adding to the general air of confusion was the fact that the whole building was in semi-darkness, there having been yet another power cut; it seemed a daily feature of life in this town. I walked up to a constable and asked if I could see the inspector. He asked me what my business was, and when I told him he nodded and disappeared into a passageway that led deeper into the building. As I waited for him to return, I continued to take in the sluggish activity in the police station, and the sense of hopelessness I'd felt as I left the collector's office returned. Even if by some miracle the inspector proved to be useful, I doubted whether these slow, paunchy, elderly policemen would be able to do anything to stop Rajan. The constable reappeared and said the inspector would see me now.

As we approached the inspector's office, I began to have second thoughts about meeting him and suddenly wished I'd listened to Noah. If Shanmugam was planning to arrest Rajan anyway, what was I going to ask him to do? Arrest him twice? The constable ushered me into the inspector's presence and left, shutting the door behind him. The inspector sat beneath a poster of the Goddess Saraswati. He was dressed in starched khaki trousers and a khaki sweater with epaulettes. A police radio crackled on a table behind him. He was a large man with a bristly moustache, and he looked impatient. He was curt with me. 'I have been warned about you, Mr Vijay. This is a peaceful town, and I hear that you have been troubling some of our most distinguished residents like Rajan sir. I'm tempted to put you in the lock-up; in fact I would have done so already if the Brigadier hadn't vouched for you.'

Taken aback, I was trying to recover my composure when the inspector's manner changed and he said in a friendlier tone, 'Let me give you some advice. There is nothing for you to write about here. It is true that Rajan sir is going to stage a peaceful demonstration outside the shrine, and soon after that I will have no option but to arrest him. We believe in non-violence here, Mr Vijay, and we will not allow anyone, no matter how important, to create any mischief. You may come to the Tower of God at noon tomorrow if you would like to write about the incident. I have had a biodata of myself prepared for you, also a photograph. Does your magazine print photographs in black and white or in colour?'

'Black and white,' I replied automatically, quite stunned by the speed and direction of the meeting.

'That's good. Passport size will do?'

I nodded, then tried to steer the conversation back to the subject of Rajan.

'Inspector,' I began, 'It's good that you will be arresting Rajan, but ...' I stopped there, for I had nothing else to say, or rather nothing I could say to the inspector without being clapped into a prison cell. Why did he bribe you? I thought as I looked into the inspector's face. What is he planning? Do you know? Or has he outsmarted us all?

It was only as I was walking down the path carved out of the red earth of the hillside that I realized I had completely forgotten to ask the Inspector's permission to hold a peaceful procession of my own. I consoled myself with the thought that it wouldn't have done me any good; even if it had been allowed, there was no way we could have organized it in the space of a few hours. Before I got in the taxi, I stopped at a little open-fronted restaurant and bought a dozen fresh vadais and chutney for dinner.

Just short of the point where the road branched off to the cemetery, I spotted Noah by the roadside. I asked the driver to drop me off and said I would walk back home later. When we got to the open ground in front of the cemetery, Godless bounded up barking and slobbering. His master grinned and asked me to toss the dog a vadai. 'Bloody unsentimental bastard,' he said, as the pack followed their leader out of the shadows. 'But in his case I guess it pays to be one. One of his bitches dies this morning and is replaced in the evening by five others.'

'Perhaps, like you, he sees no difference between the living and the dead. For all you know, he's got a bunch of spirit dogs mingled in with the living ones.'

He looked at me sharply, and muttered, 'Maybe ...'

Then, as the dogs converged on us, he asked me for a couple more vadais, threw them at the pack, and then said, 'Let's get out of here.' I followed him into the cemetery, and we made our way to the peepul tree.

⁓⁕⁓

6. A couple of years ago I was working on the penultimate draft of this book in K—, where I was on holiday, when I had to take my mother to see the ophthalmologist, as cataracts had clouded over the vision in her left eye. To explain what was happening to her, the doctor pointed to a bronze sculpture of a reclining man on his desk, and said that whereas a normally sighted person would see the depth and subtlety of the figure, to my mother it would seem flat and one-dimensional. He said that with surgery he could restore her sight almost fully. As we left his clinic I remember wondering whether our ability to see the nuances in a situation is similarly affected when we are in the grip of an obsession or fear or panic. In Meham I was beginning to be assailed by all three, and if that hadn't been the case, I doubt that I would have talked to Noah as I did that night. It is something that I will regret all my life – all I can say is that it was not given to me to see in advance how he would react.

As soon as we had finished our vadais, I launched into my attack. The day had gone badly, I had accomplished nothing, and the despair and frustration that had been gathering within me made me speak more stridently than I had intended. 'So are you going to help me or not?'

'Hey, nothing's going to happen, I know my Meham.'

'But you don't know Rajan, have you met him recently?'

Noah said mildly, 'Relax, da, if Rajan's going to have his way, he's going to have his way; there's nothing you or I or God Almighty can do about it. Fuck, I haven't had a smoke all day – want a drag?' He pulled out a joint and lit it. Seeing him like that, so utterly relaxed, leaning insouciantly against the bole of the peepul, finally set me off.

'What the fuck is wrong with you?' I screamed into the quiet of the cemetery. From across the wall I heard the sound of Godless's deep bark. Once, twice and then he was quiet. 'You can take the

223

trouble to bury some stray mongrel, but you don't seem to care that within twenty-four hours friends of yours, Brother Ahimas, Menon, others you must know, will all be dead or wounded ... Come on, man, aren't you in the least bit concerned?'

'So what if I was concerned? What do you expect me to do?' I think it was the fact that he continued to remain calm in the face of my anger that provoked me even more.

'Well, a lot more than just run away from the problem.'

'Easy, Vijay,' he said, still unflustered, but with an edge to his voice now. I told myself to calm down.

'OK, I'm sorry I shouted at you, but, you know, it's so frustrating. I still feel something terrible might happen tomorrow.'

Noah didn't reply, just continued working on his joint.

'I was thinking of turning up at the Tower of God at nine or so, to help in any way I can. I want to be there in plenty of time for Rajan's arrival. Will you come with me?'

'Look, Vijay,' he said. 'We agreed that I'd come with you today and that would be it.'

'I know we did, but I'm not asking you to *do* anything, just come to the shrine with me tomorrow.'

'That's how it all starts, doesn't it. I learned a long time ago that the best course of action is to stay put, mind my own business.'

'Do you really think you'll be safe when things start to go wrong? First, it'll be the shrine, then something else. Rajan will never stop until he has put every one of us under. Have you any idea what he thinks of us?'

'Don't look at me,' he said. 'Speak for yourself. I hang out quietly in this cemetery, with the dead for company for fuck's sake – you can't get more inoffensive than that.'

'Oh, come on ...' I said irritably. 'I've heard that once upon a time you were quite a guy, fearless, would take on anybody, anything. What happened, Noah?' The anger was starting to build again.

'Listen, Vijay,' he said, putting out the joint and getting to his feet. 'Come here, there's something I want to show you.' He led me by a path to another corner of the cemetery from where we could see a slim dagger of light between two hills. He pointed to it and said, 'That's Coimbatore, the first city on the plains. Beyond that lie

Bombay, America and all the other exciting places that I've lived in and voluntarily left behind. Do you know why?'

'You said something about not fitting in.'

'Right, but do you know how I realized that and why I live my life the way I do now? Remember Dom Moraes, the poet?'

'Yes, I do, he's famous. Why?'

'Know why his poetry is so great? Not just because of the craft or the lyricism, the guy had a way of looking beneath the surface of things that could really make you think. One day I was actually present at the making of one of his best poems. I'll just recite the relevant part, won't take long.

> Choose your rock, seamate, stay with it.
> Lose your shadow, it's of no use.
> The last bronze bird puts you down,
> Tidier than a horse, final.
>
> Ashes and marred walls deface you.
> Where is this wind from,
> Sinbad, defining its own course?
> Some of us never know home.

'On the night that inspired the poem, we had been drinking in Dom's flat in Sargent House. I had just quit my job and didn't know what I was going to do with myself, there was nothing I really wanted to do. At around ten o'clock the booze ran out, so we walked across to the Harbour Bar at the Taj and continued drinking there. Dom had just been paid for some major article he'd written, he always asked to be paid in cash, so he kept hauling these wads of hundred-rupee notes out of his trouser pockets and handing them to me to pay for each round. He was too drunk to count the money, but so was I, so I kept shoving these fistfuls of rupees at our waiter, who grew kinder and kinder as the evening wore on.

'And we drank and we talked or rather we drank and I talked because in addition to quitting my job I had just broken up with my latest girlfriend, and between bouts of cursing her for being a stupid bitch, I would tell Dom about all the women I had ever romanced or slept with. And we would drink some more, and I would rant some more, and he would listen patiently, murmuring "my dear boy" at intervals, and at some point we must have left the bar and somehow got to his flat in Colaba, where I passed out. Two days later, when I visited him again, he handed me a poem that he had just typed out on his old manual typewriter, saying in his understated way, "I thought this might interest you." It was "Sinbad" and I read it and was so taken with it that it would keep coming back to me as I thought about my life, and within the next couple of months I had left Bombay, and had come back here to this place.'

'So what are you trying to say?'

'I'm saying that I've tried pretty much everything I wanted to try; nothing quite worked, but now I think I've found my rock, and I'm going to cling to it.'

'Haven't you listened to one word I've been saying, Noah? Men like Rajan don't think people like you and I belong here. You can cling to your rock all you want, but you won't be able to escape.'

'I'll worry about that when I have to.'

I felt the anger rise within me, a clean, powerful emotion born of frustration and a sense that I had nothing left to gamble with.

'It'll be too late by then, you useless piece of shit. You'll be swept away and nobody will care. Why can't you stand and fight, instead of cowering behind your rock? Are you still blaming yourself for Karan, Maya, Iva, all the things you've lost? When are you going to redeem your miserable life, Noah, just tell me that?'

Noah's reply was brief. 'I want you to get the fuck out of my place, Vijay. Get out and don't bother coming around here again.'

⤙ ❧ ⤚

7. Later that night, just before I turned in, I went out into the garden and looked up into the clear night sky, trimmed at the edge with stars. The moon was more than half full, so I could see every detail of the landscape around me. At any other time I might have paused to reflect on its beauty, but that night all it evoked in me was despair. I had shut down every option open to me, most of all Noah, and the diamond-bright night I was gazing at demolished the last obstacle

that might have deterred Rajan. It promised to be a clear sunny day tomorrow.

⁓❧⁓

My sleep was restless and furred with dreams. In the early hours of the morning I was pulled into a nightmare, not the recurring one from Bombay, but a new one born of this place. I recognized the iron-black stone of the Tower of God, rising against a sky the colour of blood. It was the Tower of God yet it was not, for it was hollow and within it was another cylinder of stone joined to the outer shell by three great walkways. At the end of each walkway was a throne, and the central pillar was surmounted by a throne as well, and I understood the structure was a version of the Ibadat Khana, the great hall of philosophy built by Emperor Akbar. All the thrones had occupants and now their faces became clear to me. Ashoka, Akbar and Gandhi were seated on the three thrones on the periphery, and even as I recognized them, their faces faded to be replaced by my own face as well as those of Noah and Mr Sorabjee. The face of the occupant of the central throne was hidden from view. All of us were shouting and gesticulating, obviously greatly exercised by something, and our rage was directed towards the occupant of the throne in the middle.

The pillar that supported the central throne began to revolve slowly, and I suddenly knew who its occupant was. Unmoved by the commotion around him, Rajan's mouth opened in a terrifying gape, and he began saying something to me, only I couldn't hear it because I had woken up screaming.

14

Death of a rioter

I had come to these Blue Mountains, shrouded in mist and the spirits of the dead, to rest and had found only more conflict, the very thing I was running away from. This shouldn't have come as a surprise, I realize that now, because we are drawn to the things we obsess about, no matter how hard we try to escape them. Meham had much to offer, the magic of its gardens, the desolate beauty of its landscapes, the peace of its isolation, but none of these held my interest. I suppose, in other circumstances and if I had been a different sort of person, I might have been able to ignore Noah, Rajan, and the disturbance over the shrine, but that was not be.

Today, as I write this account of my brief sojourn in the Nilgiris, I can't help wondering if things might not have turned out differently if I hadn't meddled in them. Or had I made no difference at all, would events have followed their destined trajectory no matter what?

The passage of time has given me a certain perspective on the events that took place on 5 January 1994, but it has erased none of the detail.

❦

I found it difficult to go back to sleep after my nightmare. In the early hours of the morning I finally managed to drop off to, incredibly enough, the pulse of rain on the roof. I wasn't imagining it – Meham's unpredictable weather had closed in and I began to relax. Not even Rajan would attempt to get to the shrine in such conditions. When I awoke the house and garden were shuttered by mist. The rain had stopped, but this was even better. There could be no demonstration now, I was convinced of that. I had a leisurely breakfast and, Mr Khanna's driver having finally shown up, ordered the car for eleven in the morning. The inspector had told me to arrive at the shrine by twelve, so I had plenty of time. When we set off, the mist had already begun to disperse, stirring in the folds and wrinkles of the surrounding mountains. I wondered as we passed the road leading to the cemetery if I should try to persuade Noah to accompany me, but I put the thought firmly out of my mind – after our altercation, I wondered if he would ever want to see me again. As we neared the Tower of God, the mountains that guarded it looked more tremendous than ever, cowled and shadowed by mist, part of a landscape that belonged to the first light of Creation. As I looked upon the view, my sense of peace heightened. How insignificant our human struggles seemed when set against the vast, unchanging presence of the mountains.

But the peace I felt was based on an illusion, for events had moved on in my absence, and the situation was far worse than I could have imagined. I have often wondered why we are frequently lulled into an immense calm before we experience disaster. Is it because God, that ruthless autocrat, wishes us to feel the edge of His lash more keenly?

⌘

Even before we got to the starting point for the climb to the shrine, I could see that something was terribly wrong. A mob was milling about in the staging area, and there was a thin line of khaki at the very edge as the few policemen at the scene tried to hold people back. The Tower of God was still obscured by mist and cloud, but everyone's focus seemed to be on what lay in the deep chasm beyond. I told the driver to stop the car, got out and pushed my way through the crowd. Mingled among the ordinary people from town were a large number of Kadavul Katchi members, easily distinguished by their saffron bandannas and the banners and trishuls they carried. But none of them seemed in any way threatening; if anything, they looked bewildered and shaken. There were a smaller number of young men holding up placards in support of the shrine (so Menon had managed to organize a few people, I thought fleetingly), but neither group seemed to be interested in each other. A few of the KK men were arguing with Shanmugam, the police inspector, who had stationed himself in front of the steps leading down from the staging area. 'Too dangerous to go down there. We will start our investigation once the weather clears up,' he repeated over and over again. The men arguing with him did not seem to disagree, for their protests seemed desultory and they were making no attempt to push the policemen aside, something they could have done with ease, given their superior numbers.

The precise details of what happened on the morning of 5 January will never be known, for the two people who were involved, Noah and Rajan, are both dead. The only other people present, two of Rajan's associates who accompanied him on his last journey, were too far behind, and wholly preoccupied with picking their way up the slippery steps cut into the Tower of God to have actually witnessed what went on. They did speak at length to the four journalists present at the scene – of which I was one – the police, KK party members and anyone else who would listen, but as their tales grew wilder and more outrageous, it became evident that they were unreliable. As a result, most of the news stories that appeared in the immediate aftermath skimmed over the actual details of the 'accident' that resulted in the deaths. In any event, the incident was deemed of so little importance that the majority of newspapers in the country devoted only a paragraph to it. The three longer accounts, two in Tamil and one in English (besides the report I filed for the February issue of *The Indian Secularist*), appeared in local newspapers and all three dwelled on the career of Rajan, mourning the loss of one of the state's most dynamic young leaders. All three papers were known sympathizers of the KK cause. Mine was the only report that had anything at all to say about Noah, although Sakshi had to excise two paragraphs at the last minute to accommodate an advertisement. For the purposes of record I am reproducing the piece in full.

DEATHS IN MEHAM

```
By R. K. Vijay
Meham, 5 January 1994
The Feast Day of the Shrine of the Blessed Martyr in
```

the Nilgiris District witnessed the deaths of two people when a demonstration outside the shrine reportedly turned violent. According to eyewitness accounts, the trouble started when D.P. Rajan, 44, Bombay businessman who was affiliated to the Kadavul Katchi party, with its headquarters in Coimbatore, led a group of party workers to the shrine in order to demand its return to the Hindus, to whom they alleged it belonged. Right-wing Hindu parties say that a temple dedicated to Lord Shiva once stood on the spot, before it was demolished by a satrap of Hyder Ali in the eighteenth century, following which it was taken over by a Christian saint, but historical evidence in support of the Hindu claim is scanty.

According to Nallapan, 29, a long-time associate of Mr Rajan and one of those who claims to have witnessed the accident, bad weather had forced the demonstrators to delay their march upon the shrine. Some of the processionists who belonged to the district had advised Mr Rajan to postpone the demonstration, but as he was scheduled to return to Bombay the next day, he decided to stage a symbolic protest. Instructing the rest of the demonstrators to stay where they were, Mr Rajan proceeded up the rock formation (known locally as the Tower of God) with Nallapan and another associate who had accompanied him from Bombay. As the three men neared the summit, they were stopped by a local resident, Noah Yesudas, 36. An altercation broke out between Mr Yesudas and Mr Rajan and the eyewitnesses allege that Mr Rajan was attacked by Mr Yesudas without provocation. Others, especially a small group of volunteers who had gathered in the shrine to 'protect' it, insist the reverse is true. The police refuse to confirm either version of the incident, merely stating that an investigation will begin immediately. What is clear is that an argument took place, followed by a scuffle, during which the disputants lost their footing on the slippery path and plunged to their deaths.

The dispute over the shrine dates back to the 1920s, when the first claim in modern times was made by a Hindu right-wing party. Over the years there have been sporadic demands that the shrine be handed over, but the agitation only gained momentum in the 1990s with the heightening of Hindu militancy across the country. On the first anniversary of the demolition of the Babri Masjid, a group of demonstrators led by Mr Rajan attempted to repossess the shrine but they were dispersed by the police. At the time Mr Rajan announced that he would lead a peaceful dharma to press for 'restoration to the Hindus of one of their most important sacred sites in South India'.

Ironically, the shrine is one of the few places in the entire district where people of all faiths gather to worship. Its custodian, Brother Ahimas, is credited with miraculous powers of healing and the saint who founded the shrine is revered by Muslims, Hindus and Christians. Since the tragedy the shrine has been cordoned off indefinitely. The Nilgiri District Collector's office said in a statement that this measure was necessitated by the fact that the matter would need to be fully and thoroughly investigated without any evidence being disturbed. At the time of writing, this correspondent has learned that the local MLA has petitioned the Tamil Nadu Government to set up a commission of inquiry to thoroughly evaluate the dispute over the shrine.

That was my objective report, neatly bracketed by caveats and disclaimers, which would be quickly extinguished in the minds of my readers by the avalanche of newer stories that would fill the magazine.

But there was another story that germinated within me, that visited me during the early hours of the morning when I could not sleep, and that is the story I am attempting to narrate. It is a story that stretches back centuries, a story of sultans, soldiers, saints and ordinary men who felt the dead weight of God in their bones, urging them on to acts of folly that could only end disastrously. What madness had led to the establishment of this place of worship in such a remote and inaccessible spot? Had it originally been a temple dedicated to a Hindu deity? Had it been demolished by a Muslim sultan? Had it been founded by a Christian holy man? No matter what the truth about the origins of the shrine might be, there was no question that it existed under the gaze of an indifferent God, heedless to the passion and tragedy of the men who sacrificed themselves in his name. Noah and Rajan were only the latest victims but there would be more, many more, who would perish, not just at the Shrine of the Blessed Martyr but at many other places of worship in this land corroded by religion.

According to Mansukhani, who was exceptionally indiscreet and forthcoming because I interviewed him soon after the tragedy, Rajan had woken very early that morning, and as was his habit had had a bath in cold water although the temperature outside was close to zero. Dressed only in his veshti, his upper body bare, his hair still wet from his ablutions, he spent a long time in the puja room of the house, preparing himself for the day ahead. He alone knew what he had to do that morning, he hadn't confided in even his most trusted followers. All that his men were aware of was that there was to be a demonstration outside the shrine and that it was designed to attract as much media attention as possible. There was to be no violence. So soon after Ayodhya and Bombay, any injury or death would bring too much heat to bear upon the Bombay branch of the national political party Rajan was affiliated to, and the senior leadership did not think the rewards would justify it. And although they liked the idea of expanding their sphere of influence, they considered Meham too isolated and unimportant to be much of a draw. However, as Rajan seemed very keen to lead the agitation on behalf of the Kadavul Katchi, he was permitted to go ahead as long as he was cautious. Accordingly, Rajan had been entirely truthful when he had assured the Meham inspector that neither he nor his followers intended to be violent during the demonstration.

Having finished his puja, Rajan dressed quickly and told his host that he wanted to get to the Tower of God early to ensure all was in readiness. He declined the breakfast of iddlis and sambhar that had been prepared. Accompanied by his Bombay associates, he set off for his destination.

As he drove through that whisper-soft morning of mist and cloud towards his fateful encounter with Noah, I wonder what he was thinking about. He was used to dealing with death and intimidation, he was a good planner, and he knew how to use the specifics of any situation to his advantage, but I remember something the Brigadier had said to me in his home – apparently when he set out on a combat mission, all the rehearsals, operations-room briefings and strategies would disappear, to be replaced by a keen awareness of his physical self and the environment around him, everything accentuated by the fear and adrenalin coursing through him. Did Rajan look around, feel the mist sliding off the windscreen? Did he think of calling off the project on account of the inclement weather? Did he worry that his kohlapuri chappals were inadequate for the climb? Did he think that the Shiv lingam wrapped in saffron silk might fall from his grasp as he ascended the Tower of God? If the Brigadier was correct, these are the things that would have preoccupied him, his mind would have been emptied of everything else, including any prospective encounter with the defenders of the shrine.

At the steps leading to the shrine Rajan met a small group of men who had been instructed to meet him in advance of the main body of demonstrators, who were expected to arrive a few hours later when the demonstration was officially scheduled to begin. Rajan told the men that he wanted them to follow him after an interval of an hour and then wait at the base of the Tower of God for further instructions.

It was nearly seven and the first traces of morning were beginning to infiltrate the mist. Rajan and his two closest associates set off down the steps that led to the path that would take them through the forest, past the Shiva temple and to the base of the Tower of God. Even on this short flight of steps, Rajan almost slipped and fell, the thin soles of his kohlapuri chappals offering him little purchase on the moisture-slick stone. One of his lieutenants offered to go back and get him a pair of thick-soled boots but Rajan refused. In defiance of the elements and the terrain, he had dressed in the garb of a Bombay politician – white kurta-pajama and chappals – his one concession to the Meham weather a shawl thrown around his shoulders. His single-mindedness and self-belief would have it no other way; he was Rajan, the powerful politician who would bring the shrine to its knees, he was not about to hide behind boots and sweaters. But after he slipped again his companions were able to prevail upon him to discard his unsuitable footwear. The kohlapuris were found later in the day next to the little stone bridge leading into the forest, perfectly aligned, for Rajan was a fastidious man.

Rajan still did not opt for sensible shoes. Instead, he decided to make the rest of the journey barefoot. 'Sahib said this was an act of pilgrimage, and it was only proper that it be carried out in bare feet.' This was the moment Rajan chose to reveal his audacious plan. He had decided to approach the shrine with only two companions in order not to alarm the custodian. Once he got close enough, he wanted his men to create a diversion while he sneaked around on the little-used path to the old entrance of the shrine. He expected to get into the chapel undetected. Once inside, he would install the lingam behind the cross, quietly ascertain how many defenders were present and then slip out to rejoin his men, who would summon the reinforcements waiting at the bottom of the Tower. When they arrived he intended to march boldly into the shrine and ask for it to be searched for any signs that it was a Hindu place of worship. When the Shiv lingam was discovered, his men would swiftly overcome the defenders of the shrine. He didn't expect much resistance from them, they would be country people, small-town people, who would be no match for his ferociously committed rioters. By the time the police arrived on the scene the shrine would have been converted into a makeshift temple to Lord Shiva with a minimum of fuss. It was a precisely thought-through plan but it hadn't bargained for one eventuality – Noah.

I'd like to think that Noah spent the evening before his death reading one of his beloved modern European poets, Rilke maybe, thinking about Maya and Iva, listening to Jimi Hendrix tearing music from his guitar, smoking dope – it would somehow have been appropriate for his inspiration to have come from something that was diametrically opposed to the forces that drove Rajan. But that is something we will never know. All that we can verify is that sometime between my argument with him and evening prayers, Noah arrived at the shrine. Its occupants marvelled at his ability to negotiate the Tower in such treacherous conditions and poor light, but Noah was a child of these mountains and he told them it had been no trouble at all. In addition to Menon and two full-time volunteers, the custodian had permitted six young men from town to spend the night at the shrine in order to defend it should it come under attack. They were unarmed, for Brother Ahimas wouldn't allow weapons in the place. Their choppers and lathis were left outside.

When Noah had announced his intention to stay, Brother Ahimas had tried to dissuade him. There were enough defenders, not that he expected the shrine to be attacked. There had been demonstrations before, but they were usually held outside its precincts and had never been a threat, only a nuisance, so he didn't expect this one to be any different. Noah had apparently told him that Rajan was an adversary who was more dangerous than any the shrine had been threatened by before, and he was adamant about staying on. The custodian had relented, and space was found for Noah to stay the night. He hadn't spent his time sleeping, Brother Ahimas told me; instead he had talked to the old man into the early hours of the morning, when the custodian had excused himself to go to his own quarters.

Noah stayed awake, wrapped in a borrowed blanket, looking out into the blank white emptiness of the rift from a ledge that overlooked both approaches to the shrine. At first light, as people began stirring, he drank a cup of tea, refused the simple communal breakfast of poorie and potatoes, performed his ablutions and returned to his post. 'It was almost as if he was waiting for something,' one of the young defenders said to me later. As Brother Ahimas and the others assembled in the chapel for morning prayers, Noah saw Rajan walk out of the mist and head for the little-used approach to the shrine. Seeing that he was alone, Noah didn't alert the rest of the group, but got up, picked up a lathi and quickly walked around the shrine and on to the path from the opposite direction, so he would come face to face with Rajan.

If Rajan was surprised to see Noah, I'm guessing he didn't show it. He would have been single-minded in his objective and now that he was so close to achieving it, he wouldn't have flinched even if he had found commandos in full battle gear confronting him. As there were no reliable witnesses to their encounter, we'll have to guess at what happened next.

As I had discovered, the old approach to the shrine that wound around the rock was so narrow that there was barely enough space on it for two people to walk abreast. A single strand of wire was all that stood between anyone on the path and a drop of thousands of feet; indeed the protection afforded by it was so inadequate that on festival days volunteers would prevent people from taking that route for fear of an accident.

Rajan had already advanced a fair way along the path when he realized he was not alone. His two followers have steadfastly maintained that it was Noah who initiated the attack, although it is clear that they would have no means of knowing this, but both of them agree that any altercation the men might have had was short. From my knowledge of the two, I'd say it was Rajan who made the first move, once he realized that Noah had no intention of getting out of his way. It was an attack that stood no chance of succeeding, but the darkness that had been building in the two men through their entire lives had settled in them, rock hard and unyielding, and it would exact its price. Rajan and Noah met in the middle of the approach, grappled briefly and silently, lost their footing, slipped and fell; their momentum was arrested for a moment by the guard rail before it gave way, then they pitched headlong down the yawning blue throat of God.

Noah's body was never recovered. Search parties were only able to make the perilous descent into the rift three days after the accident because the weather had turned particularly severe with heavy rain cutting off all access to the Tower and its approaches. When army jawans and the police finally lowered themselves into the chasm, they found Rajan's shattered body – which was quickly cremated – but of Noah there was no sign. The tattered remnants of his Jimi Hendrix T-shirt were discovered on the branch of a tree and it was surmised that it had been ripped off as he hurtled to his death. Once the police had finished with it, I had it interred in a cheap plywood coffin in the cemetery in which Noah had lived. Moses, the priest, graciously gave me permission to bury the coffin there, although the cemetery had long been abandoned; parishioners of the church were now buried in a new cemetery, further up the hillside.

At the funeral service there was one face I didn't recognize, a short weathered wisp of a man, who came up shyly after it was all over and introduced himself as Arumugam, Noah's long-time accomplice. None of the working-class people from town and the surrounding countryside made an appearance. I guessed it was because they were intimidated by the thought of attending a church service along with the sahibs and dorais, not that any of Meham's elite bothered to attend. As he shook hands with me, Brother Ahimas said he would hold a special service for Noah the coming Sunday – his friends would get to bid him farewell after all. After the funeral I asked Moses if he had seen Godless, and he said the dog was tethered to a tree behind the parsonage. Arumugam had asked for him and would be taking him away in a short while. We walked across, and the long black form of the great hound flowed up from the ground and regarded us silently. I had never petted him before, and I hesitated to do so now. Finally, I did nothing, but made a namaskaram to Arumugam, which included Godless, and went off with the pastor. I had a couple of questions which I hoped he'd be able to answer before Mr Khanna's driver took me to Coimbatore to catch my train.

The priest cleared up a little more of the mystery surrounding Noah. He told me he wasn't related to him in any way. However, as he had known his father, who had once been the pastor of the church, he had decided to help when he found Noah sleeping on a bench in the Meham bus terminal a decade or so ago. Noah was homeless and jobless at the time and was scavenging for food from the town's rubbish dumps. The priest had told him he would pay him a small salary to be the caretaker of the old cemetery and look after the parsonage's vegetable garden. Noah had never given him any trouble besides occasionally borrowing his scooter without permission, but that was a minor infraction outweighed by the benefits – his family had never had to go to the vegetable market in all the time Noah had tended their garden. He showed me the gatehouse that he had permitted Noah to use. Its interior was very clean, and besides an old blanket and the trunk I recognized from my visits to Noah, the only other thing in the room was a rough-hewn plank of wood attached to the wall on which there were a handful of paperbacks, many without covers, all well used – books of poetry by Rimbaud, Rilke, Pessoa, Moraes, Eliot, Auden and a dozen others who were new to me. The priest said I could have the books if I wanted, but I demurred saying I had no taste for poetry, then changed my mind and took a few volumes, those that Noah had quoted from.

I don't remember much about the journey back to Bombay, except that during the early hours of the morning, when we were still an hour from the city, I drowsily recalled the one trip that Noah and I hadn't taken while I was in Meham. Noah had said to me that if I'd had more time, he would have taken me to see the Toda land of the dead, the ammunor, which lay beneath the western edge of the mountains. One of the things he liked most about Toda culture was the fact that their afterworld closely resembled the everyday reality of the Nilgiris. In my waking dream I picture him walking west towards the Kundah Hills, along routes clearly marked for the convenience of those who would cross over. He crosses the Avalanche River and reaches a stone which the dead are expected to touch so that they can forget the world of the living. Further on he will reach another stone which he will touch to rid himself of all earthly infirmities. Whole and healthy, he will take a path through the jungle until he reaches a rope bridge over a deep ravine. The Toda believe that if a man or woman has led a good life they will negotiate the rope bridge safely; otherwise it will give way and they will fall into the leech-infested ravine below. Noah crosses the rope bridge safely, passes the other obstacles that trip up sinners and enters the land of the dead. It is a world I am sure he will be welcomed into; the dead look out for their own.

15

The Last Truth

Bipeds, especially those from southern climes, are not meant to walk upright in ice and snow. A South African friend who has lived slightly longer than I have in Canada taught me how to negotiate the slipperiness of winter by walking like a penguin – feet splayed outward, gait flattened and rocking from side to side. I always feel faintly ridiculous walking like this, but as the alternative seems to be either falling backwards every few steps or crawling on my hands and knees, I put up with it, and maybe one day it will come naturally to me.

I have lived here for seven years now, and it has helped me to heal. The locals think of their city as bland but I prefer to see it as a kind city, hospitable and welcoming to those of us who have fled traumas that we would be unable to deal with at home. It is exactly what I was hoping to find when I tried to put as much distance as I could, both physically and mentally, between myself and the tragedy in Meham.

I work as a cashier in a bank. The job is undemanding and unwavering, as is my daily routine. I live alone in a one-bedroom apartment in an inexpensive part of town, and besides my twice-monthly forays to Gerrard Street to stock up on supplies – Indian spices and poppadoms, and occasionally mangoes from the sub-continent – I go nowhere and see no one. My parents have given up on me, they doubt that they will ever see me 'settled' as they put it, but I don't think that's for me, at least for now. I prefer my solitude and have guarded it obsessively in all the years I have spent writing this book. The only time it was broken was when I was briefly involved with a waitress at the local Tim Horton's. The affair lasted less than six weeks, and I wasn't tempted to let anyone into my life after that.

❧ ❧

One of the lessons Mr Sorabjee taught me was that in a news story there should be no loose ends, and keeping that dictum in mind I will do my best to tidy things up, knowing full well that this is not a news report; when you are trying to reconstruct a life or lives there will inevitably be questions that remain unanswered.

I cannot, for example, tell you exactly why Noah's death came to mark me so permanently. Anyone would have been traumatized by the violent death of someone they were close to, and felt they were in some way responsible for, but most people would, I think, have come to some sort of acceptance of the tragedy and moved on.

I didn't because, through some mysterious process, it became the defining moment of my life. Most of us actively search for this key moment, which is why we look for love, for achievement, or whatever it is we think will lend a certain weight and permanence to our days. But for some of us such moments come unexpectedly, as happened to me in Meham, and we have no choice but to configure our lives around them. What we do with the experience is up to us. The heroes in Mr Sorabjee's book used it to change the world around them for the better, but for most people that is not an option; what we are led to do is infinitely more humble. I, as you know, decided to bear witness. I began the book at Mr Sorabjee's suggestion, he said I would find the writing of it therapeutic, but along the way it became much more than something I was doing to heal myself. And now that it is finished, I am slowly beginning to take an interest in the world once more. The other day in the bank, when wind chill and freezing rain kept customers away, an unexpected thought came to me – perhaps I should go back to my own country, there was work to be done. I reckoned I had done with all that, it was why I had left India, but I did not immediately suppress the thought as I might have done in years past. I would have liked to have talked things over with Mr Sorabjee, but sadly that was not an option for he had died a year into the new century. No, I would have to make up my mind on my own. There is no rush, though, the wars inspired by the gods will be with us for a long time to come.

All that remains for me to do now is to complete the story with a quick recap of the aftermath of the tragedy. I busied myself with routine for the first few days after my return to Bombay, filing my story for the magazine, giving Mr Sorabjee a slightly more detailed account of the incident, and generally immersing myself in the tasks that were allotted to me. I didn't feel able to talk to Mr Sorabjee about his book or the part it had played in the unfortunate events that had taken place, so I put the manuscript in an envelope, along with a short note saying that I liked it very much and hoped it would be successful, and gave it to Mrs Dastur to pass on. Mr Sorabjee did not bring it up with me, not that I had expected he would.

On my first weekend back I took to my bed at the hostel feeling slightly feverish, but it wasn't my physical health that was the problem, it was more that I was consumed with guilt over Noah's death – my final argument with him kept running in a continuous loop through my head. I told myself that if I hadn't pushed him so hard he would still be alive, and I was furious with myself for straying beyond the boundaries of the assignment that had taken me to Meham. I bottled all of this up, and as my obsession with Noah's death grew, my health suffered, the nightmares returned and the days crawled by, huge and oppressive, embroidered by thoughts of the calamity. I began to neglect my work at the magazine, even to question our mission. What was the point of fighting on? I asked myself; people would continue to die in the name of God no matter what we did. Even Mr Sorabjee's decision to keep going after the bombs had gone off no longer res-onated with me in my grief. What did it matter if one person was convinced of the message we were trying to propagate, when even the sacrifices of people like Noah would really change nothing? Yet I didn't want to let Mr Sorabjee and my colleagues down. I knew they believed in what they were doing and I tried to keep on as best I could, but finally I knew it wasn't working and I resigned. Mr Sorabjee didn't attempt to change my mind, but when I came to the end of my notice period, he courteously enquired if I was free to have coffee with him at the Taj.

⁓✢⁓

We settled into window seats in the Sea Lounge which offered a view of the verminous ooze of pigeons spreading over the cobblestones of the Gateway of India and boats stacked like driftwood in the harbour, but I didn't see any of this; my gaze was focused inward on a disused cemetery deep within the Nilgiri mountains where a cold river of mist floated angels free of their gravestones. The reserve that I had maintained ever since I had returned broke down, and my remorse, grief, guilt and doubts poured forth, unstoppably. I told Mr Sorabjee in great detail about the disaster, and I asked him insistently why things had transpired the way they had. I talked about his book at length. I told him how I had used the final chapter to bolster my resolve, although in the end it had been of no use. I told him I considered myself a failure because I hadn't been capable of doing anything to defuse the situation at the shrine or prevent the death of Noah, I hadn't been able to measure up when it counted, I hadn't been capable of the final 'kick' my father had told me about. I asked him why Noah, ignored and discarded by the world, had been able to do what no one else had done, and most of all I asked him if he thought I was guilty of my friend's death.

Mr Sorabjee's response was measured and caring. After expressing his grief over both the deaths in Meham, he told me that I wasn't responsible for Noah's final actions, he had acted of his own accord. I might have nudged him towards something he had been waiting for his entire life, but that did not make me guilty; he would have done something similar sooner or later. He explained that we spend our early untried lives floating around in a fog of doubt, making our mistakes, having our certainties eroded, and in this wise finally come to a sense of ourselves. But once we come to that knowledge, sooner or later, depending on the luck or tragedy of our lives, we act entirely on our own where truly important matters are concerned.

He said that I shouldn't consider myself a failure, I had done everything I could, and in so doing had enabled Noah to find within himself what he felt called upon to do. He called Noah a true hero, an Emperor of the Everyday, and quoted Western philosophy and Eastern scripture and myth in support of his definition, saying that while most of us, after a period of youthful rebellion or flight – such as my escape from K— – devote ourselves to burrowing into society, building safety nets, surrounding ourselves with barricades like family and possessions against the unsettling nature of life, mavericks such as Noah retain the lightness of unburdened youth; it is this that enables them to soar up above the rest of us and perform feats that we would find impossible. Our role, he said, was to provide the springboard, usually unbeknown to ourselves. He said it saddened him to accept my resignation, but he understood why I wanted to leave. We talked then about what I might do next. I said I wanted to return to K— for a while to think about things, spend some time with my parents, before I got on with the rest of my life.

Towards the end of the evening we returned to the subject of Noah. He said, and this seems a fitting note on which to end the book, that it is only when people close to us die that we begin to learn how to live as we should. No matter how much we think we know about how to cope with the death of those we love – through the experience of others, our reading and our faith or lack of it – nothing quite prepares us for it. It is impossibly shocking and we feel it's the first time death has ever occurred. But sooner or later we begin painfully to engage with it, and eventually move past it, and onward. And without our realizing it, imperceptibly, the one who has passed on fuses with us, and we become a different person altogether. It is a condition of life that our beloved dead will never be forgotten.

Acknowledgements

I am deeply indebted to my wife Rachna who helped at every stage of the writing of this novel. My father Eddy Davidar gave me the benefit of his vast knowledge of the Nilgiris where much of the action takes place.

My agents David Godwin, Nicole Aragi and Kerry Glencorse were brilliant as always.

The editorial suggestions of some of the best publishers in the business – Kirsty Dunseath, Doug Pepper, Ravi Singh and Thomas Abraham – helped improve the book, every writer should be so lucky.

Four friends – Bipin Nayak, Nirmala Lakshman, Kiran Desai and Ramachandra Guha – went out of their way to assist, it's something I'll always be thankful for.

For helping in a myriad different ways I must thank Vinod Gideon, Yasmin Kotawala, Colonel Raghu Shastri (retd), Noor Mohammed, Air Vice Marshal Gurunathan (retd) and Ravi Matthews in the Nilgiris; Ruth and Rajendra Swamy in Madras; Aparajita Pant, Bena Sareen, Diya Kar Hazra, Hemali Sodhi, K.D. and Nini Singh, Mooma, Mallika and Arjun Nath in Delhi; Katie Hambly, Pia and Dilsher Sen in London; and Lisa Rundle, Nicole Winstanley and Ashley Dunn in Toronto.

And, finally, I am grateful to John Makinson and Allan Reynolds for their support.

My understanding of sectarianism, secularism, pluralism, as also Ashoka, Akbar and Gandhi was deepened by the following books and authors: *The Great Transformation* and *The Battle for God* by

Karen Armstrong; *Identity and Violence* and *The Argumentative Indian* by Amartya Sen; *Secular Common Sense* by Mukul Kesavan; *On Identity* by Amin Maalouf; *The Good Boatman* by Rajmohan Gandhi; *Gem in the Lotus* and *The Last Spring: The Lives and Times of The Great Mughals* by Abraham Eraly; *The Bastion of Believers* and *Sacred Spaces* by Yoginder Sikand; *The God Delusion* by Richard Dawkins; *The End of Faith* by Sam Harris; *No God But God* by Reza Aslan; *Early India* by Romila Thapar; *The Concerned Indian's Guide to Communalism* edited by K.N. Panikkar and *Hindutva* by Jyotirmaya Sharma.

Grateful acknowledgement is made to the following for permission to reprint previously published material:

Penguin Books India, New Delhi, for the excerpts from:
The Weaver's Songs by Kabir, translated by Vinay Dharwadker; and *Collected Poems* by Dom Moraes.

Penguin Books Ltd, London and SLL/Sterling Lord Literistic Inc. for the excerpt from the poem XXXIII, from *A Little Larger than the Entire Universe: Selected Poems* by Fernando Pessoa. Edited and translated by Richard Zenith. © Richard Zenith.

W. W. Norton, New York for excerpts from *The Collected Poems of C.P. Cavafy*, translated by Aliki Barnstone.

The Navajivan Trust for excerpts from the *Collected Works of Mahatma Gandhi*.

This is a novel about the misuse and misinterpretation of religion so I have taken extra care not to offend any religious community or faith. In order to avoid unnecessary controversy I should also state explicitly that with the exception of actual historical events that find a place in the narrative such as the demolition of the Babri Masjid and incidents from the lives of Ashoka, Akbar and Gandhi, this is a work of fiction and that names, characters, places and incidents either are the product of the author's imagination or are used fictitiously, and any resemblance to actual persons, living or dead, events or locales is entirely coincidental.